SPINDOC

STEVE PERRY

ACE BOOKS, NEW YORK

This book is an Ace original edition,
and has never been previously published.

SPINDOC

An Ace Book / published by arrangement with
the author

PRINTING HISTORY
Ace edition / February 1994

All rights reserved.
Copyright © 1994 by Steve Perry.
Cover art by Barclay Shaw.
This book may not be reproduced in whole or in part,
by mimeograph or any other means, without permission.
For information address: The Berkley Publishing Group,
200 Madison Avenue, New York, NY 10016.

ISBN: 0-441-00008-8

ACE®
Ace Books are published by The Berkley Publishing Group,
200 Madison Avenue, New York, NY 10016.
ACE and the "A" design
are trademarks belonging to Charter Communications, Inc.

PRINTED IN THE UNITED STATES OF AMERICA

10 9 8 7 6 5 4 3 2 1

*For Dianne once again;
and for the new men in the
family, the Eilenbergs:
Larry, David and Ben.*

ACKNOWLEDGMENTS

Virtually everybody I've ever approached for help in writing a novel has been quick to offer it. Most people I deal with are like that in general, willing to do what they can if you but ask in the right way. The list this time includes those who were gracious when asked, as well as some who helped without even being aware they did so. Thanks to: Don Williams, Vince Kohler, Michael Reaves, Jean Naggar, Ray & Jean Auel, Dennis & Ann Chapman, Bruce Campbell, Nancy Henry, Carol Tabb, Dick & Ann Tilden, and, of course, the usual suspects: Steph, Dal, LeAnne and the lovely Dianne. Appreciate the input, folks.

"The greatest lies always contain hidden somewhere within them the greatest truths."

—R. Howell Harding

"I'm better when I move."

—The Sundance Kid
(Courtesy of Wm. Goldman)

ONE _____

SILK WAS IN the shower when his work console began screaming, loud and strident geegaw hooters filling his entire cube with the racket.

"Shit!" He grabbed a towel and ran dripping and naked to the office. Technically, he was off-duty, but it never fucking failed, the minute he stepped into the shower, the console lit up like Las Vegas after dark.

He rounded the corner. "What?!"

"Class Two Dropbox Emergency," the computer said, her voice calm. They said dislinked biopathics didn't have an intrinsic sense of humor but he didn't buy it. He could hear the laughter. She knew she'd interrupted his shower, Silk was sure of it. He called her "Bubbles," when he was in a good mood. In bad moods, he got real creative with names for her.

He must have left the bug screen turned off last night; a gecko sat on top of the console. When it saw him, the gecko hustled back toward the window and the Maui sunshine, front and back legs on each side moving in together, almost touching, so the thing looked like a quick series of alternating, back-to-back parentheses as he moved. Or maybe it was a she. A female gecko and a femvox computer, sharing secrets.

Silk shook his head. Brain wasn't working yet. Not enough shower, no coffee. What he got for staying up so late, actually thinking he would have a free day off to laze around. Better get it in synch.

A second-class E, that was a shuttle in imminent danger, no threat to populated areas. The joy of codes.

"Jesus. Give it to me." He put the towel on the chair, sat, and slipped the thin conduction frame onto his head. The memory plastic slid tight against his temples, the eye loops moved into heads-up his vision, the bonefones pressed in snug behind his ears.

"Line info or virtual?"

"Line first."

The holoproj blossomed in front of him, a thick ghost that allowed him to see through it to the console. Names, numbers, stats, charts, all flowed across a multilayered optic feed, the levels also color-coded for quick acquisition. He focused on the nearest layer, all in red, which slowed to match his eye shift as he read.

Dropbox #113, the liner-to-ground shuttle *Star of Hawaii,* had suffered a major control-surface malfunction, the starboard and aft aerodynes were off-line and the ship was tumbling as it reached atmosphere from orbit. Backup control comp was inoperable and crosslink to the forward and port computers was down. Any attempt to boost out of the well would be futile, power would just as likely shove them down as up. The crew had tried and it had just made things worse. Bad news.

The stats flew past. Four hundred sixteen passengers, six crew onboard. All about to become past tense.

"We have incoming calls from the media," the computer said.

"That didn't take long. You leaking?"

"Not I," she said. "All opchans are patent, my pipes are clean. Cycle and hold the calls?"

"Yeah. And give me virtual."

The computer put up a new image, optically generated, based on file memory, comsat imaging and feed from the dropbox itself. The *Star of Hawaii's* communications circuits were still operable and the tight-beam radio transmission went straight to the Port of Maui's receivers on the other end of the island from Hana, where Silk now sat naked on a damp towel. Maybe somebody had bored into the tight beam, it was doable if you knew where to look. The company dropboxes used coded and variable-pulse shift gear but what one computer could hide, another could find. It happened all the time.

The 'box was essentially a kind of rounded cone with wings and a tail, extra heat-absorbing plates on the under surfaces. Tumbling as it now was, it was creating a lot of friction on places where it wasn't supposed to. A faint orange glow, brighter yellow in spots, lit the dark spuncarb hull. Silk dropped and watched the crippled ship as if he were right next to it. It fell out of the sky like a big rock, a big *hot* rock.

"What's the 'box's internal temperature?"

"One hundred and seventy-four point nine C. Going up."

Silk blew out a breath. So much for the passengers. It was an oven, even if God suddenly decided to grab the ship and set it down easy, they'd all be cooked anyway.

Jesus. What a mess.

"Where and when will it hit?"

"20 degrees 36 minutes North, 154 degrees 45 minutes West, in approximately 208 seconds, at 0831 hours local time."

"Virtual off, back on infoline. Give me a map."

The computer obeyed.

The images shimmered and changed. A map of the Big Island appeared, the numbers and figures flowed. Silk shook his head. Not even nine o'clock on his day off and already he had a major management crisis. Looked like it was going to hit about a hundred klicks north and slightly east of Hilo, well away from any land mass. InterIsland Traffic Control would have already warned surface vessel off, somebody would have to be real unlucky to get smacked in any event, but you never knew. Some guy's cube got hit by a chunk of space debris the size of a fist last year, killed him next to his wife while they lay in bed, didn't hurt her at all. She heard the chunk punch through the ceiling, felt a jolt and a splash of hot gritty wetness. She turned over and saw his head was mostly gone. Fifteen or sixteen centimeters the other way, it would have missed them both. Ten million to one he got hit, that was the supposedly unspun version Silk got from a buddy on the Flash. The antispace-stay-home groups had a fucking field day.

Wake up, Silk, this is work, not a flit down memory lane.

"Get me the Liar."

"This is an unofficial designation and the corporation desires that its operatives discontinue its usage," she said.

"Jesus, Bubbles, don't quote internal flack at me! Connect me with the damned Maui Port Authority Biopath. And don't give me that white-haired grandma holoproj the bastard uses, leave the screen blank, print-from-vox only."

"Port Authority Biopathic Computer is now on-line."

The voice, when it came, was warm, feminine, just a touch of age to lend it wisdom. "Ah, M. Venture Silk," she said, "I was expecting you to call."

Yeah, I bet. "You have the feed from *Star of Hawaii,* right?"

"I have. Such an unfortunate accident. How tragic for the passengers and crew and their families."

Still three minutes away from splash but it was a done deal, Silk thought. Shake and bake and say hello to Davy Jones, folks. "Right. Give me the spin parameters."

The computer's words continued to crawl up the invisible screen Silk's own computer generated for him upon the air of his office. The print appeared at the same time the vocals did. There was a funny smell in the office. Silk wondered if the gecko took a dump or something. What would gecko shit smell like? The little lizard was on the sill now, but hesitating. Wonder the place wasn't filled with moths, how could he have forgotten to turn on the screen? Or maybe Mac had done it before she left for work. She liked to feel the ocean air coming in without the ions being screwed up by the screen.

"The two possibilities are one, accident, or two, deliberate sabotage," the Liar said. "Under the first are equipment failure and human error or a combination of both. Equipment includes mechanical, biopathic, electronic, software and all subsystems."

Silk shook his head. The stupid fucking Liar went through this shit every time. He knew what the goddamned physical excuses were, all he needed to know was what the company wanted him to use, the at-the-moment spin the quasi wanted on the incident.

"—Human error includes on-ship crew, off-ship crew, orbital controller, passengers, unauthorized personnel—"

Christ, you'd think they'd know he could do his damned job by now. At thirty-two, he'd been a spindoc for the quasi for five years. He could manage the media, any other quasi who stuck their noses in, even the government if need be. Venture Silk was, by his own reckoning, one of the best spiders in the business. He could keep the lilies fat, dumb, and if not happy, at least not alarmed, did it concern anything to do with the Port of Maui, the second largest spaceport terminal in the SuePack

Interlink. Stupid bastards at the company just had to tell him what they wanted, he didn't need a basic class every fucking time—

"The *Star of Hawaii* has impacted," his own computer cut in. Her voice was quiet, matter-of-fact.

"Shit," Silk said. The eyeclowns would pore over the input from the dead ship's computers and maybe, maybe not, they'd figure out what really happened, why the control surfaces failed. That was important, of course, they didn't want more ships dropping out of the skies like rain—but what was really important at the moment was what to tell everybody meanwhile. Already the media were hammering at his door, figuratively, at least, and Silk needed to get on with it. If the Liar would get through its either-or drone and get to the CT— current thinking—he could do his job and maybe still get in a few hours of free time. It was too bad about the passengers, he felt sorry for them, but he had work to get done, information to manage. The truth was like a lump of gold, it could be hammered flat, bent, stretched folded or spun, whatever was needed. The truth was very malleable in the right hands. If the Liar would get its finger out of its butt, Silk might turn this into a triumph. Or if not a victory, at least not a stain on the company's sterling rep.

If they would hurry, he might still get in a swim or maybe even some crossbow practice. Come on—

The Liar finished his differential.

"And . . . ?"

"Sabotage," the Liar said. "Accidental overkill."

"Got it. Discom."

The translucent screen faded.

"Bubbles, get me a passenger and crew list on the 'box, cross to any criminal records, anybody related to anybody with a criminal record, anybody who knows anybody with a criminal record, felonies only."

As the info began to line in, Silk crafted a scenario. The trick to being a good spider—yes, the term was derogatory but it didn't bother him—was to use the truth as much as possible. Give the lilies something they could verify on six points, they'd usually buy the seventh, they ever got that far. There might be speculation, of course, but with as much info as was released into the system every second of every day, nobody had time to run it all down.

"Bryce Xong from the Flash has joined the media queue,"
Bubbles said. "He is number sixteen."

"Awful slow of him," Silk said.

He scanned the infocrawl. There was an assault case. No, not
if there was something better, assault was pretty lame . . .

"Perhaps M. Xong knows you favor him and is therefore
less inclined to hurry," Bubbles observed.

Probably so, Silk thought. We feed each other our predi-
gested tidbits. Besides, Bryce was a pretty good chess player,
he and Silk were never more than a couple of games ahead
of each other before the other one caught up.

Hmm. Here was a colonist once arrested for being under
the influence of chem and disturbing a public meeting. No,
not enough.

"Internal Editing is calling."

"Fuck them. They can wait." Come on, Silk, when the
butchers notice something before you get the scenario built,
you're getting as slow as old Xong—

Ah! There it was! One of the crew members had a brother
who'd been arrested for drug dealing. Illegal drugs scenario
was always a good spin. That was it.

Quickly Silk laid it out for Bubbles. She could run it past
the butchers for a final draft, but the main part of it was clean
enough. The butchers had to do something to justify their jobs
and so they'd change a word here or there to show they were
paying attention, but he could live with that.

"Okay, put Xong through. And give me a read on the
copy."

He read the draft of the statement while he waited for
Bubbles to have Xong's computer page him. The reporter
must have been in the loo, it took almost a minute before he
came on-line. He was about Silk's age, but where Silk was
tall and lean, Xong was short and plump. Most exercise the
reporter got was probably walking to his cooler for another of
the microbrewery beers he favored. Xong's hair was naturally
black, with a few streaks of phosphor-green here and there,
what Silk thought was probably an attempt to attract a younger
set of lovers, male or female. Xong was not particularly fussy
on that point.

"Ven, howza boy?"

"Same old, same old, Bryce. It's supposed to be my day
off."

"Life's hard, kid. This is where POM's comp sent me. So, howcum the port's feeding such spendyspendy chow to the fish off the Big Island?"

Silk chuckled. "It's a tax write-off. We put a couple more down, I get a nice bonus."

"Missed your calling, kid, shoulda been a comedian. But the public wanna know and my window is two minutes away from closing, I want to make the nets. Whatsza skinny?"

"Sabotage, I'm afraid, Xong-dong. According to our information squeeze, one of the assistant pilots is heavily into illegal chem, family biz. She must have stepped on some Yak or Moff's toes. We're backrunning it to be sure, but it looks like payback. The ship just happened to be wrapped around the woman when it got delivered."

Xong clacked his tongue. "Too bad. Serious shit, even if it was only colonists. Squirt it my way."

"In the pipe."

"I am getting first look, am I not?"

"You wound me, Bryce. Even if you were sixteenth in the queue, why do you hurt me like this?"

The round-faced man smiled. "Like shit. You have armor like a battlecruiser, dorkola. Weren't for Mac, nobody would even talk to you. Pawn to king three and discom."

The image faded. Silk smiled. To Bubbles he said, "Give him two minutes and squirt the others, in the order of their calls. And start a new game, Xong moves his pawn to king three."

"He plays a boring game," Bubbles observed. "Always opens the same."

"Hey, he beats me almost half the time."

"You play a boring game, too."

"I need this from a biopath. I'm going to finish my shower."

He stood, mostly dry by now. The warm sunlight played over him as he turned to leave. The sea air smelled clean, whatever stink the gecko had brought with it was gone. On the street below, a bus full of tourists climbed the incline toward the Fagan Memorial, the old block cross atop Lyon's Hill. A few of the passengers noticed him behind the large open window and gaped. He waved at them. Before their tour was out, half of them would be running around naked, enjoying the tropical air, getting burned in patches where they missed sunblocking themselves. He turned to leave.

"You have a nice ass," Bubbles said.

"That's true, but how would you know?"

"That's what Mac says. Do you take it as a compliment?"

He laughed. "Yeah. And I am going to go finish washing it, if you don't mind, and then I am going to the range and then maybe swimming after that."

"Take your com."

"It is my day off."

"Take it anyway."

He made a rude sound and went to finish his shower.

TWO

THE HANA ARCHERY range was just off the bus line about four kilometers south of town, toward the Seven Sacred Pools. The road got a little tricky past the range, kept in artful disrepair by the Tourist Board, and it took more than an hour for the buses to wind the eleven or twelve klicks past the range to the lower pools, jolting the passengers around like popcorn all the way. The tourists loved it. The first white men had misnamed the place, there were three or four times that many pools during the rainy season and nobody had ever determined they had been made particularly sacred by the natives. There were tiny red shrimp who thrived in the crystal water of one of the grottoes, supposedly the blood of an Hawaiian princess who had been killed there by a jealous husband or somesuch. The tourists loved that, too. According to the Board, which doubtlessly spun the numbers up, more than seventy-eight thousand people had made the trip and snapped holos with their mostly cheap recorders during the 2117–2118 season just past. Probably that wasn't too far off.

"Hey, dickless, how's it going?"

Silk pulled his thoughts away from the tourists and smiled at Coffey, the range officer. Coffey was a big man, seemed almost as wide as he was tall, mostly native stock, dark, flashing white teeth, hair going from black to gray. He was ten or fifteen years older than Silk, forty-five, maybe, and as genial a man as Silk had ever met, even though he favored a god-awful cologne that smelled to Silk like fermenting cherry juice.

9

The pass-through kiosk into the electrically fenced range was little more than a roof on thick supports. The building had rain curtains that could be dropped when it got blustery but Silk had never seen Coffey use them. Past the gate was the line, also covered but open-sided. The only enclosed areas were the toilet stalls and the armory proper. This latter was an armored box that looked much like an old-style bank vault, and it was where the bows and supplies were kept. You had to have a license to own a full-power crossbow in any of the three major disciplines, and even so, the bows and bolts usually stayed under lock at the range when you were done.

"Hey, Coffey. I hear your woman bought herself a scanning microscope to try and locate your pecker, that right?"

Coffey laughed a throaty rumble. Some men played chess, some insulted each other's dick size.

"I'll check you out a target, Silk, bring it back when you're done, yah? No point in wasting it, next guy comes along can use it since you won't put no holes in it."

"If I remember right, I beat your last week's posted high score, old man."

"Sheeit, I was shooting left handed, both eyes closed and you only barely beat me anyhow."

The two men smiled at each other. The greeting ritual done, Silk pushed his ID card into the scanner slot and the steel mesh gate slid open. Coffey walked with him to the armory, comboed the door, and fetched Silk's crossbow, ten darts, and a stack of paper practice targets. "Use lane five," he said, "I got the high school team coming in at eleven."

"Thanks, bro'. *Mahalo.*"

Silk walked to the lane, put his gear and bag on the table. He walked out to the bales to set up his targets. Once the bales would have actually been made of packed straw; now, they were thick slabs of artificial material much like the turf used in sporting arenas.

Over the years there had been a number of variations of the crossbow shooting sports but they had settled down to three main ones, two of which were in the Olympics. There was Precision, in which seated shooters loosed at airgun targets set at ten meters. The targets, backed with plates of spandoplast, had a scoring area smaller than a saucer. The crossbows used in Precision were slim, shot thin, lightweight bolts, and were popular with people who tended to be anal retentive. You fired, reeled the target in, pulled the dart, reset the target and repeated the process. It was not uncommon to see five shots put into a hole the size of a demistad by a decent shooter. The best crossbowers could use the same hole for all ten darts, on a good day.

There was Stock Class, in which only a basic crossbow with open sights was allowed. There were severe limitations on such devices and a marksman soldier from the fourteenth century armed with a period arbalest would fit right into this group.

Silk's discipline was Open Field Class. This was more akin to regular archery, in that targets were set at various ranges, from twenty-five to a hundred and fifty meters. The modern unlimited-grade crossbow used in such competitions bore the same resemblance to the fourteenth century's weapon as a maglev flitter did to a wooden ox cart; both could get you there but there were big differences.

Silk's basic chassis was a Kohler stock, skeletonized for balance, of cast Nihhon naigroceramic with an orthogel butt pad. The bow itself was spun carbonex fiber, pressure-molded and machined to microscopic tolerances. The string was stabilized cloned-spidersilk with a braided polymer core. There was a battery-powered Auel mechanocock, supplemented by a manual lever for those who felt the need to do it themselves, or who let the rechargeables go dead. The crossbow had a forty-kilo draw, plus or minus twenty grams at sea level with the humidity at fifty percent. The trigger was a Wilson Infinite, which could be angled to match the operator's finger and adjusted to any pull from one hundred grams to three kilograms. The sighting system was a heads-up full-holoprojic six-dot colorshift Tasco grid. It was a simplified variation of the same system used at major ports to land suborbital ships. The darts used in competition were the same as those used in practice; the shafts were titanium, the tips and buttcaps of stainless steel, the fletching of aerodynamic memory plastic.

Taken as a whole, a modern full-race crossbow was nearly as accurate as any firearm. Silk's system had cost him more than two months pay. He was not quite Olympic caliber, but with another year or two and a shitload of practice, maybe. On a good day he could outshoot anybody on the islands. Coffey sometimes pushed him a little, Coffey and that goddamned high school kid from Oahu who Silk suspected was part machine. Kid was sixteen and once he learned a little more patience, he was going to walk off and leave everybody on the planet behind. Silk was twice the kid's age and he could see the bell curve for his own ability. The champion shooters were all younger than thirty-five or -six. By the time the kid was as old as Silk was now, Silk would be almost fifty and probably ten years shooting in the old farts' class.

He reached the bale and put his target into the frame. Ah, well, energy was going to run down someday and the universe was going to die, too. No point in worrying about the future. *Today* was what counted. Look at what happened to that dropbox full of offworld tourists—probably none of them got up this morning knowing it was their last day.

Silk didn't usually spend much time thinking about similes and metaphors, but if pressed, he would have said his life was much like crossbow shooting: precise, controlled, on target. Everything in its place and going right where it should, in a logical, reasonable manner. He was a dart on the rise, not yet at the top of his arc, climbing, racing, right where he wanted to be.

He walked back over the neatly trimmed grass to the next set of bales, the hundred-meter ones. As he set another target, he noticed that the wind was kicking up a bit. The sky was mostly clear, only a few clouds, but he would pay attention to them. Shadows played hell with sighting, even with the polarizers. The wind gauge at the line would help, but shadows were something else.

A cricket or grasshopper bounced up in front of him as he moved back toward the fifty-meter backstops. Sometimes one of them would light on a target while you were shooting. The Precision guys good enough would plink one now and then. Hitting a bug at ten meters was a little beyond him. Then again, the Precision shooters who won medals were older. Maybe it was because they got to sit down . . .

He set the final target and went back to the line. With field crossbow you started with the outermost targets and worked your way in to the closer ones. Supposed to replicate the conditions of an actual battle, though that was pretty far removed. On a world where most serious diseases had finally been eliminated and accident was the leading cause of death behind old age, homicide was greatly frowned upon. Coffey was busy watching an entcom cast on the 'proj because Silk was the only guy on the line. If anybody else came to shoot, the big man would start acting like a range officer, he'd be watching things very closely. If anybody got shot accidentally, Coffey was going to get part of the blame and either pay a stiff fine or do some locktime along with the careless shooter. Silk thought it was a pretty good system himself. When you passed the responsibility around, it made people careful, it made them think before they did anything stupid. He'd had to take a twelve-week course after work before he had ever been allowed to touch a full-power crossbow. That was a good idea, too.

When he got to the line, he put on his shooting glasses and gloves. He went through his breathing exercises, centered himself, and spent five minutes or so clearing his mind. Nothing was supposed to intrude on a shooter's concentration, he wanted to get a decent score.

When he was ready, he picked up the crossbow.

He finished before the local school team arrived. Coffey, who had been pretending not to watch, looked up from his 'proj.

"You hit anything?"

"Not much. The wind was blowing, clouds rolled in, bad conditions."

"Right. And your arm was sore and your finger was tired, too."

"Fuck you."

Coffey grinned. "With what? I hear you have to call Surf Rescue to help you find it just to pee. Come on, bro', what'd you shoot?"

"Oh, a lousy four-ninety-eight."

"The hell you did. Fuck you and your lying dog, too."

"Well, the wind *was* blowing."

"Yeah, sure, musta been a kokua wind, blowing your quarrels right into the target. Four-ninety-eight my ass."

Silk grinned. It was a master class score, he'd shot better a couple of times, once a clean five hundred on the mainland, tied with Endo Spirelli, and had to go to a two-hundred-meter shoot-off, which Spirelli won. Of course, he was NorAm champ, he speared all six bennies, but Silk hadn't embarrassed himself, he'd hit four. And today's shooting wasn't quite that good but it wasn't anything to be ashamed of, either.

To rub it in, he said, "I need a new string. The old one's throwing them crooked."

"I just got in a dozen new. You want me to do it?"

"Hah. You'd string it so I'd be putting them in the ocean. I'll do it."

With the discretion of the RO, you could take your bow from the range for repairs. You weren't supposed to keep it more than a day or two and no quarrels, of course. Silk had fifty practice darts at home he was refletching, not to mention a pack of razor-tipped hunting heads Mac had given him for his collection. Those things were a hundred years old, carbon steel antiques, still sharp enough to cut yourself if you weren't careful when handling them. He wasn't a major collector like some of the shooters he knew, but he had a few nice pieces, including a wooden arrow from the 1880s with a stone head that was certified as having been made and owned by an Amerind in North Dakota. *That* little jewel had cost him almost as much as his crossbow had.

"Thumb the plate," Coffey said.

Silk did so, and the scanner duly noted his print. Coffey punched in the serial number of the crossbow. "Now, don't run around killing the tourists because you are upset about your lack of manhood, Silk."

"Hey, I didn't shoot a four-eighty-four last week, bro'. *My* manhood is secure."

"And your fucking dog," Coffey said.

Silk got off the bus at his cube, stashed his crossbow and gear, grabbed a towel and his swim pack, and hiked over to the Red Sand Beach. He had to use the old trail past the big hotel, a route most tourists never seemed to find. There were never more than a handful of swimmers at the Red Beach, mostly snorkelers.

He made his way down the incline to the water. The red sand was more like red gravel, but the color was right. There was a rocky outcrop in the water that formed a quiet pool where four or five people now snorkeled back and forth, most of them still tourist-pale; one was dark enough to be a local or somebody with enough free time to indulge himself.

Silk stripped, put on a swim strap and his silicone eyeshells, sprayed himself with sunblock and waded into the water. Though it was November, the ocean was warm. He took a

few breaths, picked out a lane, and started a lazy freestyle
crawl. The wave action was mild, hardly noticeable here. He
could see the bottom, even when he got into deeper water,
and several hand-sized tropical fish darted about below him.
When he'd first started doing his laps here, he'd swum nude,
figuring the mesh swim strap didn't hide anything anyway, it
was basically nothing more than a pouch and a couple of loops
of elastic string. The first time he'd paddled through a school of
convict tang had cured him of swimming naked. The damned
little fish liked to nibble and dangling things were apparently
a favorite. That wasn't so bad, but there were bigger creatures
in the sea, a couple of parrot fish who hung out locally and
made him leery. So, the strap.

Silk swam back and forth, making a fifty-meter loop, moving slowly at first and then speeding up as his muscles loosened
and grew warmer. He managed to miss the snorkelers, though
he nearly ran over one fat man a few times. Damned tourists. During the holiday season you couldn't move without
tripping over one and if you fell there'd be one under you
and five more to complain about having to walk around you.
Of course, being able to swim in the ocean in the middle
of winter, when people on the mainland might be wading
through a meter of snow to get to their bus, well, that made
up for it some. They got rain here, but it was warm rain,
you could wander around in shorts most of the year. Silk's
cube didn't even have a heating unit in it. In the five years
he'd lived in Hana, he'd never needed one. Or a cooler,
either. A fan stuck in the window on calm days was usually enough to do it, though Mac complained she was going
to buy herself a portable air cooler every time the winds
dropped off.

He finished another loop. Glanced at his chrono, saw he'd
been swimming for nearly twenty minutes. Another twenty
and he'd pull up. Grab himself some lunch, hell, maybe take
a nap. Mac wouldn't be home for another four hours. They
could roll around, take a shower, go out for dinner. Aside
from that one emergency this morning, it had been a great
day so far.

Silk passed the fat snorkeler again. The man was waving
his feet up and down, splashing his fins out of the water
and wasting a lot of energy for not much motion. Taking
holos of the bottom, the fish, and every now and then a

woman who had chosen to swim nude, save for her eyeshells and fins, and who was attractive enough in a slightly-too-voluptuous way.

Silk grinned. He wondered what the poor people were doing.

THREE

SILK WAS DOZING when Mac came home, lying naked on the bed in the beginnings of an erotic dream that involved a recslide and a canola fog machine.

"Must be nice," Mac said.

Silk slid up from the dream greasy with imaginary oil. "Huh?"

"I'm out there healing the sick and making the world safe from *ausvelter* plagues, working my fingers to nubs, and here you are in bed dreaming you're a flagpole."

Silk glanced down at his erection and grinned. "I was dreaming of you, Gemma McKenzie-Ryan. You want to play doctor? Or better, flagpole sitter?" He waggled his eyebrows at her, pointed meaningfully at his penis, and made it jump.

"Such muscle control," she said. "My. I can hardly restrain myself from tearing my clothes off and impaling my tender hot wetness upon your mighty sword."

Silk was not slow. "But you can restrain yourself."

"You forgot, didn't you?"

He ran a rapid scan of his memory. With the surge in mentation, his flagpole developed a list, first to starboard, then to port, deflating like a balloon with a slow leak. "No, I didn't forget," he said, stalling. What? What was he supposed to remember? Come on, Silk—

Mac glanced at her chrono. He looked at her. She was tall, only a few centimeters shorter than his own 185; mesomorphic, with muscles kept toned by a daily hour in the stimgym. Long legs, a trifle wide in the hips, but that was useful, raven hair,

17

slightly crooked features that gave her character to go with the beauty. And a full MD, with a mind as sharp as an ultrasonic scalpel.

Hurry up, Silk.

"I just thought we'd have time to play before we left, that's all," he tried.

"If you can move like a hamster," she said. She shook her head. "And if I don't take a shower, in which case I get to walk around the party smelling like pussy."

Party! Damn, the Medical Associates new employees party! Shit, that was tonight.

"Wouldn't bother me any," he said, sitting up. He held his arms out to her. "I like the smell. Besides, I'm fairly certain your boss knows you do it with me. We could confirm it for her."

"Her and everybody else. Get up and get dressed, Silk. I'm going to go shower."

He shrugged. "Your loss."

"You did forget, didn't you?"

Automatically he reached for the truth and spun it. "Come on, give me a break. You think I would forget the social event of the season?"

"No doubt in my mind at all."

He laughed as she walked away, watching her strip her whites away and letting them fall to the floor. "You are a slob," he called to her as she made it to the fresher. "If you weren't such a good fuck I'd throw you out!"

From inside the fresher, she laughed.

He liked that, being able to make her laugh.

He heard the water start and he swung his legs over the edge of the bed. He looked down at his limp rod. "Sorry, pal," he said. "But it's your fault I forgot the damned party anyhow. Suffer."

As a medic on staff for Offworld Quarantine, Mac had a few perks. They drove to the Hana Hotel's new ballroom in one of those perks, a Byers E-cart, a wheeled electric four-seater that would cost more than Silk made in six months if he were foolish enough to want to buy one. It was a nice toy, of course, but even a cheap electric cart would cost more to license every year than it did to buy in the first place. Unless you were rich—or got a perk from your employer like Mac did—you took pubtrans if something was further away than you wanted to walk or bike. For anything in and around Hana, Silk rode the bus or his recumbent bike. And the Byers wasn't cheap. With the spuncarb frame and rotolin engines, the cart could hit a hundred kilometers per hour on a straight stretch. Not that there were that many straight stretches of road around here, but on the brighter side of the island, there were places you could do it. And even here in rainy Hana, you hardly ever had to plug it in for a recharge; park it in a sunny spot and the solar inducers would fill the batteries from dead empty in a couple of hours.

They drove with the top retracted and the cooling evening air tried to restyle their hair.

"Where did you go?"

He blinked at Mac. She looked great in her spidersilk jumpsuit and cape, all in shifting blues. His own outfit was mostly charcoal-gray, the most conservative cut of the half dozen suits he owned. It was a polypropylene unitard under a knee-length tunic, with matching slippers. His undershirt was also gray, but darker, the cotton showing only as puff sleeves and from under the tunic's V-neck. The outfit was tropical weight and cool enough for evening wear, though it would certainly be too warm for sunshiny use. Mac liked him to look respectable when she took him to OhQue functions. He would smile, behave himself, stay sober. She was on a fast track to Medical Supervisor and a stoned partner spilling his drink on a higher-up would be a major faux pas.

"Yo, M. Flagpole?"

"Oh, sorry. I was just thinking about maybe getting myself one of these babies." He patted the instrument panel a couple of times as if it were a dog or a small child's head.

"Hah. Right. And what do you plan to do for rent money? Or to eat while you drive around in your status symbol?"

He waggled his eyebrows at her. "Why, escort work. I could turn pro. Lotta women tourists would pay a bundle to have me show them what's what."

She laughed.

"Or you could keep me."

She kept smiling.

"Well, I could also get promoted. Old lady Perkins is slowing down. She does a couple more crooked spins like the twirl she put on that Oahu Water Taxi deal, or the old bomb that killed the tourists on Molokai, they could be looking for a new Chief of SuePack."

"Sure," she said. "And you are what? fourth in line? Perkins fucks up, Bevins, Stark and Kinya all drop dead, you're a shoo-in—if they don't look outside."

"Well, you never know."

"That's true. I suppose I could win the Nobel in medicine, too."

"I wouldn't be surprised," he said. "And how was your day?"

"Interesting. You remember that *ausvelter* I told you about? The one with the hemolytic dyscrasia?"

Silk nodded absently. Medicalese didn't do much for him and truth be known, he hardly ever paid any attention to what Mac brought home from work. Sick people and offworlders bored him. "Um." He didn't remember but that reply sounded neutral enough, he thought.

"Got some more intriguing stuff back on the scan on him. Very interesting. I didn't have time to lock it down today but I'll play with it tomorrow."

"Lucky scan," he said.

A few insects buzzed past with the evening air, some dying on the windshield, others escaping to risk the next bus full of tourists. The hotel was just ahead, and the lot was half-full when Mac pulled the cart in and parked. Most of the carts on this side of the island would be there before the night was through, it was a big social event, and if not of the season, at least of the month. Silk saw the Maui Corp's CEO's Jag, the Medical Director's homely-by-comparison Mitsubishi van— though he had *three* children, even if one of them was adopted. There were laws and then there were laws, Silk knew. The set of laws for the rich and powerful had, like gold, quite a bit more flexibility than those the rest of the Earth lived by. Of course, you could have all the children you wanted, if you didn't mind shipping fifty or a hundred light-years away to E2 or Fuji or Hock Miete or any of the other *ausvelt* planets. Right, and get to live in the techo equivalent of a mud hut with all the little brats.

Well. Maybe that was a little overstated; still, Silk liked it here on the homeworld and he wasn't all that hot to have little squawlers messing up his personal landscape anyhow.

Maybe someday he and Mac could make themselves one but not just yet.

"You sleeping over there again?"

Silk shook himself back into the here and now. "Nope, all ready to be charming and witty. I'll have you running the center before the night is out."

"Just don't puke on the CEO, that'll keep me happy."

"Me? Come on. You suppose they'll have those boiled shrimp on ice again? I really like those."

"You and everybody else. Come on."

Inside, the crowd was pretty much local well-to-doers. A few up and coming types from the West End were there, even a couple from Honolulu and the mainland that Silk recognized as hotprops. Mostly the gathering was of local doctors, upper-level techs, and admin people attached to the Hana Offworld Quarantine Station. Offworlders arriving in this hemisphere spent thirty days at one of the three stations in SuePack, the local one being a man-made peninsula jutting from the shore between the spaceport and Old Town.

Mac went to speak to her supervisor and Silk gravitated toward the food tables. He spied the shrimp, big, thumb-thick pink beauties already peeled and deveined, artfully placed on trays of shaved ice. A dozen people milled around the display, trying to look as if they weren't impressed or too greedy as they speared the shrimp with long, colorful toothpicks. Must be five, maybe six hundred stads worth of the seafood already out and probably that much more stashed in the kitchen for late arrivals.

Silk selected a long purple toothpick and a mushpaper plate and napkin and went to join the throng. He and Mac enjoyed flesh foods now and then, between the two of them they made pretty good money, but mostly it was chicken or rabbit. The Ausvelt Plague of 2060 had killed six million people but had also wiped out nearly all the world's cattle. Eating beef now was technically illegal except for certain rare exceptions. If you owned a cow and it died of a heart attack or something else the vets could certify as accidental, you could eat the remains. Like everything else there were ways to get around the prohibition. He'd heard there were people who specialized in scaring cows to death, for the right price. Silk had tasted hamburger four times in his life, had once had an entire chunk of roast, almost thirty grams, to himself. Seafood was still available, but at fifty or sixty stads a half kilo, shrimp were seldom-indulged treats for most people. He'd heard that on the planets of Ujvaros and Ventoblanco the wildlife was so plentiful you could step outside your cube and hit it over the head with a stick; that there were restaurants where meat or fish or fowl was the main course in *all* the entrees. Must be nice.

Then again, he thought, as he speared a fat boiled shrimp, there was that mud hut, alien disease, and all the other discontents of frontier life. No, thank you.

Ah, God, the shrimp was good! Four, he would have at least four. And if nobody was looking, hell, maybe five.

By 2200 the ballroom was full. Party walla rumbled around the room, people talking, laughing, discussing business.

One of the doctors who worked with Mac cornered Silk and asked about the dropbox crash.

"Sabotage? Really?"

Herr Doctor Klein was a fair-fat-forty MidEuropean who totally avoided the sun and was thus as pale as a corpse. That made for healthy skin, Silk knew, but looking like bread dough where you bulged the seams of your unitard, nearly filled the puff sleeves, and your neck lapped over the collarless ring of your tunic sure didn't make up for a nice epidermis.

"Handled the report myself," Silk said. He had already had his limit of three drinks, the shrimp on the ice bed were all gone and he knew Mac wouldn't be ready to leave for another hour. So, Herr Doctor Klein.

Well. Into each life a little crap must fall.

"Really. A shame about all those people."

Silk glanced surreptitiously at his chronograph. "Yes, it is a pity. Still, what can you do? Things happen."

Klein nodded, his blond hair moving as a single piece. Jesus, what did he use on it? Shellac?

Mac arrived and saved him from the doctor's prattle.

"Ah, there you are. Would you excuse us for a moment, Hans? I need to show Ven off to somebody."

"But of course, dear colleague."

When they were a couple of meters away, Silk said, "'Dear colleague'? People actually talk like that?"

"Be grateful I saved you from him."

"I am, I am. How can I show you?"

"You could have saved me one of those shrimp, you greedy pig."

He grinned. Held his hands out, showed her the palms and then the backs.

She raised her eyebrows.

"Ta da!" He pulled the napkin from his tunic's breast pocket with a flourish and unfolded it to reveal two shrimp.

She laughed. "I take the greedy pig part back."

"These were the largest two on the tray. I risked my life to obtain them."

"Gimme."

He tendered the napkin. She took the shrimp, smiled at him, and put half of one into her mouth. Moved it in and out as if fellating it.

Silk stared. "Whoa."

She bit the shrimp in half and chewed slowly. Licked her lips.

"Christ, Mac."

"I think it's about time we left," she said. "Don't you?"

"While I can still walk without tripping over myself? Yeah."

"You wish, braggart."

"Wait until I get you home and we'll see who is bragging."

"I don't know if I can wait that long."

"Out. Now," he said, grinning.

FOUR

BY THE TIME Mac had the cart started and rolling, Silk had his hand between her legs; he nibbled her earlobe as they left the hotel parking lot. He stuck his tongue in her ear as they approached the stop sign at the bottom of the hill, and she went through the intersection without slowing.

"Quit that! You want me to wreck this thing?"

The wind and the bugs sped past in the night. "I don't care." He rubbed her mons with his fingertips. Surely that was dampness under that spidersilk?

She laughed. "Okay, M. Silk, let's see how brave you are."

They were rounding the curve by the new banana plantation Miyamoto had cultivated for the tourist trade. The patch was bounded on both sides by assorted lush vegetation; during the day it would have been a study in green, from spring to olive, a dozen different shades. In the dark, it was much more monochromatic.

Mac pulled the cart off the road and down the service drive for Miyamoto's. The broad leaves of the banana plants hung limp in the starlight, unlike Silk's own pendant. Mac parked the car behind the storage shed.

Silk reached for her, but she pulled away, hopped out of the car.

"Mac . . ."

"Come on, goat-boy. Catch me if you can."

She turned and ran.

Silk leapt over the side of the cart and sprinted after her.

She got as far as the nearest patch of mini-jungle. He caught her as they were enveloped in the foliage of a giant hanging vine with heart-shaped leaves the size of Silk's head. He grabbed her from behind, his hands cupping her breasts. She laughed and spun to face him.

The kiss was long, hot, they chewed on each other's tongues. When he could hardly stand it he was so excited, she dropped to her knees, jerked open the cro-flypatch on his unitard and took him into her mouth, slid him in and out rapidly, urging him in with one hand on his ass, the other encircling him so he wouldn't go too deep.

Silk groaned, felt himself gathering pressure. It felt unbelievably good, but he gently moved her head away.

She grinned up at him. "What's the matter? No control?"

"Let's talk about that in a minute. My turn."

He squatted, pushed her backward, and started trying to get her out of her clothes.

"Goddamned jumpsuit!"

She laughed.

He managed it, finally. Spread her knees wide and bent to kiss her. He used his tongue, felt that tiny spot grow hard under his lips.

Thirty seconds later she began to throb rhythmically. She clutched at the back of his head, fingers pulling his hair.

"Oh, God!"

When her orgasm ebbed from surf to a gentle wave, he grinned up at her over her damp pubic patch. "Hey, I was just getting started, you can't be done yet. Now that you're warmed up, let me show you what I can really do—"

She laughed again and shoved his face away from her mons. "Like hell. You come up here."

He smiled and started to slide up her.

"Wait a second," she said. Looked over her shoulder at him. "This is the woods' position. Come in from behind."

Silk hurried to do just that.

He slid into her—she was completely wet—and was captured by her warmth and tightness. "Oh, man!"

"I certainly hope not," she said.

He began pumping, intending it to last for a long time, hours, days, years. He tried to hold back but managed all of eight or nine strokes before he came, expending himself in her, trying to pull himself deeper with his hands on her hips, driving in the final thrust as far and hard as he could.

"Oh!"

He stayed on his knees for another five seconds, then toppled, pulling them both over onto their sides on the soft ground, still joined together.

"Oh, *boy!*" he said.

They both laughed at that.

After a minute, she said, "I don't suppose you brought a towel or something to wipe off with?"

"Me? This was your idea."

"Oh, I see. And you weren't interested?"

"Well, okay, I confess I was."

"Good. We'll use your tunic, then."

"Hey!" But before he could move, she rolled away and off him and had his tunic pressed between her legs.

"See how *you* like smelling like pussy."

Silk laughed again.

Here he was, lying on the ground under a bush in a semitropical garden in the middle of civilization's best approximation of paradise, his belly full of expensive seafood and fucked mellow by a witty and beautiful woman.

Silk didn't see how it could get much better than this.

FIVE

TWO BUSES FULL of tourists crashed into each other near the port and Silk was spinning the relatively minor accident—nobody was hurt bad—when the call came in on his personal line. It was just past noon.

"It's Bryce Xong," Bubbles said.

"Just a second."

He finished his spin and had Bubbles ship it to the butchers. "Okay, put Xong on."

"I'm so damned sorry, Ven," Bryce began. He looked grave.

Silk blinked, wondering what Xong was talking about.

"I'll miss the hell out of her. If there is anything I can do, anything at all."

Silk's belly clutched, went cold all the way to the end of his bowels. "What are you talking about, Bryce?"

"Oh, shit, you don't know?"

"Discom this," Silk ordered his computer. "Get me Mac at Offworld Quarantine."

Too many heartbeats went past before somebody answered his com.

"This is Dr. Klein."

"Hans, this is Venture Silk. I need to speak to Mac."

There came an endless pause. The universe flywheeled itself apart to total chaos, energy ran out, entropy claimed all hope. Oh, God—

"I am sorry, M. Silk. There has been an . . . accident."

Oh, no!

"Dr. McKenzie is—ah, she is in . . . surgery," Klein began.

He was lying. Silk was too good a liar himself not to hear that. Even if Xong hadn't called.

"No, she isn't. She is dead," Silk said. "Save the spin for somebody who'll believe it, Doctor, and better you should leave it to the professionals—you don't have the skill for it."

Silk broke the connection. Thought of all the favors he had owed him and which ones he could call in the fastest. He put his computer on it, and stared stupidly at the wall as his biopath burrowed her way through the prevarications to as much truth as he was going to get for now.

In the end it was as bad as it could be:

Mac was dead.

And she had been murdered.

SIX

DEPARD KING WAS angry.

He had been angry most of his life and much of his anger was now directed at himself. His temper again. He had lost control and now look what he had to show for it. Wonderful, simply wonderful.

He stood on the corner, the golf course behind him, the doctor's cube across the narrow street. It was just after 1800 and the service workers were changing shifts. People walked or rode bikes or filled the shuttle buses that zoomed past King trailing faint mechanical scents, scorched lube and motor flux. King wore baggy, colorful shorts and an equally colorful shirt. Hiking socks, also somewhat baggy, were tucked into his walking sandals. Around his neck he had slung a cheap holocam and a tourist purse. A hat woven from palm fronds by one of the locals completed the disguise. He looked like a thousand other visitors, nothing to set him apart, only—

None of *them* had killed anybody today.

He glanced at his chrono. It wouldn't be dark for a while yet and he couldn't stand out here for several hours, that was strange behavior even for a tourist. There was a small restaurant down on the bay, a couple of blocks walk. He turned and started that way.

A woman as brown as stained boot plastic went past him up the hill on a recumbent bike, naked except for raggy shorts. She flashed white and even teeth at him in a smile. *"Mahalo!"* she called out.

King forced a smile and waved back, striving to look innocu-

ous and touristy. He was a big man, not huge, and he tried to
hide his well-developed musculature under his baggy costume
as best he could. The trick to blending into a local scene was
to become that which you imitated. Like an actor in a role, you
not only wore the clothes, you learned the moves, the lines, the
attitude of your character. Tourists were easy, King had been
them a hundred times over the years while working for Terran
Security. The Scat, the field ops liked to call it, a nickname
arrived at in the roundabout way such things sometimes came
about. Terran Security was TS, which was all too easy to make
into "Tough Shit," and thus Scat. King had done his tourist so
often the characterization had become imbued with a life of his
own. Maynard Isaac Clark—call me Mike—who had a condo
in Kansas City, a job at Tarnover Financial where he was an
Assistant Comptroller. His ex-spouse was bleeding him dry,
his good-for-nothing son was playing that weird bondoAfrican
music in some scuzzy band in Little Miami and spending what
little money he got for that on offworld tattoos, and Mike had
saved for three years to take this vacation. Even gone to the
gym to get in shape for all the walking out here in the sticks.
Hell, when a man hit forty as he had just done, he had to start
taking care of himself, didn't he?

Another pair of tourists passed him going the other way and
he exchanged smiles and nods with them. Two women, and he
might be expected to admire their new tans and local shirts if
he ran into them in a restaurant line or on a bus to one of the
attractions, but passing on the street didn't require that. He
didn't want to leave any impressions in anybody's mind at
this particular location.

The line at the restaurant was fairly long, but that didn't
matter, he had plenty of time to kill—

Damn.

Even after all the training, the years of martial arts and
calming meditation, the assorted therapies he had indulged in,
he still could not completely control his violent nature. It had
cost him his job with The Scat, his temper. He had tried for
years to get a handle on it. Yes, he was much improved over
what he had been, and he had usually been careful to cover it
before he improved, but the bottom line was, he had a ways
to go. If that stupid woman had been cooperative, if she had
listened to reason, it would not have happened. Some of the
blame must rest on her.

Another bus went past, blowing up a wake of dust and grit. Mike would turn his head and shut his eyes against this minor attack and King did so.

Certainly he had deleted other people in his career, even though such was frowned upon unless absolutely necessary and unless such deletions could be made to look like accidents or the blame laid elsewhere. On today's Earth, violence against citizens was a major crime. Murder was worth full stasis for life, a most unpleasant prospect. They put you in a box and into a medically induced trance in which you did not dream; life support kept your body functioning but for all practical purposes, you were brain-dead until you finally died for real. It was civilization's answer to capital punishment and to most people worse than deletion itself. Certainly King thought so, and Mike did, too. If you wanted to knock heads and brawl, you emigrated to the other worlds; on Earth, you joined a dojo or boxing gym and signed a waiver, or you kept your hands to yourself.

He made it to the restaurant line.

Stupid woman.

It had begun well enough. Mike had approached her after she left her cart. The carts were parked in the sunlight for recharging and her slot was far enough away so she had a nice hike to her building. There was a short cut through a thickly forested area, the local flora being rampant where it was allowed to grow as it would, and McKenzie was one of the few people at the OhQue center who used the path through the woods. Mike had been waiting there for her since before dawn. Nobody had seen him arrive and he had picked out an exit whereby no one would see him leave the area. A careful man could keep out of sight by using the foliage and while Mike would blunder around carelessly, Depard King was a careful man indeed. Except that he had a violent temper . . .

"Dr. McKenzie?"

She started at his voice, but relaxed when she saw his Mike persona.

"Could I have a word with you?"

She stopped. They were in the thickest part of the woods, long vines hanging from the tall trees, dense bushes rising up two meters from the ground, invisible to anybody who wasn't within a few meters.

"Certainly," she said.

Her eyes narrowed, though, and he was aware of her guard going up. Obviously a fairly bright woman, he thought. She sees a tourist, but one who has addressed her by name and in a place where none ought to be.

"I have a proposition for you," he said.

She had listened to his pitch all the way through without interrupting, nodding to show she understood, and, he thought, was willing to consider it as a serious proposal.

Wrong.

When he was done, she smiled, then actually laughed. *Laughed!*

"You are out of your mind," she said. "If you will excuse me—"

She started to move past him.

He grabbed her arm. "Wait, you don't understand—"

Somewhere along the way somebody had showed her a trick. She twisted free of his grip and stabbed at his eyes with her extended fingers. There was no real chance she would have hit him, but if she had, he would have been blinded. He moved easily to one side, not even bothering to parry or block the thrust and that should have been the end of it.

Should have been the end of it. He was a pro, there were other ways, he could have shrugged it off and walked, shucked Mike and regrouped.

But—no.

That this stupid woman would try to poke him in the eye—

His rage blossomed and enveloped him. How *dare* she!

The problem with being trained to kill with one's hands to the point where it was useful was that the moves became almost reflexive. With control gone, a skilled man was dangerous. Deadly dangerous.

King stepped in and swung his right fist up and over and down. There were many names in many arts for the technique. In kendo the stroke was called *shomen*; in chan gen, it was named the Hammer Fist. When he had trained in the TS school, the students had called it the Pile Driver.

The bottom edge of his fist smashed down on top of the woman's head. She dropped, unconscious as she fell, and even then it was not too late. But King was set for a follow-up by the time she sprawled, and it was the heel kick to her temple that crushed the thinner bone there and ruptured the membranes covering her brain. That was the strike that killed her, even though it probably took some time for her to die.

Cursing her and himself, King stared at the crumpled woman for a moment, then turned and ran. Dammit!

Dammit—

"Party of one, sir?" the hostess said.

King blinked. He'd reached the front of the line waiting to be seated. He'd lost Mike, that was bad. "Huh? Oh, yeah, that's me, party of one."

"Would you mind being seated with a couple from . . ." he looked down at his computer flatscreen, " . . . from Boise?"

Mike wouldn't.

"No problem."

"Right this way, sir."

As he followed the hostess, King put the killing out of his mind. He was going to be having dinner with a couple from Boise and he was Maynard Isaac Clark—call me Mike—from Kansas City. Murder would be the last thing on his mind. Hell, he'd saved three years for this vacation . . .

SEVEN

"EVERYTHING LOOKS FINE," the medic said. "You can get dressed now."

Naked on the exam table, Zia Rélanj offered no reaction. It all ought to look fine, given the training, workouts and surgery she'd had in the last four years to make it so. A team of E2's best psychologists had designed her to be attractive to the most number of basic-stock humans sexually oriented toward normal women. She wouldn't appeal to those who liked them fat or ugly or with amputations, but she was sthenic, mesomorphic, with long blond hair, wide shoulders, narrow hips, and long legs. She looked athletic but not too muscular—her breasts were slightly larger than average and you didn't get that if your bodyfat were too low; even so, they'd had to tweak the hormones some. At 173 centimeters she was slightly taller than an average terran woman; at 58 kilos, probably a bit less than average weight for her height. Her face had been sculpted to be slightly less than perfect, almost beautiful but not quite. According to the doctors, really beautiful women made many terrans uncomfortable and they didn't want that. She was twenty-five in E.S. years and they left that alone because it was old enough to be an adult and young enough to be the most attractive. Aside from her looks, she had been trained to be quick on her feet physically and mentally, and she could converse intelligently on several thousand topics as the need arose. She hadn't had the Treatment yet, but she was first in line when she got back, that was a guarantee. That alone made the trip worthwhile.

For the business she was in, her programming was perfect. Zia Rélanj was a spy.

She slid off the table and began to dress, coolly pulling on her silks without any false modesty. Too many people had seen her naked too many times for her to be bothered by it anymore.

The medico watched, trying to maintain his professional detachment but not quite pulling it off. He had a thing for blondes, especially when the pubic hair matched the rest as hers did. Zia knew because she had done a background on the doctor before she came in for her exam.

She arranged it so that she had turned to face him when she pulled her pants up. She dragged the waistband up slowly and gave it a little back and forth move when she reached her pubes so the fine hair there danced a little. She could almost hear his erection begin, feel his mouth go dry. She might need something from him when she got back from Terra, no point in letting the opportunity to set the hook pass. It was a simple trick, but effective.

The doctor was married and had four children, another one on the way, and if he had ever played around on his monogamy contract, New Earth Security Agency couldn't find it. But Zia knew that he would get out of his own clothes fast enough if she indicated she was interested in playing. It was her business to know that and to use it.

She finished dressing, checked her face in the mirror on the wall, nodded at the doctor and left. She had a sparring session and a weapons class this afternoon but a couple of hours off until then. She decided to walk to the restaurant where she was planning to have her midday meal.

It was warm and mostly sunny, with a few clouds clumped together over the mountains to the northwest. The spring air held a high tang of butterflower pollen and the big bees zipped past on their way from the flowers to the hives and vice versa.

Beagle was the biggest town on the Lower Island and it bustled with activity: the streets were thick with alcohol-powered carriages and little fuel-cell scooters that sounded like angry sewing machines. Pedestrians tromped along the wide plastcrete walks, staid old grannies and kids running and laughing. Buildings loomed, some reaching up five or six stories. Almost two hundred thousand people lived here in the second largest city on New Earth, only Touchdown was bigger, with nearly a quarter million.

Of course, you could put the entire population of the planet, just over a million altogether, into one corner of New York City on E1 and probably nobody would even notice the addition. There were almost seven *billion* people on Terra.

It was hard to imagine. Even though she'd done the training, walked the ersatz holoproj streets of London and Tokyo and New Madras, it still didn't seem real to her. Why would anybody want to live like that? Like rats stuffed into a too-small cage? It just went to show that some of what her instructors taught her was valid: they must all be as crazy as dung flies back there on the homeworld.

The restaurant, the Big Dog, was only a couple of streets ahead. Zia took in the sights and smell of the city, the looks she got from men and a few women, the joy of being young and strong and in peak shape, striding along in eight hundred stads worth of green silk, in control of her life. This assignment had been a plum, every op in the biz worth anything wanted it but she had gotten it. When it was done, she was going to be in big demand, it would be a deep notch in her gunbutt. No doubt about that at all. And it wasn't even that tough an assignment, just pick up the package and bring it back. Easy as falling into bed. Another of her many skills, that.

She reached the Dog and strode inside. The harmless old guy behind the counter smiled and began setting a place for her.

"Hey, Drellie," she said as she slid onto the stool.

"Hey, Zia. Usual?"

"I think I want to try something different today. How about the Steak Dianne?"

He grinned again. "You got it, kid." He went to make the dish.

She was a little surprised at herself. Raw meat? That wasn't something her programmers would have built in, now was it? Maybe there was still some of what she used to be left, under all the cutting and pasting. It was possible—not that it mattered. What mattered was the job, doing it well, getting it done right.

Whatever it took.

EIGHT

SILK COULD HAVE done it over the net, could have had his computer connect him with the police, but he wanted to go himself. He felt impotent sitting in his office at home, talking to an image in the air. He needed to see real people, to be able to pick up on their body language, to cut through the crap.

So it was that he sat in the waiting room of the Hana Police Station, waiting to see the PR flack. They didn't have their own spindoc on staff here, local crime didn't much warrant it. Drunk or stoned tourists, petty theft, domestic disputes, those were the things the Hana police usually had to deal with. There hadn't been a serious crime here in five years, and SuePack Security had taken care of that one, an ADW on a corporate honcho from offworld by a jealous wife. SuePack would be sending a team in to investigate this, too, but they hadn't arrived yet, or if they had, nobody was letting that out.

The room had a stale smell to it and the paint on the cheap fibercast walls had peeled in spots, revealing the ugly mottled grain under it. The plastic chair Silk sat upon sagged, having flexed too many times under too many heavy bodies. In his years in town, he'd never been inside this building before. No loss in that.

"M. Silk?"

He looked up to see a bald man of fifty, deeply tanned, dressed in the khaki shirt and shorts the local law officers wore.

"I'm Sergeant Lennox," he said. "I'm sorry for your loss."

Silk stood. "What happened to her?"

The man looked uncomfortable. "Policy doesn't allow me to get into the details of that, M. Silk. All I can say is that Dr. McKenzie was assaulted on her way from the parking lot to her building this morning. She expired from her injuries."

"Look, Sergeant, I understand your position, I'm in the business, but this is my contracted we're talking about. We were together for four years. She's dead and I have to know why."

Lennox looked around. Aside from a woman sitting at one end of the waiting room and the desk officer, they were alone in the room. "Let's take a walk," Lennox said.

Outside, the evening had just begun to claim the day. A cool breeze brought a slight fishy smell inland. The smell of decay. Of death.

"This is off the record and you never heard it from me," Lennox said.

Silk nodded.

"One of the *ausvelters* broke quarantine between the bed check last night and assembly this morning. A New Earther. OhQue doesn't know how he slipped the wards and got out but he did. We'll find him, he can't get far without logging onto pubtrans, but for the moment, he's out of reach. We think Dr. McKenzie must have run into him as he fled. The guy panicked and there was a struggle. You know how *ausvelters* are, they're violent, stuff like this happens all the time out on the frontier. It was unfortunate, she was in the wrong place at the wrong time. I'm sorry."

Silk stared at the man. How could something like this happen? To Mac?

"We'll pick him up soon enough and he'll get a fast ride to brainsleep. I know that's not much consolation, but he'll pay for what he did."

Silk didn't know what to say. Was this the truth? Lennox sounded sincere, but Silk had heard bigger lies with straighter faces behind them. He had done it himself. The OhQue squirt was that Dr. Gemma McKenzie-Ryan had died as a result of an accident, a simple fall that had been made fatal due to a freak landing, could have happened to anybody. Whatever SuePack's investigators turned up would follow that line until they had a better story. If they caught the killer, then it would be learned that the information released to the media had been structured

to lull the assassin into a false sense of security until he could
be apprehended. If by some miracle he was not captured, if
he swam to the mainland or stole transportation and eluded
the authorities, they'd stay with the accident story. Silk knew
how it worked. The truth was like gold, too valuable to give
out in major chunks; the truth needed to be melded with lesser
metals, alloyed because it was too soft to wear well without a
harder adulterant. The lilies didn't need to be upset, life was
tough enough already.

He thanked the sergeant for his help. After the man went
back into the station, Silk wandered to where he had parked
his bicycle. He didn't feel like going home yet, the cube would
feel too damned empty without her.

Ah, fuck, Mac, why did you have to die?

He climbed onto the recumbent bike and pointed it in a
direction. By the time he had gone half a klick he was in
high gear, pumping as hard as he could, fairly flying along
the darkening road. Bugs bounced off the small windshield,
some of them clearing the rim to smack into his face. He didn't
bother to wipe them away. They made wet spatters on his cheek
but that didn't matter, his cheeks were already wet.

The worst part was, he hadn't realized how much he had
really cared about her. He was a spindoc, oh-so-cool, above all
the lilies because he was behind the scenes, in the know, sophisticated, clever. Only now, Mac was gone and he was alone, his
life wrecked, his plans, everything.

Fuck. Oh, fuck.

King wore silicone slippers and surgical gloves as he used the
pickgun on the cube's lock. It was dark and he had unscrewed
the bulb in the security lamp two seconds after its motion sensors
flicked it on, but he didn't want to be standing around out here
for long.

The pickgun vibrated, the delta-shaped knob of the thin metal
strip clattered against the pin tumblers of the old-style deadbolt
lock. He twisted with the torsion tool at the same time. It was
a long twenty seconds before the door opened. It had been too
long, he was out of practice. Dreadful how the skills went if
you didn't exercise them. If there wasn't a key hanging on a
nail or something just inside, he wasn't going to be able to
lock the door when he left, but that wasn't important, not if
he found what he wanted. If there was a key, King would use

it. If the guy came home and the door was locked, he'd think he must have lost the key somehow. As the door swung open, he reached up and tightened the security lamp.

Inside, King quickly used his suppressor to lay an electronic blanket over the cube, in case there was an alarm system. The boyfriend was a spider and his office was here, so he'd have a computer and it could well be set up to cast a cry for help. The suppressor was a very nice toy and if the technogeeks in The Scat knew he had this one, they would be most upset—this particular paean to the electronic geniuses who created it was supposed to have been destroyed in the big L.A. quake three years ago. True enough, King's cube had been flattened and him nearly with it, but he had known even then his days would be numbered with the agency. So they'd issued him a replacement for the suppposedly crushed device—he'd cobbled together something that wouldn't pass a close look by anybody who knew anything about such circuitry but that had easily convinced his supervisor. When he was "retired" he naturally turned in all of his officially issued gear, but the stolen suppressor, though highly illegal, was worth its weight in diamonds.

King relocked the door behind him and looked around. Aside from the gloves and slippers he was still in his Mike costume, but he would certainly play hell trying to explain how he had wandered into a securely locked cube. He shoved the suppressor and pickgun into his purse with the torsion tool and pulled the little fléchette pistol out in exchange. He lit the inside lights at the control panel. People expected to see lights in a house after dark, not the beam of a battery torch probing around. Using a flashlight in an empty house was amateur stuff. If he had to use the weapon, it would probably not be fatal—the myoelectric charge the little darts carried were supposed to stun and not kill, but sometimes a weak heart might cause problems. If he had to use the gun, he was probably in dire trouble and he needn't worry about such things. The contracted lover was out and the driveway was a long one. If he came home, King would have plenty of warning from the squeal, enough time to escape. But King also thought it likely the boyfriend would be away for a time. That tended to be the pattern of those who had just lost a loved one, especially if they otherwise lived alone. Home was where the memories lay in waiting.

King started his search.

The obvious he checked first. He'd read *The Purloined Letter*, it would be naive to think everything of value was locked away in a vault somewhere. People sometimes left precious gems and wads of cash lying on a table; once, he had come across a shoebox full of platinum coins next to a trash bin under a sink. Of course, that for which he now searched was worth a lot more than mere platinum.

Much more.

And if the deceased doctor had been clever and paranoid, he would play hell finding where she'd hid it. Vast amounts of information could be shrunk to the size of a period, did you have the proper tools, and hidden in the middle of a thirty-volume hard-copy encyclopedia, becoming virtually impossible to locate. Not that he thought the woman had access to such tools or expertise offhand; still, many things were possible. His belief—and hope—was that the doctor had not had sufficient time to do more than hurried work.

He opened the refrigerator and pawed through the blocks of frozen dinners. He didn't have an awful lot more to go on at the moment. The doctor was dead. The *ausvelter* had run, not very bright, but in his shoes King supposed he would have done the same. Given what the man had done, he was certainly going to become an historical footnote as soon as anybody who knew what was going on found and finished with him. With the spin put on the situation, King and his alter ego were in the clear, so he wasn't worried about that.

Frozen cabbage. How awful. Who could eat such stuff?

King continued his search.

Zia Rélanj arrived at the port almost an hour early. She had time to make certain her personal gear was checked through, to get a bite of what would probably be her last real food until she got back. Ship food was awful, and all the Elers ate was grass or some variation thereof, flesh foods being frowned upon and very expensive. Not that she had to worry about money, Nessie's account was fat enough and she wouldn't have any trouble drawing what she needed; still, a good agent didn't draw attention to herself and dropping big stads on expensive dinners when you were trying to be unobtrusive wasn't too smart. Whatever else she might be, she was a good agent. She had spent weeks working on her accent; she could pass for a native Spanglese-speaker, including a Hong Kong lilt that ought to fool a local. She'd start out using her cover, that of a New Earth teacher come to sightsee on the homeworld, but there might be times when she had to shift out of that in a hurry. Her cover was thick, she could recite it backward and forward all the way to her great-grandparents, and any check from offworld would go straight to Nessie's comp to be vetted. She had microspeck documents for half a dozen identities under the fingernail polish of her right pinkie, complete with valid credit lines. Using a common holoproj camcorder, she could impress any of those IDs onto a blank card or cube and instantly become somebody completely different. That was an unlikely event, but part of what made her a good op was that she took care of those little details.

Terrans probably assumed everybody from offworld was a spy. Zia thought that was the real reason they stuck everybody into a thirty-day quarantine the minute they touched down, the disease stuff was only a cover. It would give them a chance to check out every person who wasn't a native. Fine, let them look, it wouldn't matter, she would come up clean on any scan. If it went as planned, she could make her collection while she was still quarantined—she would change liners twice along the way so that the dropship she wound up falling to E1 on would land at the same processing center as her quarry. Everything was arranged, she had good reasons for making the trip that way, fake relatives to visit, scheduled sights to see.

A tall man with more muscle than average smiled at her from two tables over as she finished her steak. She mechanically returned his smile, but shook her head and pointed at her chrono. He shrugged and spread his hands. Mutual regret.

Well, not really. Quick sex in a port sleepbox wasn't her idea of fun. Actually, fun and sex didn't go together for her. Sex was part of her business, something you did to loosen tongues or bind somebody to you. It was a tool, nothing more, and if you needed that release, you could do it better by yourself, with a lot less risk.

Silk glided toward his cube from up the hill, coasting the last hundred meters. He switched his bike's lamps off halfway down the street and rolled across the yard, not bothering to use the driveway. He was exhausted, both from the emotional drain and the physical effort he'd put out in the last hour. He'd probably covered twenty, twenty-five klicks, nearly running into several tourists and almost getting hit by a bus once when he ran a blinking light at a busy intersection. It didn't matter.

He climbed off the bike, let it fall onto its side. Started for the stairs.

A methodical search of an average cube could take days. Certainly there was a veritable plethora of things that could remain undiscovered in a hurried look of only a couple of hours. Even so, a professional operative developed a kind of extrasensory perception about such activities after doing dozens of them. This one did not feel as if it were going to be successfully resolved just at the moment.

King was rummaging through a drawer full of woman's clothes in the bedroom, feeling less hopeful all the time, when he heard the creak of the wooden stairs.

Damn! He hadn't heard the electronic squeal he'd set up at the end of the driveway! Who could that be? Somebody coming to visit?

He moved to a window and peered out carefully. With the lights on, he'd be visible from without, so the glance was quick and mostly covered.

There climbed the contracted, his bicycle lying on the ground behind him.

King felt a flash of adrenaline, a hot jolt that strobed him like a lightning bolt. He would not be able to exit in time, not unless he were willing to leap from a second-story window and even then not likely he could manage it without being seen. But it was hardly reason for panic. This would not be the first time such a thing had happened. There were contingency plans. There were always fallback positions and he had already marked several such in his mind.

Depard King went to hide.

Silk unlocked the door and stepped inside. The small kitchen gleamed under the overhead lights, empty, sterile, as if mocking him. He enjoyed cooking—had enjoyed it—but the idea of food nauseated him. He had eaten something this morning, though offhand he could not remember what the hell it had been.

It didn't matter.

He trudged into the bedroom, almost sobbed when he looked at the empty bed. All the lights in the cube seemed to be on, he couldn't remember doing that, but it didn't matter. He sprawled on the bed and stared at the ceiling. He was tired but not sleepy. He lay there for a long time, and all he did was stare—and grieve.

King sat on the floor of the dead woman's closet, dozing in spite of himself. The contracted had been home and lying on the bed with all the lights on for almost four hours. From his breathing and small movements, King knew the man was awake—or had been the last time King himself had been fully so—and if he didn't go to sleep soon, King was going to have to urinate into whatever container he could find in the dark closet.

But the sound of the man's breathing had changed. It was deeper, slower, even. Good. About time.

Carefully, moving so slowly as to seem almost motionless, King slid the middle-hinged door open a crack. He angled himself so he could see the bed.

Asleep, for certain.

King breathed an inward sigh of relief. Now he could depart safely. The man would never know he'd been here. True, he had not accomplished what he had set out to accomplish, but he could return on another occasion and continue his search. Though he was relatively sure that would be a waste of his time here, he knew better than to assume such and let it go. If when he finished he had not found that which he sought, then it would be time for other avenues. King was a student of history, had in fact been a professor of such before he had been induced to join the agency. He knew that great mistakes had often arisen from tiny errors. Yes, he had a bad temper that caused him grief, but he was not a stupid man because of that.

He moved the door with great care and extreme slowness, opening it only enough to allow himself to edge past without touching it. He stayed on the floor on his hands and knees and slid along as quietly as he could. Once he achieved the bedroom's exit, he felt much bet-

ter. Now he stood and started for the cube's door—Came
then the sound of the man in the bedroom stepping onto
the floor.

King darted toward the kitchen and dropped behind the
counter. The cube's exit was in sight of the short hallway
leading to the bedroom and the fresher and it was his guess
that the man was going to the latter—unless King had made
some kind of noise . . . ?

But—no. The footsteps went into the fresher. The sound of
urine splashing into the chembowl was loud in the quiet cube.
King envied the man. If he didn't void his own bladder soon,
he was going to be *extremely* uncomfortable. And unless the
man wanted a late night snack, he would likely finish and
return to bed in a moment.

Still, King held ready the small fléchette pistol. Just in
case.

Silk stood over the bowl, pissing, leaning against the wall
behind the toilet with one hand supporting him as the piss
flowed. He'd been dreaming of peeing, that's what woke
him up.

He finished. Put the seat and lid down automatically before
he realized it didn't matter. Mac wasn't going to give him a
hard time for leaving it up.

That was the thought that did it. He sobbed, lost it, began to
cry. He hadn't cried since he'd been fourteen and his dog had
been squashed by a mail truck, but he made up for it now. He
sat on the closed toilet and it flowed from him, tears and sobs
and wordless keening.

King heard the man break down in the fresher, heard him
begin crying. He nibbled at his lip. It was not his fault. If the
woman had been *reasonable,* she could have been rich instead
of dead. If she hadn't tried to hurt him . . .

Reason stood little chance against the truth, however. He
had lost his temper. Had he maintained his calm, he would
not be here, listening to a man he did not know giving vent
to his emotion alone in a fresher.

Well. There was nothing to be done for it. Things had
happened as they did, time's arrow had yet to be reversed
by humans, done was done.

Did a man spend his life looking over his shoulder at every

possible branching of his path he *could* have taken, he would never accomplish anything. One must learn from history so as not to repeat it, but one must not waste one's energy or time worrying about what *might* have been.

Sorry, King thought. But people die every day and the galaxy continues on quite well without them. Consider yourself lucky you are one of those as yet unselected by the Fates, crying man.

In his career he had caused more than a few people pain and that was part of how things must be. Like a medic or a social worker, King had learned how to distance himself from too much involvement with the feelings of those with whom he had to interact. That way lay his own emotional stability. One must consider one's own self first.

Finish your tears, he thought, and go back to bed. My bladder will thank you.

It took him low and it was probably not finished with him but the grief ebbed. Silk wiped his face with a wet towel, took a couple of deep breaths, and went back to the bedroom. He sat on the edge of the bed and stared at his lap. He supposed he could undress.

Go back to sleep, King thought. Or your kitchen will be puddled with urine—wait. Here was a thought. The sink was directly behind him. He could stand and use it. He had to do something, the cramp had turned into a real pain and he was worried that soon he might get to the point where he couldn't pee at all, hold it long enough and that was possible. He couldn't be seen from the bedroom. Yes.

The thought quickly became the deed. King stood, untabbed his shorts, and took aim at the wall of the sink so that the urine would run down it quietly . . .

The sense of relief as the flow began was exquisite.

Silk had started to undress when he heard water gurgling down the sink in the kitchen. Odd. He didn't hear the pipes— this was an old cube, the plumbing was crappy—but there was definitely liquid flowing in there. All the fixtures in the cube were connected and what happened in one you could hear all over the place. He and Mac had laughed about that—

Don't think about Mac.

Curious, Silk padded quietly to the doorway and peered out. Couldn't see anything. Probably just his imagination. He moved a meter or so up the hall—

Jesus! There was a tourist pissing into his sink!

NINE

FOR A MOMENT, Silk was frozen, unable to think past the obvious. What was a tourist doing there, draining his lizard into the kitchen sink? How had he gotten in? Was this a drunk so desperate for a toilet he would climb a flight of stairs and use a sink?

Silk's built-in editor grabbed that one and ran with it:

Wouldn't a guy who had to pee that bad just do it in the yard? Behind a bush somewhere? What kind of guy climbed stairs to piss in a sink?

"Hey! What the fuck are you doing?"

The man spun, slinging a line of piss across the kitchen in a long arc. He reached for something on the counter—

There was nothing wrong with Silk's vision. He'd seen enough entcom action-adventure vids to know a gun when he saw one. Even as the tourist brought the little weapon up, Silk scrambled backward toward the bedroom.

The gun made a not very loud *whump!*

Something thunked into the wall a few centimeters away from Silk's head.

"Shit!"

Silk spun and nearly dived at the bedroom. He slammed the door behind himself—Christ, he had never realized how thin and cheap the plastic door was before—set the pitiful latch and his mind went into full fight-or-flight mode: Run!

There was nowhere to go except out the window.

Fuck it, it wasn't that high up here, the ground was pretty soft, do it!

The window was cheaper than the door. He pulled on it. Panic made him too strong. The force of his frantic tug buckled the thin aluminum frame around the plastic and it jammed in the track, open only a handspan. Fuck!

The other window opened over the driveway, a fall to the plastcrete might break an ankle, but the fucking tourist had a gun!

Yeah, and even now he might be coming this way to use it on you. The door won't slow him down, he'll shoot you in the back as you climb out!

Panic geysered. He was going to die.

He was looking right at his crossbow where it lay on the antique table Mac had made him buy and it seemed like hours—like years—before what he saw made any sense. Because he was a target shooter, he seldom thought of the thing as a weapon, but it was, countless thousands of soldiers had died from being shot with a quarrel from one of these things! The quarrels he had were only target arrows, the points were just pointed metal caps, but even so, they'd be effective at close range.

Silk lunged for the crossbow.

King ran for the cube's exit. This was burned, the guy had seen him and in his own panicked reaction, he had fired a fléchette, and worse, he had missed.

The mark of a civilized man was knowing when to leave the party and this one was over. It was time to leave, and quickly.

Silk heard the door shut. Had the tourist left? Had he been frightened off? Silk supposed he should go and check, but he stood in front of the closed bedroom door with the crossbow loaded and pointed right at the middle of it, afraid. What if the guy had just slammed the door but was sitting out there with the gun aimed right where his head would be when he came through the door? Silk had a quick vision of his skull exploding like a bad entcom vid's villain. No. He was going to stay right here.

"Bubbles!" he yelled. "Open a com to the local police!"

If his computer heard him, she did not answer.

Well. There was a comset next to the bed. He would call manually—

He heard the sound of footsteps on the driveway.

Silk moved to the other window and without thinking slid it open. Saw the big man running toward the street a dozen meters up the drive.

"Hey! Hey!"

What the fuck are you doing? He has a fucking gun, *you stupid asshole!*

The running man turned slightly, looking over one shoulder. There was enough ambient light for Silk to see him snap the gun up. A couple more of those compressed air *whumps!* rose up to Silk's window.

Duck, asshole, duck! He's shooting at you again!

But without conscious thought, Silk brought the crossbow up. He put the sight dot on the man's upper back—it was hard to keep there, the running man was bouncing around—and fired. The twang of the bow was quite loud in the bedroom.

The fleeing man fired his gun again at the same moment. Something stung Silk at the base of his neck and he felt an electric jolt that spasmed him into unconsciousness . . .

King's pain was laced liberally with rage. The man had shot him! With some kind of long dart! He could feel the point of it grate against something as he ran; he had reached back and felt it lodged in his back just below his right shoulder blade. It hurt, but it didn't feel as if it were dangerous. If it had been charged, the charge must have been depleted, and if it were chemmed, the medication had not taken effect during the time since he'd been hit, at least two minutes.

He had to get back to his room unseen and deal with this. Damn it all!

When Silk came to, it was through a haze of body aches, as if he had been swimming for hours and was sore from the exertion. His head also hurt, throbbing, and there was something jagged stuck in his throat, and what the hell was he doing lying on the floor—?

It came back to him all of a moment: the tourist with the gun, shooting at the man with his crossbow . . .

Holy shit.

He pulled the tiny dart from his neck and stared at it. It looked almost like a kind of squat arrow, all metal, some kind of electronic device smaller than a speck embedded under a clear window of plastic near the tip. The speck looked like a superconductor capacitor—there was a similar one in the sight assembly of his crossbow scope—must hold some kind of high-voltage charge. Just like in the fucking vids, a stun gun fléchette. Jesus!

"Bubbles?"

The computer still wasn't answering—he remembered calling out to her before—maybe the tourist—tourist, hell—the burglar had damaged her.

Still holding the dart, Silk hurried into his office.

The computer looked okay. "Bubbles?"

No response. He pulled the keyboard out of the drawer and punched the manual power-up. Nothing. Damn, there was some kind of lock on the system, and there was a way to clear it, but it had been so long since he'd had to use it he'd forgotten what it was? Power and push down the little cloverleaf key? Yeah, that was it . . .

"Logging com to Hana Police," Bubbles said suddenly.

"What happened? Why didn't you do that when the cocksucker was in here shooting at my ass?"

"I was suppressed. Electronic jamming."

"Hana Police Department," came a voice. No visual.

Silk stared at the computer console. "Suppressed? That's not supposed to be possible."

"Hana Police, may we help you?" Visual sparkled on. It was the desk cop Silk had seen earlier. How much earlier? What time was it now? How long was he out—?

"Sir?"

"Oh. Sorry. This is Venture Silk. I've just had a burglar break into my cube."

"Is he still there?"

"No."

"Well, we'll send a unit over—"

"But he shot at me with a fucking dart gun before he left." Silk held the little fléchette up in front of the com's camera.

"Damn!" the policeman said. "Stay right there, there's a scooter on the way!"

The two uniformed officers were excited about the break-in, that was easy enough to tell. First they ran around the yard, checking to make certain the burglar was really gone. Both carried stun wands loaded with hot-sleep spray. Silk had heard that stuff was nasty, it made your eyes and nostrils swell shut and then it put you into a coma from which you awoke in a few minutes puking up everything you had eaten since you were born. Both of the policemen had their wands out waving them, looking—and obviously hoping for—a target.

"No sign of 'im, bro'," the older of the two said. He was tall and skinny to the other cop's short and stout.

The stout one picked up the crossbow and shook his head. "You shot at the guy with this?"

"Yeah."

"You not supposed to have this here, bro'," Skinny said as Stout handed him the bow.

"It's legal, I checked it out yesterday for repair. License is on file under my ID."

Stout shrugged. "Didn't see no arrow out there."

"It would be buried up to the fletching in the ground if it hit the yard at an angle," Silk said. "It hit the plastcrete, it could have bounced all the way across the street."

"Or it could have maybe turned the guy into a luau soyroast," Skinny said. He gestured with one finger extended, mimicking a turning spit.

Silk shook his head. He didn't know if he had hit the guy, and if he had, how would that make him feel? It ought to make him feel sick, the idea of skewering another human being and hurting or maybe even killing him. Ought to, but didn't. The guy had been shooting at him. Fuck him.

"Investigators are on the way," Stout said, touching the complug in his left ear. "Fuckers."

"Not your guys?"

"Goddamned SuePack assholes. We're lucky, six months from now we get a report about this, it don't say nothing anyway."

"I got the statement recorded and the pix of the scene," Stout said. "We'll stick around until the SuePack guys get here."

"Not like the entcom vids on the holoproj, being a peace officer," Skinny said. "You cite tourists for piddly shit, maybe break up a fight now and then between two drunks. Anything bigger than that, SuePack sends in the heavyweights."

Silk nodded but didn't care. Maybe it wasn't all that exciting for the cops but his night had been a fucking entcom drama.

Space travel was about as exciting as riding a ferry from Frogtown to the Offshore Islands on a calm day in the fog,

Zia thought. Maybe not even that interesting—in the depths of Empty Space, there wasn't anything to see. No windows and even if there had been, all that was out there was a flat and dead grayness.

Zia stood in the small bar on the upper deck, watching the fifteen or so patrons sip or toke at their chem. Of this particular group, there was a couple celebrating their sixtieth anniversary by taking a trip to the storm resort on Ventoblanco; three or four single people who had indicated they would not be averse to spending some time in bed with her, thank you, no: assorted business or minor political types on boring missions to Shinto or Ujvaros or Hock Miete.

She sipped at her beer, a mildly bitter brew that would not win any prizes, except if maybe they gave one for bland. Of the three hundred or so travelers onboard, she was probably the only spy.

Still, you never knew. Virtually any of the others could be in her business. If she were going to pick somebody to cast in the part from this crowd, she'd go with the older couple. They were just past normal middle-age at eighty or so, all covered with smile wrinkles and heads full of naturally white hair. The last people anybody would suspect of being spies. Which probably meant it would be better to go with somebody else—paranoid authorities sometimes figured the last people they would ordinarily suspect should be the ones they ought to worry about the most. Maybe the fat produce salesman going to try and do business with the Paradisians. Or the young woman with the plain face and dumpy body who was off to see a dying relative.

She took another sip from the benign beer. It hardly looked as exciting as the interstellar transit ads tried to portray it. Travel across the galaxy on one of our beautiful starliners. Get from New Earth to York in less time than it would take to drive from Beagle to Candu City in your personal motorcoach. Visit exotic planets by slipping the bonds of space and time and outrunning light as if it were standing still . . .

What Zia knew about the Rhomberg-Morrison Pull Through FTL Drive was enough to get by in a conversation with any-body else who was less than a fairly bright physicist, but that wasn't much. Somehow the drive allowed a vessel containing it to move light-years in hours and that was all most people knew or cared about. And since a trip between any two of the

eleven inhabited worlds in the Seven Stellar Systems where
humans were able to set up shop took only a few days at
most, nobody had spent a lot of money turning most of the
standard starliners into homes-away-from-home. There were
luxury vessels for those who had stads to burn, but the teacher
Zia was supposed to be wouldn't be traveling first class. The
ships that flew the big void were inside a lot like ocean liners,
you could move around, but it was also much the same as
being in a medium-sized apartment plex, which was to say
not the most interesting place in the galaxy.

It hardly seemed like they were moving. The gravity mostly
worked, though it would sometimes have these unexpected
little microfluctuations that made your stomach roil. The air
was stale and always smelled like whatever cleaner they used
to filter out the more obnoxious stinks; the food was crappy,
a lot of processed stuff that would stack neatly in storage.
The sleeping compartments were not much bigger or better appointed than those on a basic maglev train. Even on
this particular ship, the *Pride of Mchanga*, you could get
a larger room but not that much bigger and for a whole
lot more cost. Oh, to be sure, they ran vids in the little
theater or on your compartment's proj, you weren't socia-
ble; there was a library and a gym, but Zia was prevented
from using those as she would have back on E2—her cover
went into effect before she boarded. The somewhat-shy and
altogether too-prim-for-her-taste teacher she was supposed to
be would hardly read retro-Nihonnese samurai novels even if
they were available in the ship's library, which they weren't,
nor would she beat anybody she was likely to freestyle spar
with in the gym's fighting ring because she wouldn't spar
with anybody in the first place. She probably wouldn't even
shuck her clothes to swim naked in the miniscule pool with
the other travelers. Still, it was part of the job and while
it might be boring, it was going to pay off big when she
got done. It was like a role in a play or vid, you became
your character and who you were in real life went away—
you weren't supposed to think of things that your character
wouldn't think of. There'd be plenty of time for that later.
Plenty of time.

So, for now, she would play the role and think about the
rewards waiting when she got home. But she had had enough
of this lousy beer for now, thank you.

She left the pub and went to explore the ship. In the manner of a shy prim-ed teacher, of course.

Depard King had a decent aid kit he had come by while working for The Scat. He had picked it up from a medical center he'd infiltrated as an orderly and it was as good as such things got, for its size. There was an adequate diagnostic computer that would accept vox or keyboard input for symptoms, enough medication loaded into the assorted dispensing chambers to treat a busload of ill patients, and various probes and sensors easily programmed and utilized by someone with even a rudimentary knowledge of the hard- and software. After pulling the shaft of the dart from his back—no small accomplishment in itself—he had pressed a sensor patch over the wound. The computer had done its work silently and announced that he had a puncture wound through the epi- and dermis, muscles whose names he couldn't recall, several torn or cut blood vessels and a chipped scapula, but no major damage. King allowed the thing to pump whatever pain blockers and antibiotics it deemed necessary into him, then had it staple and seal the wound. It would leave a scar, but he could live with that; a plastic surgeon could revise that at some later date, did he wish it so. For now, it was sufficient that he be repaired.

With the pain blockers operative, he felt sufficiently better to chide himself for the unhappy events of this entire business. In his hurry to acquire that which he sought, he had become sloppy indeed. The prize had been too rich to do his usual methodical background investigation, in this race there would be no second-place winner, one must be first or last. So, he had leapt in, thinking to strike quickly, trusting to his experience and skills to make up for his lack of preparation. So much for that thought. He recalled what his instructor in Escape and Evasion Tactics had said on the first day of class back when he had been younger and—apparently—wiser: "People, we operate on the Six-P Principle here: Proper planning prevents piss-poor performance."

Despite the fubar situation in which he was now embroiled, King had to smile. Certainly the piss part of that old homily had come to pass. If his bladder had a larger capacity, it was likely he would have escaped from the woman's cube unseen by her paramour.

Ah, well. There was nothing to be done for that. As much as he would like to revise that history, he knew full well it would not come to pass, at least not for some considerable time. Later, perhaps, when he was at a far remove from this debacle, he could cast it in a different light. For the moment, he had to recalibrate his instruments and seek another method to secure that which he sought. The contracted had been alerted, he had seen King's Mike persona, and thus Mike would have to disappear. The man was violent, dangerously so, and doubtless would be feeling some worry after the violation of his home. He would therefore be somewhat more likely to take precautions, so returning to the scene of that crime would be risky.

King, drifting a little in the chemical fog of the medications, considered the contracted. He would have to do some research on the man. Perhaps the relationship the man had enjoyed with the deceased doctor was such that she entrusted him with her secrets?

That was certainly one line King should follow. Yes, the fellow had shot him with a barbaric device, and to be sure, King would repay him in kind did the occasion arise, but he was a professional. The job had to come first, the goal was much more valuable than beginning a vendetta. What was the old saying? Living well is the best revenge?

Yes. That was true. Once he had what he needed, the dead woman's lover would mean nothing.

He could kill him then without a qualm of regret.

That thought made him smile again.

TEN

THE SUEPACK INVESTIGATORS were too slick and too smooth for Silk's taste. Yeah, they were supposed to project an aura of competence but they were so condescending and on-top-of-things he wanted to trip one of them just to see how he'd handle the surprise of a sudden fall. As he had with the two local cops, Silk looked at these two in terms of physical attributes. Here, though, both were perfect, tall, fit, clean-cut, well dressed. Both of them had brown hair. The differences in their accents were negligible—they spoke in well-modulated tones, standard midwestern holoproj announcer's popvox. They could have been brothers. The only difference in their demeanor was that one smiled constantly, flashing his bright and perfect teeth, and the other didn't smile at all.

"I hardly think you have anything to worry about, M. Silk," Smiles said. He flashed his insincere grin yet again. "It would seem a simple case of a less-than-able burglar."

"My contracted was killed this morning," Silk said. "And tonight a man breaks into my cube and shoots me. If you were me, wouldn't you worry?"

"An unfortunate coincidence," Serious said.

"What about the *ausvelter* who broke out of quarantine?"

"From your description, M. Silk, it is obviously not the same man."

"He could have changed his clothes."

"But not likely his height and weight and general build, not in so short a time. Besides, why would he have come here?"

Silk didn't have an answer to that. He didn't have an answer to anything.

"Did you find the bolt?"

Smiles took that one. "The local police are still searching for it. It will turn up."

"We appreciate your concern," Serious said, "but we have everything under control. We'll no doubt collect the criminal in short order and find out the reasons for his visit here."

"You haven't caught the *ausvelter* yet."

"We will, M. Silk, we will." Serious almost cracked a smile of his own. "Criminals are generally inept, they wouldn't *be* criminals if they were well-adjusted members of society."

"He was adept enough to have gotten his hands on a gun," Silk said.

"Which he did not use particularly well," Smiles said.

Silk rubbed at his neck where the paramedic had sprayed a small blob of statskin over the tiny wound. "He managed to hit me with it."

"But only once out of several attempts, the first of which was at a much closer range. A lucky shot."

Silk shook his head. These guys weren't going to let anything he threw at them stick or even leave a smear.

"Why don't you just try to put this behind you?" Serious said. "Nothing was stolen, you haven't been permanently damaged, the criminal is probably halfway to the mainland by now. We'll catch him eventually and you'll be notified when we do."

Smiles and Serious exchanged quick glances.

Smiles said, "I think we have all we need here, M. Silk. If you think of anything else you might have neglected to tell us, you can reach us through any South Pacific interlink, just mention today's date and location and it will be routed to us."

If he smiled one more time Silk thought he was going to scream, but for once the man did not show his expensive vat-growns.

End of interview. And as Silk knew from his own experience in such things, also the end of his involvement as far as they were concerned. He was a lily to them, a civilian, and he didn't need to know anything more than they had told him. Not now, not ever.

He watched them walk down the stairs. The night was shot, dawn wasn't far away, and he wasn't going to be doing any more sleeping anytime soon. Too many questions rattling around in his brain: Mac, dead and why? The man who had come to pee in the sink, who was he and what had he been doing here? For his contracted to be killed and then his cube broken into within a day smelled of more than simple coincidence. What did it mean? What was going on here? Which god had he angered to be treated so?

Silk watched the pair of look-alike agents enter their electric cart and leave. The two local policemen were still moving back and forth, using metal detectors set to locate the stainless-steel tip and butt plate of the missing quarrel. Maybe he had hit the running man. If so, he was glad of it. That didn't make him feel good about himself, but there it was.

What did it all mean?

King watched as the travel bag full of Mike's identity splashed into the deep hole over which he had the small rental boat idling. There were enough pieces of volcanic rock in with the clothing and ID so that the bag disappeared quickly. The water here, according to the chart he had consulted, was nearly eighty meters deep. It was unlikely a tourist diving to see the fish would happen across it on the bottom and even if one should do so, there was no way to link the bag to King's new identity.

The morning sun sparkled on the water. The air carried a distinctly fishy odor. A clump of seaweed floated past. Rest in peace, Mike.

King turned the boat and adjusted the siphons so that it began to move at a stately pace. He was a new man now, and he looked very little like the Maynard Isaac Clark persona on its way to the bottom of the ocean. True, he was the same size, that was difficult to change, but he wore padding under his shirt and shorts so that he looked fat rather than fit. His clothing was still somewhat touristy, but less colorful than Mike's had been, more in tune with what an upper middle-class businessman from Australia would wear. His formerly black hair was now a mousy brown and shorter; he wore expensive sunglasses, his skin was three shades darker than it had been yesterday, and a mild allergic reaction to an injection of special chem had given him enough edema so that his face was slightly bloated, softening the lines of his underlying bone structure. He'd used some of the chem on his ears, ears were hard to disguise, and they too looked different. His walk was not the same, his manner altered from Mike's, his attitude more superior. Bentley Smythe was unlikely to be recognized by anybody who had ever met Mike Clark. He had a different room in a different hotel, reserved in advance at the same time Mike's room had been booked. A third room was available under yet another identity, should that become necessary, paid for in advance whether it was used or not. All standard operating procedure for an operative in his position. True, such expenses were now his and not The Scat's, but even so, he was hardly destitute. And if things went well, money would be the last thing he would ever have to worry about. He would be richer than The Scat. There was a pleasant thought with which to cruise in a small boat along the coast of Maui on a bright and balmy morning. And money was actually the least of it.

While time was of the essence and he could hardly afford to dawdle, he would arm himself with more knowledge before he did anything precipitous. The Six-P Principle had not become obsolete since first he had heard it and had he hewn to it before, he would likely be done with the endeavor by now.

Ah, well. Such was the way a man learned. Sometimes the more difficult path was the one necessary for the lesson to be absorbed properly. In a few days, at most, he would know everything there was to know about one Venture Silk and his relationship with the departed woman.

Then would Depard King move. And properly this time.

The space station in high orbit somewhere between that of Luna and Earth was one of the newer ones. It was no less shoddy because of that. Mass drivers shot partially finished construction material from the moon's surface to a place where the crews could use it, and the cheap cast plastics and hastily smelted metal that made up the station did not give you the feeling of security when you looked at the place, especially from the inside. The station was cold, the corridors narrow and held together with visible rivets and bolts. Zia felt as if she sneezed too hard it might rupture a wall. Yes, it was only supposed to be a transfer point, for those coming and going to Earth, but still. She had been briefed on the history of such places and blowouts were not uncommon. Less than four years ago a station hanging here had turned itself inside out when a big section of wall let go, and eight hundred and some-odd people had been spewed into hard vacuum to burst and freeze in little crystalline clouds of body fluids. An investigation later showed that the failed wall had been leaking air outward for a month and no less than fifty people had reported it. Some tech slapped a patch over the hole and thought that would do it. Zia wondered if the tech had been one of the ones who had gotten the big surprise when the wall shattered. She hoped so; she didn't like incompetent people taking care of dangerous business, especially when it was her beautiful ass at risk.

Then again, most of the people who had died were offworlders, *ausvelters*, and the E1 folks could really care about them. They were snobs down there at the bottom of the local gravity well, planetists who thought they were the elite, the *real* humans, and that everybody else was inferior.

She smiled at that while she stood in the line waiting for the flunky to process her visa. The terrans were certainly going to be in for a surprise in the not-too-distant future. Big surprise, courtesy of the inferior people of E2—

"Fem?"

Zia looked at the young man standing behind the counter. Don't forget who you are, girl.

"S-sir?"

"Your ID number?"

She gave it to him.

"The length of your stay on Earth?"

"Two weeks." Not counting the month of quarantine, of course.

He waved his hands over the light-sensitive input device of his computer console, fluttering his fingers in well-practiced patterns. She could see the back of the proj as the pix and stats flashed into view. He glanced at the screen, then up at her. "Everything seems to be in order, F. Kyle. Enjoy your trip to Earth." He was bored and she was supposed to give him a hesitant and slightly nervous smile. For half a second, she thought about turning the teacher's bland expression into a full heat wanna-fuck-me? look. That would jolt the poor sucker out of his doze, to see this little primrose suddenly blossom into a hothouse orchid. But—no. It would be petty, stupid and nonprofessional of her. She had to watch that, did she want to stay alive and healthy. That was the problem with walking the edge, it made you feel as if you could get away with anything, that you were sharper than anybody else. Dangerous, but part of the appeal. It wasn't worth the risk: who cared what this nobody clerk thought?

So, the little abashed grin.

The clerk was already looking past her at the next person in line when she turned away. Now, if the station didn't explode in the next few hours, she would board a dropbox to the Offworld Quarantine Station at the tiny island of Maui. So far, so good. It was almost too easy.

Silk had taken a couple of days off after the cremation. He had Mac's ashes shipped to her parents, had spoken to them and exchanged grief. They promised to keep in touch with him, though he didn't think they would. He had no particular desire to see or talk to Mac's mother, who looked too much like Mac. He couldn't see her without thinking that maybe Mac might have looked like that someday, only now, she never would.

They'd given him a week off from the port, called it sick leave, it wouldn't even count against his vacation. On the one hand he was glad—the idea of spinning straw into gold didn't much appeal to him at the moment. On the other hand, it would be something to do. Aside from practicing daily at the range and swimming until he was exhausted, he didn't have anywhere he wanted to spend his time. He ate but didn't taste it, slept but didn't seem rested, and felt an emptiness he had never felt before. It wasn't fucking fair that this should happen to him!

Imagine how the contracted and parents and children of all those people who cooked and fell into the ocean inside that dropbox must feel.

Fuck them. He didn't know them. He knew Mac.

Had known Mac.

Jesus.

He couldn't see how things could get much worse than this.

ELEVEN

GONE. HER TARGET was *gone!*

Zia sat on the cot in the tiny cubical the quarantine authorities had issued her and stared at the bare and antiseptic-white wall. The man she had come light-years to collect was not here, a major foul-up, and now what was she supposed to do?

The air was cool, smelled like a hospital back home, and offered not the slightest answer to her question. Despite her normal calm, she was irritated. Damn!

It hadn't taken her long to dig the story out, there were dozens of E2 natives here waiting for their cycle to finish so they could leave and virtually all of them had heard about it. From the eight versions Zia accessed, she put together the common elements into what she thought might be something close to the truth.

The old man from Dogleg Creek was probably as close as anybody:

"Busted himself out," he said. "Man always looked like something was behind him and gaining, spent more time looking over his shoulder than where he was going. Nervous as a pik-bird in a room fulla cats, would come a meter off the floor if somebody coughed too hard. Didn't surprise me none when he disappeared one night after bed check. Dunno how he got out, the doors are locked and there are 'orderlies' with shockstiks roaming the halls alla time, but he did it. Hell, they was dancing around like bugs on a hot skillet the next morning, asking everybody if they seen Spackler, did he say anything, like that."

Zia gave the old man one of her best questioning looks. "Really. How interesting."

"Yeah, they shitting square boulders trying to find him, that's how I know it wasn't he got hauled off by Terran Security for being a spy or some shit like some say. He busted out on his own. Musta been something real bad coming up on him."

The old man smiled at Zia. "My guess is, he left home with something that didn't belong to him, something the E2 bootshiners want back and he didn't want to be here when they showed up."

"You think so?"

"Yeah, that's what I think. I was in the Standing Army for a double-ten, I had friends in AI ops, they used to tell me stories about shit like this. No names, of course."

"Of course."

Now, alone in her room, Zia thought about what she was going to do. The simple pickup of Spackler—he was supposed to be two weeks away from finishing quarantine when she arrived—was in the recycle sewage tank. In theory, she had been supposed to connect with him, let him know who and what she was, and convince him to cancel his quarantine and take the next riser to the space station. It was not unusual for tourists to decide they didn't want to complete their time in quarantine and leave the gravity well for points elsewhere. It happened all the time, the terrans didn't care, one less *ausvelter* cluttering up the works. If he'd been here, she would have convinced him—they would have been sleeping together and if he'd made a crooked move, she would have killed him—and he would quickly know that. That would have been his choice: to die here, right now, or go home and face the legal proceedings. Of course, once he was convicted of his crime, he would have been zapped, but Zia would have convinced him he'd only have to pay a heavy fine and do fifteen or twenty years in the penal mines. Given what he'd done, what he had become, twenty years was nothing and he'd know that. In his boots, she wouldn't have believed it for a second, but she was very good at convincing people of what she wanted them to believe . . .

Not that it made any difference now. Spackler was gone, it looked as if he had killed a medic on his way out, and a whole trainload of Terran Security types would be filtering fine looking for him. Shit.

So, her choices.

She could turn around and go home and nobody could blame her. She went to collect a package and it was not there, it wasn't her fault.

She could wait out her quarantine and start looking for him herself. That would give him almost five weeks headstart.

She could do what Spackler had done, escape, and see if she could track him down. He had a few days on her, but that would be better than a month and some.

She wasn't going home empty-handed.

She wasn't going to sit here for another thirty days doing nothing.

So, that left the third alternative.

Zia sighed, but felt better. There were risks, of course, but she would rather take those and have a goal, a plan, than not. And she was one of the best in her business; if she couldn't get out of this bugtrap quarantine, she deserved whatever they'd do if they caught her.

Nessie didn't have much of an organization here on E1, but there were people installed here she could turn to once she got free, she could get a little backup—if she decided she needed any.

Yes. That was the way to go. She'd been here most of a day already. Time to move. Tonight. She would scope the layout and devise her escape tonight. It was that simple.

King, in his new persona, snapped a picture of the Offworld Quarantine Center from the tourist tram as it rolled past the complex. Their security was only fair, and designed to keep people from getting out. Given that the *ausvelter* had managed to slip the bonds and escape unhindered, perhaps "fair" was overly generous a designation. And certainly not many people had attempted to break *in* to the place.

King smiled, his eyes hidden behind the sunglasses. His research on the contracted of the woman he had accidentally canceled was going well. The man was a minor functionary for the local Port Authority, a professional prevaricator who had a few quirks, such as his crossbow hobby, but who would hardly be a major hindrance did King have to continue his efforts in that direction. Now that he knew the man's background, he would be dealt with, did that need arise. And perhaps it would not arise at all, given his latest thoughts. He was armed with a computer rascal that, while not the very latest release, was certainly sufficient to breach the security of a medical comp at a quarantine center. Perhaps the files he sought would come to light as easily as that. One could hope.

While it wasn't necessary for him to physically enter the complex for this particular endeavor, he did have to obtain certain codes before he was ready for his electronic assault. This would entail no small effort and cost, but he was prepared for that. There were other options here, things he could do. The *ausvelter* was still at large, and perhaps King might be the one to find him; the contracted, M. Silk, was a possibility; the departed medic's personal or professional logs awaited his perusal. Certainly this affair was not yet impossible to conclude successfully. A single failure did not always have to put a player out of the game.

An insect flew into the open tram, heading toward King's face. Without thinking, he snapped his hand up and caught the hapless bug, closing his fingers around it and crushing it all of a single quick move. For a moment King felt a quick rush of fear envelop him. He dropped his hand with the smashed insect and glanced around. Nobody seemed to notice, they were all busy looking at the giant carved tiki— an anachronistic and wrongly located object that certainly did not belong on this island—set there for the tourists to ogle. He dropped the dead bug and wiped his palm on his shorts. He was going to have to watch himself, his reflexes had already gotten him into trouble once. A fat executive snatching flies from the air might be unusual enough to stand out in even the torpid memory of a tourist, he most assuredly did not need that. He could not allow himself to fall prey to such things, not if he wanted the prize.

Silk had gone back to work but the challenge that had been there before, the pleasure he had taken in the subtle twisting of truth to suit his company and his own needs, were gone. He did it, he was too much the professional not to manage it, but there was no joy in it now. The company shrink they'd made him visit had told him he would feel grief, that his energy and emotions would be dimmed for a time, but those were words and this was the reality.

Bubbles said, "The media are waiting."

"Fuck them. Let them wait."

But he scanned the data, assembling mechanically in his thoughts the proper spin on the merger proposal the newshounds had sniffed out. It was easy enough, by the numbers, a first-year student intern could do it.

Why had Mac died? It had to mean something, there had to be some reason bigger than a crazed *ausvelter* lashing out. There must be a way to make some *sense* of it, but in the days since it had happened, Silk had not been able to find it.

"All right. Here's the spin. The merger will offer increased prosperity for all concerned. No layoffs are planned at this time, operations will continue as is for the time being, dividends will likely rise."

Bubbles did not speak to that, having no reason to do so.

"Feed it to the butchers and squirt the media in the order of their calls."

"Including Bryce Xong?"

Silk sighed. "No, you can give it to Xong first."

It didn't matter.

The SuePack investigators had not called again, nor had the police, which meant that the man who murdered Mac was still at large. The burglar who had broken into his cube was also still running around out there and Silk couldn't help but think there was some kind of connection between the two. He couldn't see what it might be—unless it was something as simple as what the local cops said, sometimes when people died, the bents out there took notice and tried to profit from it. You were dead, you weren't going to be home watching your stuff anymore, sometimes it was worth a shot and mostly these guys were stupid enough to miss things like whether or not anybody else lived there.

Silk leaned back, pulled the headset off, stared through the window. The glory of another Hawaiian day shined before him, breezes stirring the tropical foliage, the sun offering more of its forever summer.

He was going to have to get on with his life, he knew. Mourning Mac wasn't going to bring her back, there was no grief powerful enough for that miracle.

Silk shook his head. The words versus the reality again. Shit.

"Anything else on the queue?"

"No," Bubbles said.

"Fine. I'm going to the range."

"Take your com."
He nodded. He didn't feel like arguing with her.

Electronic break-ins were considerably less risky to one's person than actual covert operations on-site; still, King knew, there were certain risks. A few basic precautions generally ameliorated these factors to an acceptable level, though there were no titanium-clad guarantees even so.

King sat in the third of the rooms he had procured, his assault system set up on the small desk in the bedroom. The computer console was a more or less standard Sanyo mini-main portable. He had tied its modem into a three-step cellular uplink, routing it first through the restaurant line across the street—the establishment being open only for breakfast and lunch, it was now closed and the phone therein unlikely to be used. The second line was a pay telephone on the Hana Highway across from the old Catholic church. The unit wore an out-of-order sign and the receiver had been removed to further discourage would-be users. The third baffle was one he thought somewhat ironic, that of the also disabled phone in the visitors' center at the OhQue tourist stop. An expert could certainly backwalk the linkage, given sufficient time and equipment, but King doubted whether there was such an expert available locally to begin the process in time. He had his computer's timer going and it would sever the connection three minutes after it began. Even a computer wizard who knew he was coming would have difficulty tracing him that quickly.

Too, the subject of his security breach was not of the highest order, and therefore less likely to be as vigilant as it might be had it more sensitive information to protect. Who really cared if anybody poked around in the medical files of *ausvelters* anyhow?

And finally, the rascal program King would launch was very good, if somewhat dated. Doubtless a cutting-edge full-security watchman would stop his rascal, but King did not think that OhQue would have installed such a thing. One thing his experience working in a governmental agency had taught him was that funding was always less than desired and that it was usually wasted in less efficient ways than buying useful things . . .

He took a deep breath, put on his heads-up display unit, adjusted the earplugs and glasses, and smiled. "Computer, launch primary program," he said.

"Launching program."

Even through the security subrouting, it took only a second for the connection to be accomplished.

"This is the Offworld Quarantine Information Line," came the voice of OhQue's comp. "How may we help you?"

King used the keyboard to input the passby code. He wasn't going to risk leaving a voxprint, even though the rascal was supposed to prevent that on its way out.

"Files," came the voice.

Grinning, King began to type.

Zia had her plan constructed by the time it got dark. The security had been beefed up, according to what she'd found out, but since they weren't really sure how Spackler had gotten out, they had done it more or less across the board.

The locks were electronic and controlled from a central security comp, but anybody with the IQ of a dustfly could bypass one of these cheap devices with a cellular phone and a basic knowledge of tone generators, which Zia certainly had.

The increased number of human guards was more of a problem. You couldn't bet on somebody falling asleep at just the right moment, or going to the fresher, especially not after there'd been a recent breach. For a few days, anyway, the guards would be bustling around trying to look sharp.

There were cams mounted here and there and probably monitored a little better than before Spackler's run. He'd had an easier time of it, a little patience and he probably just skied past a drowsy "orderly" and into the woods, no sweat. They'd be a lot more alert now.

Then again, Spackler wasn't anybody's idea of a dream mate, either, and Zia had already spotted the guard she thought would be interested in finding a place to be alone and naked with her. She flashed her wanna-fuck? smile at him and watched the front of his coverall stir in response. Men made her job so much easier when they thought with the little head instead of the big one. And most of the fem-oriented men she had known thought that way sooner or later. She was pretty sure the men's men thought that way, too, they just had a different focus. It was something she had learned how to use, even before she had gone into the biz. By the time she was fifteen, Zia Rélanj had become an expert in

channeling that particular drive in men. It was almost too
easy sometimes.

She forced herself to be patient, it wouldn't be long now.
A few more hours and she would be out of here. Meanwhile,
she went over her conversations with her homeworlders again,
sorting useful information. There wasn't a lot of it, but there
was some. Spackler had apparently killed a medic when he
flitted, something that was out of character for him, he wasn't
supposed to be especially violent. A measure of his desperation, Zia supposed. Back most people up into a tight enough
corner and push, you could get a big surprise. That probably
meant her story of telling him things would be fine, more or
less, when they got home was not going to lift and hover too
well. The locals would zap his brain, if they caught him, he had
to know that. And if he was willing to terminate somebody to
get away, he was more afraid than she'd been led to believe.

Okay, there was always the backup scenario. She didn't
particularly want to have to use it, but it was there. If he
wouldn't come with her willingly, she had authorization to
bring him kicking and screaming, she could manage to figure
out how. And if *that* failed, there was the last-ditch fallback:
she would go home alone but Spackler would be plant fertilizer
when she did. That wouldn't be quite so glorious a victory but
it wouldn't be a loss, either. Given what her quarry had already
done, she'd have no trouble justifying killing him and making
sure the body never got found. If he gave her too much trouble,
Spackler would be history.

TWELVE

KING LEANED BACK in the cheap hotel chair and stared at the wall. Damnation! He'd spent nearly three hours in real time scanning the files that he'd stolen in a couple of minutes and so far, without any positive results. It would have been too easy for the woman to have stored them under a simple name or obvious code, he hadn't expected that, but thus far, at least, there was no sign of that which he sought. Though he wasn't finished quite yet, it did not look promising. The hundreds of pages of data that had been compressed and squirted from the OhQue comp via the modem link maze he'd constructed were all stored neatly in his own system, the link severed without any apparent notice by anyone in authority. He had gone in and come out without anyone the wiser—including, so it would seem, himself.

Well. Perhaps that was not strictly true. He did know one thing: the departed doctor had discovered the secret and latched onto it for herself. King was able to determine this by induction rather than deduction, but he was fairly certain of it. The *ausvelter* named Spackler from New Earth had ceased to exist, insofar as the medical records section of the OhQue computer files was concerned. It would seem awfully coincidental that of all the patients examined by this quarantine station in the last few weeks, the particular one King sought had been wiped from memory. No, the dead woman had tumbled to Spackler and his little secret and neatly snipped him out and hidden him somewhere, figuratively speaking.

71

So far, she had not cloistered him elsewhere in the medical impedimenta of her own computer system, not unless she was considerably better at electronic manipulation than was Depard King. He thought that doubtful, most doubtful.

He would, of course, finish his scan, would have his computer break down every file he had siphoned to be certain nothing was buried under an alias, but he had to give the woman credit. She had thwarted him. So far.

She deserved to die for that.

Well, perhaps, but would that he had killed her *after* he had prized the information from her.

Ah, well. It was history and might be subject to later revision but for now was more or less unsurmountable. Bringing people back from the dead was not one of King's talents.

He rubbed at his face and eyes, and went back to his work.

Zia had no intention of having sex with the guard-as-orderly. It wasn't so much that he wasn't appealing—he wasn't but she'd had worse—she didn't have the time to waste. All she needed was a few things and she was on her way.

First, she needed some kind of transportation. Since everybody seemed to walk or bike or bus, a bike would be good. If the guard didn't have one, he'd know where she could borrow one. She'd rather take a cart, but since those were relatively rare, that might be noticed and more easily traced. She didn't want to get on a bus, the fewer people who saw her, the better. Second, she'd need to get to a place where she could change her looks and ID. If the guard had a cube, she could use that, though she wouldn't be surprised if he had a bedmate there. And he would probably lie to her about that, assuming there was any kind of legal or understood contract with the mate—unless she asked him in a special way.

She needed to get moving. The best time to leave would be when there were still enough people running around so she wouldn't stand out. This was a resort area and so some things did not shut down at night, but it was a good idea to give yourself all the breaks you could. So she made herself available in the rec room, knowing the guard would be coming in soon.

Sure enough, the man, tall and lean save for a good begin-ning on a potbelly, leered at her when he came into the rec room a few minutes later.

Zia wore a pale green skinsilk shirt cut low in front. She leaned forward a little in her chair when he passed by, enough to give him a good view of her nipples if he wanted to look. This was out of character for her mousy teacher role, but the teacher was about to be shucked like a pair of dirty socks anyhow.

Want to see under my shirt, fella?

He wanted to see, all right.

She thought he might drool on her.

"Evening," he managed, his voice almost a croak.

She smiled. "Boring in here," she said. She waved a hand at the people watching the holoproj or playing cards or something called Ping-Pong.

"It's a nice night for a walk," he said.

"Yeah, I bet. Too bad I can't go outside."

"It could be arranged."

"Really? Oh, I'd really be grateful for that." She inhaled deeply and pushed her breasts up at him.

She thought he was going to have an orgasm right there.

"Uh . . . uh, yeah. Give me a couple of minutes and I'll be right back."

He hurried off and Zia allowed herself a tiny smile at his back. Men. They were so easy. He was running to tell a buddy to cover for him because he was going to get himself some *ausvelter* pussy. She bet he'd be back in less than two minutes.

Sure enough. Minute and a half, if that.

She followed him through the door, stood smiling while he locked it behind him, took his arm as they strolled down the corridor. Another guard smiled at her man, gave him a quick thumbs-up gesture when he thought she wasn't looking. Had to be thinking, hell, this job ain't so bad. I might get lucky, too.

Don't envy him too much, friend. Later, you'll thank your gods I picked the potbellied scarecrow here instead of you. But Zia smiled and gave the guard's arm a suggestive squeeze as they walked. "My. You certainly have a hard muscle," she said. She batted her lashes at him.

"Honey, you don't know the half of it." He led her toward

the second of two locked doors between her and outside.

She smiled, but not for the reason he probably thought. That's where you're wrong, zordo. There won't be any surprises for me, but *you* have one coming.

Silk leaned against the counter in his kitchen, staring at a pot of rice he'd cooked. He wasn't hungry now.

He looked through the window at the warm night. A little cloudy, supposed to rain later on.

He felt cooped up. Maybe he would go for a walk or a bike ride. Something. Anything to get out of here.

King shook his head, temporarily defeated. Nothing. Not a sign of the information. Well. So much for that idea.

It seemed he was going to become more conversant with M. Venture Silk after all. Ah, well. Whatever was required.

Zia smiled professionally as the guard led her toward a stand of thick shrubs on the grounds. Once they were hidden from view, he grabbed her roughly and tried to kiss her, shove himself into her through both sets of clothes and feel her breasts all at the same time.

"Easy, big guy," she said. "Let me get you out and wet you a little first."

She knelt in front of him and untabbed his pants. His erection sprang out through the opening. Nothing to write home about. He probably thought that his life couldn't get any better than this: having his dick sucked in the bushes by a beautiful and exotic *ausvelter*.

While he was still waiting and anticipating the warmth of her mouth, she came up, slammed her fist into his solar plexus in a two-knuckle punch, and knocked the wind out of him.

"Unngg—!"

She hooked her left ankle behind his feet and shoved. He fell backward, stunned and surprised, and she fell on him. Grabbed his penis in one hand and brought out the steel comb she had in her back pocket and pressed it against the sensitive flesh.

"Move and I'll saw your cock off," she said. She smiled at him.

He kept trying to breathe, shaking his head as if he couldn't believe it. She could understand how he must have felt. Those tits, that smile, Jesus and Buddha in a hammock!

"Now, if you want to leave here in one piece instead of two, I need you to answer some questions. Nod if you understand."

He nodded.

"You probably wouldn't have liked it anyway," she said. "It's got teeth in it, too."

Silk pedaled the bike along the Hana Road, zipping past the turn for the memorial on the hill and on toward Hasegawa's Resort. Hasegawa's had once been little more than a general store, but that was in the time of the current owner's great-grandfather; now, it was the most sought-after place to stay on the island. Three-year waiting list, didn't matter how much money you had, the old man didn't care, it was your attitude and manners that decided whether you got a room or not. Half a dozen people had tried to buy the place and kick the old man out because of his refusal to let them stay there, but he'd turned them all down. Plus, he had friends in high places who had spent vacations with him, so he didn't have to worry about muscle bothering him.

Silk rolled past, the solid hardplast tires of his bike making humming noises on the road. The first few drops of rain started to fall. He could have stopped and put on a rainsuit but he didn't bother. So he got wet. It didn't matter.

Zia put the guard to sleep using a choke hold—he'd struggled at the last, trying to get away, but he was too late. She used his clothes to tie and gag him, and left him in the bushes. His buddy inside would probably be thinking she was really something after a couple of hours went by and the guard didn't return.

She made her way carefully to where the employee bicycles were parked and found the one belonging to the guard, right where he said it would be. The high electric fence around the complex was guarded at the main entrance, but there was a gate the workers used when they were in a hurry. Just wave your ID at the lock and it would open. A simpleminded computer took note of your coming and going but it wouldn't try to stop you if you wanted to sneak home early.

Sure enough when she shoved the guard's ID at the reader

in front of the gate, the entrance slid open, allowing her to ride through.

Jesus. What a setup. A ten-year-old could bust out of this place, and this was after the security was put on alert. It was criminal.

She geared the bike up quickly as she rolled, enjoying the exercise. The guard had a girlfriend, sure enough, but she was visiting her mother on the Big Island until the end of the week. Nobody else lived at his cube except their cat. And yes, he had a holocam and corder at home, as well as a cheap computer.

Perfect.

Full of adrenaline despite herself, Zia enjoyed the damp night air as she rode; it was warm, full of strange plant smells and insects. Also smelled like it was about to rain, and she couldn't see the stars for the thick clouds revealed in the city glow. Still, it felt good to be out and moving, she had a goal and a plan, though that second part was a little on the sketchy side. Oh, well. One thing at a time.

King found himself walking along a path that wound about the hotel grounds, considering how best to utilize the information he had gained. Rain had begun to patter down, making gentle drumming sounds on the bushes and broad-leafed plants in the hotel gardens, sizzling where it hit concealed lights that illuminated the carefully tended foliage. There were occasions upon which rapid movement was paramount and had not the doctor been terminated, this would likely have been one of those; however, with the doctor deceased and the *ausvelter* fled, it would seem that haste was no longer quite so necessary. Given his option, he preferred careful plans, those whose parameters had been drawn with some precision. Not necessarily complex ones, simpler was usually preferable, but those in which the various possibilities had been well considered. Proper planning did indeed prevent piss-poor performance.

The rain came down a bit harder. A slight wind arose, gusted the rain into his face. King ignored it. It would be in character for him to do so. Successful Australian businessmen were not bothered by any rain short of hurricanes.

He came to the road that bounded the hotel on the west and stopped. The rain had apparently dampened the spirits of most of the tourists, since he had passed none since it began. The road loomed wet and empty as far as he could see in either direction, the hotel's lights puddled on the macadam in drop-rippled pools. No, wait. Here came a single bicyclist from the north, trailing a spray of water from beneath the rear tire as he rode quickly along. The foolish rider was apt to get himself in trouble moving at such speed on narrow tires along a wet road, King thought.

Silk pedaled in top gear, probably almost hydroplaning on the slick street. The rain spattered his face and he kept blinking it away as he rode along, barely able to see. He was coming up on the Island Wind Hotel, the lights there showing cones of glittery gray. A single tourist stood in front, drenched, not moving.

Zia saw another cyclist heading toward her from the other direction. She was in a hurry now, soaked from the rain, the back tire of the stolen bicycle drawing a muddy track up her back—the guard hadn't installed a rain flap or fender on this sucker. But she should be close to the guard's cube by now, assuming his directions had been accurate. And she was pretty sure they had been. A man who is afraid his penis will be chopped off usually doesn't want to risk lying about piddly things that might cause it.

The poor fool had thought her nothing more than an easy lay and instead, she had turned into a cold and calculating monster on him. She didn't feel particularly sorry for him; it was what she did. All part of the biz.

Silk zipped past the tourist standing in the rain. For a moment, the man looked familiar, but when he blinked away the water, he didn't recognize him. Just another tourist, too fucking stupid to get in out of the rain.

Got a lot of room to be talking, hey?

A woman who wasn't dressed for the weather biked up the road toward him. They passed at a combined speed of at least fifty klicks an hour, he guessed, and her wake sprayed him as she went by, further blinding him for a moment.

She had long blond hair and wore a shirt that looked more like paint than cloth, it was so thin and so wet. Nice tits, too.

He felt a stab of guilt at that thought. Mac—

Then he was out of the hotel lights and following his headlamps again, the rainy night closing in on him like a tunnel.

THIRTEEN _____

THE GUARD'S CUBE was a run-down unit in a complex of several dozen, a tiny one-bedroom ground-floor place that opened with a mechanical key Zia found under the doormat where he said it would be. She hurried inside and checked the place, found a meowing cat and nobody else. Good.

She stripped her wet clothes off and let them fall on the kitchen floor. Found a plastic can full of cat food in the refrigerator and dumped it in a saucer for the cat, who shut up and started eating. The cooler also had beer. She opened a bottle, sipped at it, then padded naked into the small living room where she found the holoproj and switched it on. She opened the control panel of the projector and located the input SIMM. Good, no problem with the hardware.

It took a few seconds to peel up the polish and to dig out the first of the microspeck ID chips inset into her fingernail. Tiny little sucker, she almost dropped it, but managed to catch it. She found a metal fork in a drawer, bent a tine up, and used the thing to insert the chip into the projector module. This was a tricky business even with tweezers or a pin-grip tool, but it went okay. She tapped the control panel keys in a coded sequence and watched the screen light up with her new ID stats. Everything there except the pix, that she'd have to input once she'd changed her appearance.

She went into the fresher and dug through the supplies in the mirror cabinet and under the sink. Found a pair of scissors. And the girlfriend had an old bottle of hair dye, a lucky find. Auburn, it said, and she decided it wasn't too red to use. It took a few minutes to shear off most of her hair, leaving a short cap. The dye darkened the new haircut and she dried and fluffed it until she was satisfied. She plucked her eyebrows into thinner lines, used the girlfriend's makeup to make her nose look a bit narrower and her cheekbones higher, colored her lips, deepened the shadows around her eyes. Not a spectacular change, but she looked different at first glance. The real misdirection would be elsewhere.

Zia went into the bedroom and dug through the girlfriend's clothes. The woman was shorter and heavier, to judge from what she found, but there were some loose flowered shirts and sweatpants that didn't look too baggy. She dressed, put everything neatly back into place, and went back to the holoproj. She used the cam to snap a still pix, then inserted that into the new ID.

Farewell, shy little schoolteacher. Hello, Wenda Flores, somewhat bawdy private secretary to an attorney in Miami Beach.

It wouldn't fool a cross-referenced printmach or a retinal scan, because her old ID prints and arteries would match the new ones, but if anybody got that close she'd be in trouble anyhow. It would pass a quick look, any scanner that wasn't locked into a comparable net, and that ought to be enough until she could get someplace where she'd have more time to play with the next ID.

Okay, better get moving along here.

Zia sat at the computer and logged onto a flight reservation service. Booked passage on the next hopper leaving Hana for the mainland under the name "Pia Laranj." The flight left in a half hour, the guard would probably still be trussed up in the bushes then.

Now came the hard part. She used the number she'd memorized for the E2 underground computer net, logged on using her Nessie ID number, and told the resident biopath who she was and what she wanted.

If the computer got it right and if it was half as good as she'd been told, it would break into the flight computer and insert a bit of information that showed one Pia Laranj had boarded the suborbital shuttle for the mainland. She made the reservation from here so when they backwalked it they'd buy it, but she didn't want to get on the hopper, she still had stuff to attend to here. The biopath was fairly limited, she'd been told, she couldn't depend on it for a whole hell of a lot, but it could manage this kind of thing okay. There also wouldn't be any record of her call from here to the E2 secret system. Supposedly.

She shut the system down. The rain had stopped. She stood, stretched, and headed for the cube's exit. "So long, cat," she said. She liked cats, they were independent, like she was.

The animal was giving itself a bath and didn't answer.

Outside, she headed on foot back toward a busy pub she'd passed on the way here. With any luck, she could pick up a horny tourist and have a place to spend the night. She would book a room under her new ID after that and go from there.

So far, so good.

Silk rolled into his yard. The ground was wet enough so the bike bogged down halfway across. He left it there and slogged the rest of the way to his stairs, leaving deep and muddy prints in the lawn. He was warm from his exertions but wet from the now-stopped rain and he felt like shit. The idea of a hot shower and bed sounded good, he was too tired to think about anything else. Just what he wanted.

He ought to be over this by now, it irritated him that he wasn't. He ought to be able to pick up with his life and go on, put Mac behind him and get out of this pit he'd fallen into. Should be able to do that.

Not tonight. A shower and bed, that was what he was going to do tonight.

King logged onto the GlobalCrimeNet and checked for information regarding the escaped *ausvelter* Spackler. Once he would have been able to do that using his Scat ID; now, he did it courtesy of the Panamanian State Police, using their numbers, where for a hefty fee anybody who wished could be made a Special Officer, with all the privileges such a rank conferred. In essence, such privileges were scant, but access to law enforcement computer nets was the one thing worth the price. The name King used was false, but dutifully accorded the rank of Special Officer with a plastic ID card and badge attesting it was so. A blind-drop computer postal box received the bills for air time and the annual fee and was paid from same.

If any law enforcement agency from the local police to SuePack to Terran Security had anything new on Spackler, they had not reported to the net.

King logged off and ordered his computer to shut down. He stood, stretched, bent and touched his toes, bouncing a couple of times to loosen the kinks in his low back and hamstrings. He stood. There was a gym in the hotel, a low-budget affair with a few devices, including a weightlifting station. He would go and pump the pistons for a few minutes, that would probably make him feel better. And if not, at least he would be doing good things for his physique. He took a certain pride in his body, in keeping it fit. *Mens sana, copore sano.* True, his guise of the portly businessman meant he couldn't go full out, but if nobody else was around this late, he could at least get a good pump. Better than nothing.

He pulled on a baggy sweatsuit that would hide his musculature, grabbed a towel and drapped it around his neck, and left his room for the gym.

Zia found her mark quickly enough. After two drinks she knew his life story, not particularly interesting, but that didn't matter. He was Terry M. Fontenot, from someplace called New Arcadia, an artificial island off the coast of Louisiana. He was tall, swarthy, black-haired and blue-eyed, and according to his own reckoning a pretty fair tennis player. He was also well built, young, probably about her own age, and, while part of a tour, had his own room at one of the nicer hotels. He was going to meet his fiancée in Honolulu in four days, but hell, he wasn't dead yet and that was then, this was now.

Interesting set of morals, Zia thought. Of course, she was hardly in a position to be holier-than-thou, given her business, but she would have thought that a man about to contract for marriage would be somewhat less likely to fuck around. Spies had to live by a different set of rules than civilians, but if she were going to marry somebody, she thought she would probably play it straight with him. Not that she had any plans along those lines, but maybe someday she might.

Didn't matter. M. Fontenot was exactly what she needed and they could use each other.

They held hands as they walked the short distance from the pub to his room. Once inside the door, Zia grabbed, stuck one hand down his shorts and used the other hand to pull his face to hers. She thrust her tongue into his mouth while she squeezed his already hard dick.

If their clothes didn't fall away like rose petals or autumn leaves in a fresh breeze, they managed to get out of them quick enough.

Zia pulled him down to the floor right in front of the door. The bed could wait until later, too. She got him flat, lifted herself over him, and slid down to his base in one quick move.

"*Jee*zus!" he said.

She leaned forward, put her hands on his shoulders and began pumping. Once she got the rhythm she wanted going, she sat up straight, leaned her head back, and stared at the ceiling for a second before she closed her eyes. She didn't need to see him, didn't particularly want to see him. All he was was a cock, and if she took care of that, he would do whatever she needed him to do. She put her hands under her breasts and cupped them to keep them from bouncing. Fontenot got the idea quick enough and shoved her hands aside with his. He used his thumbs on her nipples, rubbing them in quick circles.

Her nipples budded and grew hard under his touch. Hurt a little, but she ignored them. She moaned. Let him think she was the most passionate woman he'd ever been with. She lifted herself faster, came down on him with all of her weight, heard the wet sucking sound she made on him. Once, twice, three, four, five times—

He spasmed, lifted them both clear of the floor. "Oh!"

She grinned down at him, in control, feeling her own power. She clenched her vaginal muscles tight, then relaxed them, milking him.

I'm just getting warmed up, pal, she thought. *When I'm done with you, you won't want to get married to anybody else, I'm going to spoil you for other women.*

She bent down without coming off him and bit his left nipple.

"Hey, wow," he said. "You are something else, Wenda."

For a second the name didn't track, then she smiled. "Let's try the bed," she said. "I've something else you might enjoy."

He was hers. But for Zia, it was all part of the show.

• • •

Silk dreamed of a tourist who kept peeing on him while trying to shoot him. Only thing was, Mac got in the way and the guy shot her instead.

Silk came awake crying. Mac. Ah, Jesus. Mac.

FOURTEEN _____

AFTER FONTENOT WAS asleep—a worn-out stupor almost as deep as a coma, Zia figured—she used his com to call and make a reservation for a room at a hotel a few blocks away, starting tomorrow. The authorities wouldn't be looking for her to check into a hotel coming from—supposedly—off the island. If her plan had worked, they would be looking for her on the mainland under the hardly altered name "Pia." Just to be sure, she had the call routed through a comsat relay, so it would seem to come from Florida. Easy as slipping on black ice.

She lay back on the bed and stared at the ceiling. She was on top of things. Fontenot had managed to get it up four times in six hours—and she'd made him feel as if he were the best lover who'd ever lived with her moaning and crying in supposed ecstacy. She hadn't climaxed herself, she never did while she was working, that wasn't part of it. But there was no doubt he believed her. She'd leave before he awoke in the morning, wander on the beach or something for a little while, then check into her new room. After that? Well, she had to start thinking like Spackler if she was going to catch him. Where would he run? He didn't have access to Nessie's moles, he'd be pretty much on his own, so he'd be limited. He didn't know anybody on Earth, not if his records could be believed, and he'd be fleeing blind and panicky. It was a big planet, but she had read his psychological files and she could maybe anticipate him some.

Meanwhile, before she left the area, she had a couple of things to check out. Spackler had killed somebody and chances were, it was a reflexive thing done out of fear. But maybe not. He wasn't supposed to be violent. Maybe the woman he'd killed had been like Zia's guard, maybe she'd been helping him. And maybe she had known something that would help Zia find Spackler. Of course, her being dead would put a big knot in that string, Zia could hardly ask her any questions since she was either in a hole in the ground or a vase on somebody's bookshelf or somesuch; still, a quick background check was in order. Maybe Spackler left something behind.

Yeah, like a map telling where he was going. Right.

Well, okay, so probably not, but you never knew what might turn up and you wouldn't find out unless you bothered to look.

Then, once the local cops were sure Zia-Pia was elsewhere, she could book another flight and get clear of this place. Maybe by then she'd have a better idea of where that might be.

Spackler was gone, but she was out and on his trail, she had a place to stay and things to do. It was going okay. It could be a lot worse.

The morning broke easily over the tropics, and Depard King allowed himself a leisurely breakfast at the hotel's coffee shop before returning to his room. He didn't feel stalled, precisely, but he was rather at loggerheads as to his next move. He had looked in the obvious places and it seemed that the dead woman had been a bit more devious than he had guessed on first view. It was one thing to speak of taking the time to properly plan one's moves, another to be faced with the reality of a field situation. The truth be known, he had expected to uncover everything he needed before now; the truth be known, he had *not* expected to have deleted somebody and to be sitting in a backup identity with virtually nothing to show for such drastic action.

As he sat in his room, thinking about his various choices, he once again logged onto the police net, in the hopes that something new would have occurred. His computer, set to globally search for topics King thought relevant, came up with an idea he had not anticipated.

A second *ausvelter* had been reported missing from the local quarantine station.

King blinked at the sharp holoproj floating in his room, feeling the implications of the information wash over him rather like a frigid blast of arctic air.

He told himself he had known such a thing must happen, but in point of fact, he had considered it and shelved it without further thought earlier in the game. He had thought that it would be later rather than sooner and dismissed it. Another error.

A quick surge of fear bloomed in his belly, threatened to expand from his bowels and fill him. He fought it, took several deep breaths and tried to calm himself. All right, all right, the New Earthers were not stupid, they were bound to find out about Spackler and could hardly allow him to skip blithely away unhampered. They would have sent an agent after the man.

King had his computer display the description of the new *ausvelter*. Looked at the holograph of her, read the crawl under it. She was an attractive enough creature, the E2 agent, though he expected she would look less so in person, with her role in place. Not, he thought, that she would look anything like this holograph by this time.

He memorized the stats nonetheless, took special note of her facial features and ears. His advantage, if one could call it such, was that local authorities and The Scat would likely be looking for an escaped *ausvelter* without knowing who— or what—she really was. Oh, to be certain, they would suspect that she was a spy, the paranoia that riddled TSA would hardly allow them to think otherwise, and in this case would actually be justified. But they wouldn't know her mission for certain, and he did.

King considered the information. The new agent could be a problem, in that she would surely want to recover Spackler alive, but failing that would very likely have no compunctions about killing him and destroying the body. She would get in King's way, did she know he was aware of Spackler and what he represented. Fortunately, she would have no way of knowing that he knew.

On the other hand, if he could find this woman, he could use her, for she was much more likely to have information that would lead her to Spackler than anybody local would have.

She would have been given everything the E2ers had on the man and she would also be one of the more adept agents they had or they would not have sent her. He couldn't assume she would be the only one they'd shipped this way, either. There might be others and he would have to maintain his alertness for them.

Of course, terran authorities would be searching for the most recent escapee as well as Spackler, but it would hardly be a priority-one agenda item. Perhaps a dozen or so *ausvelters* managed to slip quarantine every year at various locations on-planet. Some of them were surely spies from other worlds but some of them were merely impatient fools. The quarantine itself was hardly necessary from a medical standpoint—most deadly diseases on the frontier planets had been eliminated in the last twenty years, certainly all the ones that were very contagious—so nobody was *really* worried about some Typhoid Mary running around infecting the locals. Politically, of course, the quarantine allowed tight controls that the powers-that-be were loath to give up. Sooner or later the quarantine would become a point of contention and the balance of trade would require that it be modified into something more of a token, if not eliminated altogether. But that was down the road; meanwhile, at least a few Scat-cats would be stirred enough to try to find Spackler and the woman who had come after him. King had to beat them to his quarry or lose the most valuable prize in history.

If he were an offworld spy in a strange land and he was not certain of his target's whereabouts, he would surely try to contact anybody who might put him on the trail. The official spin on the death of the medic was that she had been killed in an accident. The secondary and unofficial spin said that Spackler had slain her during his escape. The link between the dead woman and Spackler was tenuous, thready in the extreme, but there was enough there so King would have sought to explore it further, were he the E2 agent. The medic was dead and impossible to question, but her contracted, a man she might well have trusted with valuable information, was alive.

M. Venture Silk might well be the piece that would allow completion of the puzzle. King still thought so himself, and he could not assume this new player would miss the possibility.

Interesting. Most interesting. It meant he would have to become more aggressive in this matter. And that M. Silk would become at least a partial focus of that aggression.

Silk sat drinking coffee, staring out through the window at nothing. It was late, nearly noon, and there hadn't been any web-work today, nothing to keep him busy and thoughtless. He was on his fifth cup of coffee, a Kona blend that he bought by the half kilo despite the cost. Mac had picked it out—

Fuck this. Everything he thought about kept coming back to her and he was sick of it. He had a life before he met her, they'd only been together a few years of that life. He was going to have to get past this. Maybe a vacation somewhere . . .

He had to smile at that over the cooling coffee. Where does a man who lives in paradise go for a vacation? A slum? Some rat-infested back alley in Singapore or Rangoon or Little NYC?

A woman with short reddish hair walked up the street toward his cube, moving athletically along, dressed in a blue and white flowered Hawaiian shirt new enough so the fold lines still showed and blue shorts and sandals.

Silk sipped at his coffee and watched the woman. Even under the baggy shirt he could see she had nice tits—

Hmm. Something about her was familiar, but he couldn't quite put his finger on it. Had he seen this tourist somewhere before?

Trying to place the woman, he barely noticed the big fat man coming from the other direction, more or less marching along in a no-nonsense manner. He had a good seat, up on the second story, the sun shining, his view unimpeded, so he saw everything that happened next. It went so fast, like somebody spilling a drink, that it wasn't until later he could reconstruct it properly, but he caught the big splashes.

The woman turned up his driveway and started for his cube. She smiled, revealing even teeth and a pretty face.

The fat man began moving faster. When he was still twelve or fifteen meters away from the woman, who was now moving aslant to him, he pulled something from under his baggy shirt and pointed it at her.

Silk's recent experience with guns flashed him like a strobe. "Look out!" he screamed.

The window was open, the woman no more than thirty meters away. She looked up at him. Silk was on his feet, the coffee still spilling from his cup as he dropped it and pointed at the fat man. She heard him, twisted, saw the fat man with the gun.

Silk stared at the man. *It's the burglar!*

He looked different, but he was the right size and he held the gun the same way, brought his left hand up to cup it around the right hand. Silk knew how important a grip was when you were shooting a crossbow—

The woman dived, hit the plastcrete in a kind of elongated hoop, rolled up, then dived again—

The too-familiar *twang* of the gun reached Silk and he started yelling: "Hey, hey, hey! Stop it!"

The man fired three, maybe four times, but the woman was still rolling around like a demented gymnast, stopping and starting in fast jerks, changing her direction—

A two-person pedal cart came up the road and things got very complex. Silk never got a good look at the driver of the cart, but the passenger was a pale man with blond hair, also dressed like a tourist in new flowered shirt and shorts. And this tourist—had they all gone fucking crazy?—leaned out of the pedal cart holding a long gun. Silk didn't get a very good look at it but it must have been a gas-powered pellet rifle or shotgun, because it made a deep *whump-whump-whump!* when it went off, like compressed air being vented from a dive shop's tank-filler.

The shooter in the pedal cart must have hit the fat man, the fat man lurched to one side, grabbed at his right thigh with his left hand and turned his pistol on the cart and let go three more shots.

The woman came up from her last roll and ran toward Silk's door.

The passenger of the cart jerked back into the vehicle and stopped shooting. Silk couldn't tell if he'd been hit by the fat man's shots or not.

His crossbow was back at the range.

The fat man glanced up at Silk for an instant, then tucked the gun away and hobbled off quickly.

Silk said, "Bubbles! Open a com to—"

"Don't call the police!" came the woman's voice from behind him.

Silk spun to see the gymnast behind him, trying to catch her breath. "Please," she said. "I'll explain, give me a second, okay?"

Silk stared at her.

What the fuck was going on here?

FIFTEEN

IN HIS ROOM again, King found that the projectile had passed cleanly through his thigh at a shallow depth and angle, failing to expand and thus missing the bone and any major vessels. Both the entrance and exit wounds were small. He put his medical device into operation once again, listened to it hum and buzz as it worked its technological biomedical magic, and relaxed somewhat as the local and systemic pain medications began to take effect. The wound was more of an irritant than a danger in itself, but what was even more disturbing was the cause.

The spy had confederates.

King had erred greatly in assuming she was alone. He was relatively certain he had darted the one who shot him—he hoped the man had a hellacious headache when he awoke— but once again he had made a mistake, this one nearly fatal. It made him angry, not so much at the spy and her henchmen but at himself. Ten years ago he would not have been so careless, would not have assumed that the spy was without backup and an easy target. He was but forty-five, but perhaps he was too old for this business. He'd lost his edge.

He had been so busy congratulating himself on his good fortune in happening across her that he had become overconfident. He had thought it a simple matter to dart her and then carry her to his room for examination at his leisure. He could learn what he could, use her as he saw fit, dispose of her. It had never crossed his mind that it was too good to be true, altogether too easy.

Fool. But for the ineptitude of her assistants, he would be badly injured, having to explain himself to the authorities; or worse, he could be dead. That was a military-grade CO_2 rifle the shooter had wielded, however poorly. Had that metal pellet hit bone, it would have shattered his leg. Half a meter higher, it would have blown his liver or spleen to pieces.

He suppressed the rage as best he could but it was bottled in him as might be some superheated fluid trying to boil under a pressure lid. This had ceased to be an impersonal operation. He was now emotionally involved in a way that would demand a very personal satisfaction before he could walk away. Yes, the goal, of course, but now, he had a certain amount of vengeance he wished to enact upon the players opposite him. He knew it ought not to be so, but it was. A nonprofessional attitude, to be sure, but one with which he would have to deal.

They were going to rue the day they had crossed swords with Depard King.

Who *were* those guys? Zia's mind darted here and there trying to figure it out. They couldn't be TSA, they would still be coming. And why were they shooting at each other? This didn't make any sense—!

She had to think fast and yet be real careful of what she said. She didn't know who this guy was, either, other than his name and that he had been the contracted of the dead doc, but things had just turned ugly and she might need him on her side if she was going to get out of this mess without stinking. Or worse, not get out at all. She hadn't planned to meet him in this manner but here she was. The trick now was to say what would get him on her side in a hurry.

"Listen, M. Silk, you've gotten yourself in the middle of a mess." That was true enough. "If you cooperate with us, we can get you out of it in one piece." Or get me out of it, the more important thing here.

"What the fuck are you talking about?"

He was angry, she could use that. She started a story, improvising as she went along.

"That man down there, the one who shot at me. He's the one who killed your contracted."

Silk stared at her. "He doesn't look anything like the *ausvelter* who escaped. He looked like the son-of-a-bitch who broke into my cube and shot at me last week. And who was it blasting at him?"

Somebody had shot at this guy? What was going on here? Zia hurriedly altered her story before she spoke. "No, that's because he isn't the one who escaped but he's part of it. The others are part of my team, but they're also undercover."

"Listen, fem, you want to cut the dross and get to it?"

"All right. I'm going to have to trust you. My name is Trish Danner, I'm with Terran Security, sub rosa operations. We've uncovered an *ausvelter* plot, a major piece of sabotage supported by a dissident group and backed by certain factions on New Earth. I've just returned from there and that man was trying to kill me to stop my investigation." Her delivery was good, she thought, enough sincerity to make it believable. "I've been in quarantine, but in order to continue my investigation, I had to 'escape' last night. You can check it out, if you want, you'll find another *ausvelter* supposedly broke custody."

Whenever possible, it was best to use as much truth as you could in making up a cover story. If baby blue eyes here did check, he would find out that part of her story was valid, even if it wasn't quite how she put it.

"What has that got to do with me?"

Come on, Zia, he isn't swallowing it that easy, get him into the picture, fast.

"Your contracted, Dr. McKenzie, stumbled across part of the plot. She must have discovered something about the plotters when they were in quarantine, we aren't quite sure exactly what happened. They must have thought she was a threat. They had to silence her."

"Come on!"

"M. Silk, I have no reason to lie to you about this. Surely you don't buy that *accident* story? Or that she just *happened* to be strolling past when a crazed *ausvelter* escapee got loose and he killed her in passing?" As improv went, this was a pretty good line, she thought. She waited for him.

He shook his head slowly. "That didn't make any sense, no."

Now she had him. "Look, I'm sorry to have to dump this on you like this, but we are talking about a major problem here. You're going to have to help me."

"Me? Fuck that. Why don't you just call in the troops?"

"I can't. There is a leak in my organization, a spy we haven't been able to run down. Any attempt to contact my superiors through regular channels might alert him. Or her."

He still looked dubious, but he was wavering. Time to set the hook.

"Do you want your contracted's death to be for nothing? We can catch these people and punish them. Doesn't she deserve that?"

The man sighed. He wasn't bad-looking, trim, a little older than she was, maybe thirty, thirty-two, in pretty good shape. He was obviously feeling grief over the recent loss of his woman and that was Zia's biggest lever: you find the right place and you hit it hard.

"What will it take to convince you, M. Silk?" She leaned forward and the front of her shirt fell away from her chest, leaving a gap. He flicked his gaze at her breasts. She wore an ultrasheer bra, it gave her a little support but was almost transparent. He glanced away, back at her face.

She held back the smile, kept her face serious. She would convince him. One way or another.

Silk was rattled and this woman standing across from him wasn't making things any easier. All this stuff was out of a bad entcom, spies and plots and shit; and yet, Mac was dead, there was no way around that. If what this Danner woman was saying *was* true, then maybe Mac's murder meant something, maybe it was important. He hadn't thought she kept things from him, but when he thought back on it, she had said something about the *ausvelter*. She sure as hell hadn't mentioned he was a spy, but there was *some* thing. He couldn't recall exactly what it was, just that it had been part of a conversation they'd had not long before she'd been killed.

He looked at the young woman again, focused on her. She was attractive enough, despite a bad haircut, looked good under those baggy clothes. It might be true. He could check it out.

Aloud, he said, "Bubbles, on-line."

"Right here."

The woman started, looked around, realized the vox was computer-generated, all in a second or so. She was quick.

"Access police chan, check and see if anybody broke quarantine at OhQue last night."

"Channel accessed. There is a report of an unauthorized exit from Offworld Quarantine during that period. A guard is being questioned regarding the UE."

"Pix of the escapee?"

"None available."

"Identification?"

"Not available."

Silk looked at the woman.

"See?" she said.

To Bubbles, he said, "Get me Hans Klein at OhQue."

A few seconds passed. "Yes?"

Silk kept his visual transmission off, said, "Hans, Venture Silk."

"Ah, M. Silk. How have you been doing?"

"Better. Look, Hans, I need a favor. This is personal, not for public consumption."

"Yes?"

"I understand another *ausvelter* took leave of you last night."

Hans didn't speak to that for a moment. "Ah, well—"

"Look, it's on the net, official channel, you aren't confirming something I don't already know."

Silk guessed that Dr. Klein would be dialing up a visual to check that. A few seconds passed. "Well, yes, I was not on duty, but so it would seem."

"And she was from E2, the woman who got out, is that right?"

Hans must have been trying to read and think at the same time. "Yes, that's what it says."

Silk smiled at being able to rascal Hans so easily. "Thanks, Hans, I'll get back to you. Discom, Bubbles, off-line."

He looked at the woman. "So that part seems to be true. An *ausvelter* did break out last night and it was a woman."

Danner nodded.

"Let's assume I buy your story. What happens now?"

She looked at him with a serious expression. "We have to get out of here before the assassin comes back with help," she said. "Is there someplace around here where we can talk without being found?"

Silk considered it for a moment. "Yeah."

He wasn't sure about this but he was curious. It had the smell of something big, and it concerned Mac's death, he did believe that. The authorities hadn't been giving him diddly and maybe this woman had some answers. Answers he wanted.

"Come on, we'll take my bike."

With her tucked in behind him on the not-quite-big-enough passenger seat, the woman pressed against his back with her groin, her legs touching his hips. Her body was warm, almost hot where they touched, and Silk felt an uncomfortable and, lately, an unfamiliar stirring in his own crotch.

Jesus, Ven, Mac has only been gone a few days! What is the matter with you?

He put a little more energy into his pedaling, geared up another sprocket, and opened it up on the straightaway past the turn for Koki Beach, heading for the archery range.

"Nobody following us," the woman said. "Unless we've got a caster hidden on the bike. Pull over and let's check it out."

A bus full of tourists passed, returning from the Sacred Pools. Silk slowed the bike, stopped. They hopped off and went over the frame carefully, pulled the seat up, checked inside the grips.

"Looks clean, but they can make those things pretty small," she said.

God, this was hard to believe.

He was very much aware of the heat of her mons pressing against the base of his spine as they rolled along.

Jesus.

SIXTEEN

COFFEY WAS MORE than a little surprised to see the woman, Silk could tell. He had known who Mac was, of course, but she had never come to the range, crossbow or archery being of no interest to her. And here Silk was showing up with a new woman only a few days after the old one had been killed.

"*Mahalo*, Coffey."

"*Mahalo*, bro'."

"Give us a lane, would you? I don't need the equipment, I'm, ah, just giving a quick theoretical lesson here."

"Sure. Take three." He raised an eyebrow.

Well, he couldn't explain it to the rangemaster now. Maybe another time. What they needed was a safe place to think, to talk, and here was as good a spot as Silk knew. Assuming some assassin didn't cut him down, he'd tell Coffey about it later.

The woman looked around as they passed through the gate, but didn't speak until they were out of Coffey's hearing. "You spend a lot of time here?"

"Some."

They moved to the lane. Silk pointed at the backstops for Coffey's benefit. They were alone at the range, no other shooters out.

"Okay, now what?"

She looked cool, in control. "We've got to track down the *ausvelter* who escaped," she said. "He's the key to all this. We catch him, it's all over."

"And how the hell are we supposed to do that? It's a big planet and I get the impression a whole lot of people are looking for this guy already and they haven't found him."

"I have some information that should help," she said.

He shook his head. "I don't know about all this."

"Look, I can understand your reluctance, but face it, you *are* in the middle of it. The opposition has already made one pass at you. If we don't stop them, neither of us is safe."

"I have a job—"

"Make some temporary excuse, we'll take care of that through official channels later. Your planet needs you, M. Silk. And this is your chance to balance the equation and punish those who killed your contracted."

Silk thought about it. Okay, Mac was dead and he hurt but— did he want to dive any deeper into this shit? He couldn't bring her back, no matter what he did. Still, it pissed him off that the spin on her death was so cheap, and that the guy who did it might get away. Plus, as a spider himself, he had a desire to know the truth, the whole picture, not the official pap they wanted to feed him.

Danner moved in and put one hand on his arm, looked into his eyes. "Please, M. Silk. I need your help."

Her touch was hot on his skin.

King hoped his hastily improvised disguise would pass a cursory inspection. He had decided to go for ostentation, reasoning that while he would thus draw more attention, a viewer would be more apt to accept what he proffered at face value and not look any deeper. He dyed his hair a shocked blue, darkened his tan until he was the color of coffee and cream, and assembled a wardrobe of flashy, colorful offworld silks. He would stand out in a crowd and he looked—he hoped— like an aging, but fit, entcom or rockvid star, or a producer wishiwere come to spend money on his vacation. He rented a sporty electric cart, a top of the line model whose cost for a week was worth food and shelter for a small family for three months, but it was part of the image. He drove past Silk's cube as if he owned the road. He got a few stares from the natives and tourists, but they were not the kinds of looks one gave a murderer or a prior-to bumbling operative. Some of the passersby were envious, some amused, some disdainful, but what they thought was of no importance.

No police that he could see, nothing electronic made his wideband detector scream, and while he could not be certain, given the state of the art in surveillance equipment—he could be footprinted by a spysat from orbit that could read his chronograph if somebody wanted to know the time badly enough—it did not feel to him as if he were being watched.

That was both odd and reassuring. If the dead woman's contracted had not given the alarm, then he *must* have something he did not want the local authorities to know. That would serve King's interest, to be sure. Then again, if Silk were in league with the offworld spy, perhaps they had come to some kind of accommodation. That was not so good, but once again, not an insurmountable obstacle. If a man would sell something to a buyer, then he would likely sell it to another who made a better offer. It reminded King of the old joke: We have already settled what you *are*, madam, we are now merely haggling over your price . . .

The *ausvelter* woman had resources and if she had spirited Silk away to a safecube or off the island already, there was little King could do immediately. If, however, she had not yet done so, he might still locate and recover them.

The darts in his weapon still bore charges that would merely stun, but that could be rectified easily; for the moment, he still needed one or both of the prey alive.

Where would they hide if for some reason she chose not to go to ground? He had to consider the possibility.

He had studied Silk's background. He was a homebody, save when he practiced with that damned crossbow or went swimming. The Red Sand Beach was close. King would check there first. Then the archery range. This latter was not quite so pleasant a prospect. Finding his target unarmed and in a swim mesh was much more appealing than locating him when he might be playing with that blasted weapon. King had altogether too much experience with the man's expertise using that devilish device. The man had now seen him in two guises and he might be smart enough to be suspicious of anybody with a remote resemblance to either of them. There was little King could do to make himself smaller. He would have to move with caution.

He smiled to himself as he wheeled the expensive cart around a corner, forcing a pair of women tourists to step lively to avoid being run over. The women, both elderly and white-haired, cursed him as he zipped past. Very fluent in the Anglo-Saxonisms, they were. The smile was not for this, however, but at the thought of a contest. Perhaps he was indeed past his prime, but there was a certain epinephrinic thrill to the idea of a head-to-head battle with the spindoc and his new ally. A man did like to be tested now and again, to demonstrate his worth. Not that he intended to take any foolish risks, no sportsmanlike rules or other such idiocy. Like ancient samurai, the basic game in this business was simple: by your existence you were supposed to be prepared. To be or do less was your problem and not that of your enemy. Functional paranoia was perhaps the best term, and indeed it was not paranoia if someone might in fact leap out at any moment. Condition Yellow, the old gunfighters called it. You had to eat, sleep and fornicate in that mode or you might well be sorry.

King was no longer off guard as he had been. He had been clogged with the rust of disuse, cobbed in webs of hubris and ennui. No longer. Now, he was ready, and woe be to those in this game who were not.

Zia was trying to make the best of a murky situation here, and given how she'd landed in the middle of a thick fog, doing okay. The goal was the same, to collect her package or dispose of it, whichever it took. There were some new players here and she hadn't sorted them out yet, but she'd made a good start on it with Silk. He was attracted to her, she'd have been surprised if he wasn't, and he had some personal sorting out of his own to do. Now that he'd agreed to help, they had to get the hell away from this island and to a wider spot where they'd be harder to find. Maybe he wouldn't be much use to her as cover, but she couldn't take the chance that he knew something, that his woman had said or done something to let him in on stuff he ought not to know. Collecting her package was at the top of her list, but if anybody here knew what Spackler represented, that would have to be dealt with, too. Without him to verify it, knowing didn't mean a whole lot, but if the suspicion was thick enough, that could cause certain problems. Whatever else they might be, terrans had been at the spy biz a lot longer than anybody else. They might be a half step slow because they were old and stale, but they had deep pockets and a network that put all the outworlds to shame.

Zia was going to make sure if these beans got spilled it wasn't going to be her fault.

"What now?" Silk said.

"We need to get to the major land," she said.

"Mainland," he corrected.

"Whatever. To Los Angeles."

"L.A.? Why?"

"That's where we'll probably find Spackler."

"Who?"

"The *ausvelter* who escaped. The renegade from E2."

"Oh."

"Can we get to an air- or orbitport on that bike from here?"

"Yeah. I'll need to pack some stuff—"

"Not a good idea," she said. "Better if we pick up what we need along the way. The government is paying, M. Silk."

"Call me Ven," he said.

Zia flashed her professional smile, but she felt it this time. *Gotcha.*

SEVENTEEN _____

SILK HAD THE bike moving along pretty good, in tenth or twelfth gear on the straight stretch a klick from the range, doing maybe thirty-five or forty kilometers per hour when an oncoming cart crossed into his lane and came right at them.

"Fuck!"

He had time to see the driver of the droptop before he took the bike off the road. A dark-skinned man with blue hair, dressed like a goddamned macaw. Christ, he must be stoned to the hairline—!

Then he was off the macadam. The bike slewed through the loose gravel of the road's shoulder, the back end came around in a fishtail, but straightened as they bumped and bounced into the rocky field. Danner grabbed tight around his waist but didn't move otherwise, which was good, because if she shifted her weight, they would probably fucking roll—

"It's *him*!" she yelled.

Silk was busy trying to keep them upright, but he managed a quick glance backward. Danner was looking behind them at the cart, which was skidding through a fast turn of its own as the driver braked and tried to do a one-eighty.

"What?"

"The guy at your apartment, the shooter," she said. Her voice was remarkably calm, considering.

He found a fairly flat patch of ground and brought the bike to a halt.

"Move," she commanded. "Head that way, for the ocean!"

"What?"

"We'll never outrun him on the road."

"Yeah, and we won't outrun him on the ground, either, that cart's got better suspension than this bike and a lot more power."

There was a narrow ditch fifty meters ahead, a runoff trench cut to keep the low spot in the road behind them drained when the rains got heavy. It was only a meter or so wide and half again that deep and it snaked back and forth in a sharp meander on its way to the sea. They wouldn't be able to cross that on the bike.

The guy behind them wouldn't be able to clear it in his cart, either.

"Run for the ditch," Silk said.

They ran.

The sound of the cart's electric motor increased behind them. Silk heard the gravel from the road's apron clattering against the underside of the vehicle. As he ran, he was struck with a sudden thought: The owners of the rental were going to be real unhappy with the driver for treating the cart that way . . .

The two of them reached the ditch. Silk never broke stride, but leapt, and in his peripheral vision saw the woman beat him by a half step.

If the shooter wanted to chase them any further, he'd have to leave his ride behind. Maybe he wouldn't be able to stop in time and he'd crash. The rental people would *really* love him for that.

They were still sixty or seventy meters ahead of him. Silk hoped that was outside of shooting range for that goddamned little handgun the guy had.

Funny, he wouldn't have recognized the guy in the bird-of-paradise silks if Danner hadn't seen him and called it. Could have walked right past and never spotted him.

Worry about that later, though. Now, getting away was the important thing.

King cursed, tried to drive and pull his pistol, did neither well. The automobile jounced around, lifted him clear of the seat as he hit partially buried rocks in the field, rattled his teeth painfully. The gun's front sight caught on the expensive cloth of his shirt and he ripped both the shirt and his own skin as he jerked the weapon loose.

The man and woman stopped the bicycle, leapt off and began to run. Too far for a dart, but he was much faster relative to the runners now, he would gain another ten meters in a few seconds and could risk a shot—

Damn!

A crevasse loomed ahead, he saw it at the same time the running couple leapt over it.

King dropped the pistol on the seat next to himself and grabbed the steering wheel with both hands as he trod heavily on the cart's brake pedal. The wheels locked, skidded, unlocked, relocked, the cart slid to one side, the rear end broke traction and came partway around. King released the brake and turned into the skid. The cart straightened. He braked again, and the vehicle came to a stop four or five meters short of the trench.

King looked down at the seat. The gun was gone. It must have fallen to the floor, bounced under the seat. He didn't have time to look for it now. He leapt free of the stopped cart and gave chase.

The fleeing couple was thirty meters ahead of him now and gaining. He hopped over the narrow ditch and ran. He was in excellent condition, he could overtake them—

After a sprint of a hundred, perhaps a hundred and fifty meters, however, he realized they must also be in good aerobic shape. He was able to maintain the distance but not to close on them.

Still, the sea loomed half a klick or less and unless they planned to dive in and swim across the ocean, he *would* overtake them when they ran out of beach. The rocky shore along this coast did not allow for straight travel, cliffs came down and jutted into the surf in many places. It would be only a matter of time. True, he was not armed, but his fighting skills would suffice. The woman spy might be trained in defensive tactics, but he was larger and stronger and that usually told, all else being equal; the man had no martial arts prowess and he was not carrying that crossbow now. King was confident he could defeat them both.

He sucked at the warm sea air, his lungs burning, and concentrated on maintaining his stride and balance.

Zia wished she had a gun or a knife. Might as well wish for a squad of riot troopers while she was at it. The big man was still back there, not catching up but not dropping back any, either. The beach was just ahead and if they ran out of that, he was going to be all over them real quick. Where were the tourists? Shit, they were all alone out here!

Maybe the two of them could take him—

Yeah, he'll just stand still and let you without pulling the dart gun you know he's got.

Ahead, the beach slanted to their left and ran for three or four hundred meters before a black cliff sloped into the water and made a broken wall that extended fifty meters offshore. They'd have to swim around that, and that surf didn't look real pleasant the way it crashed against the rocks and blew spray and foam high into the sunny air.

Damn.

Wait a second, wait—!

A small boat rounded the end of the rocky beach, heading parallel to the shore out past the breaker line. Looked like one guy in it, probably a fisherman or something.

"The boat!" Zia managed to say, nearly out of breath.

Silk stared at her.

"Swim out to . . . the . . . boat!"

He nodded, saving his own wind, and they angled toward the waterline.

Silk hit the water in a clean racing dive. The water was shallow but his speed carried him through the wave's foam and into the following trough. Danner's dive was not so perfect, she hit crooked, but straightened out quickly.

Silk timed his strokes, dived beneath the next big wave, paddled underwater through the surge. He got to deeper water, began a powerful crawl. There was a rip here, and he used it, let it carry him away from the shore. He was aware of Danner swimming next to him, but half a body length behind him. The boat was still out a ways and approaching from the north. Maybe the guy chasing them would give it up, maybe he couldn't swim.

Silk came up for breath and looked back at the shore.

The big man ran into the surf, splashing up sheets of water as he ran, and fell forward into a clumsy belly flop of a dive.

They were still way ahead of him. The trick was going to be getting out far enough to reach the boat and having it get there before the man caught up with them. If it was just the guy and Silk in the water, he might wait to take him on. He was a strong swimmer, could hold his breath for almost two minutes, and he could fucking try to *drown* the son-of-a-bitch. But a gun would probably work fine if it were wet, who knew what the fuck else the guy might have, a knife, whatever, and Silk had no desire to be crab food.

So Silk swam as hard as he could.

Zia was a decent swimmer, she'd been on the team in secondary ed, but this guy was leaving her in his wake. Unless the guy behind them was part fish, they should be able to get to the boat before he caught them.

It was okay to be worried but not to panic, not just yet.

King was furious. He thrashed at the water, never very good as a swimmer, but making up as much as he could in power for what he lacked in technique. He saw his quarry's intent and did he not hurry, they would escape.

No. He couldn't allow that. He had been thwarted too many times already, he couldn't allow them to outmaneuver him yet again!

The briny taste of the sea sloshed into his mouth and nose and he coughed it out, trying to avoid inhaling it. He allowed his rage to fill him, giving him strength, damping the pain from his burning muscles and aching lungs.

He would kill them for this alone if nothing else.

When they drew near the boat, Silk saw a man in a face mask pushed up on his forehead, a snorkel attached. Skin diver, he realized.

"Hey, could you give me a hand?" Danner called out from behind him. "I've got a cramp!"

She bobbed up, pain on her face.

The man in the boat peered at them but used the little electric motor to maneuver the blue plastic craft closer.

Danner treaded water and moved closer to Silk. "Get ready to move," she said.

"What?"

"Just get ready."

The boat approached.

Silk looked back. The big man was not in sight, but he was there somewhere, hidden by the waves.

The diver reached out. "Gimme yuh hann," he said in a thick southern accent.

Danner reached up. Silk saw her brace her feet against the side of the little boat. What was she doing? All they had to do was let this guy give them a ride and they'd be safe—

When the diver caught her wrist, she reached up with her free hand and caught his wrist. Silk heard her grunt with effort as she jerked the diver out of the boat and over her head.

"Shit—!" he began, then he hit the water.

Danner was already clambering into the boat. "Come on!" she yelled.

Silk obeyed.

By the time he was halfway over the side, she had the electric motor control turned up. The little siphons blew seawater out and the boat started moving faster.

It wasn't a speedshell, but no unaugmented swimmer was going to keep up with it.

The diver surfaced. "Hey!" he yelled. "Motherfucker, that's mah boat! Hey, y'all, stop!"

Silk rolled all the way into the boat. Took two deep breaths, then sat up and looked back.

The assassin was still twenty meters away from the diver. He stopped swimming and stared after them for a moment. Then he turned and started back toward the shore.

They'd made it.

"Which way to the airport?" Danner said. Her clothes stuck to her like thick and lumpy plaster, hiding little.

Silk was exhausted from running and swimming and fear. He was rattled, this was not part of his world. How the hell had he gotten here? And for some reason he could not understand, what Silk wanted to do right now more than anything was to leap on this woman and fuck her brains out.

He shook his head. Jesus.

EIGHTEEN _____

THE BOAT TRIP was more or less uneventful. Because the port was mostly on an artificial peninsula that jutted from the shore into the ocean north of Nanuele Point, much like the OhQue complex, Silk and Danner were able to get fairly close. They put ashore, their clothes more or less sun-dried, and caught an electric that delivered them to the Aloha Airlines terminal. None of the tourists on the bus paid them any attention; most of them were leaving paradise, going back to civilization, and they wanted to enjoy their final views through the open windows.

At the terminal, Silk hung back as Danner bought tickets.

"Congratulations," she said as she returned to where he stood waiting. "You and I are just contracted. M. and F. Wm. Danner, going to visit your new in-laws—my parents—in Seattle."

"Seattle? I thought we were going to—"

"We are, but not directly. If somebody strains all the passenger lists with a decent computer—and they will—they'll eventually happen across the fact that the Danners left the island without ever having officially *arrived* here, assuming they check the local population rolls. They are looking for a woman alone, and they'll double check for glitches, but sooner or later when they don't find me, somebody will probably want to have a word with us. The Danners will be history shortly after we land in Seattle, but better anybody wanting to find them should look there and not Los Angeles."

Silk nodded. If he'd thought about it, maybe he would have come up with that reasoning, but the truth was, it wouldn't have occurred to him. This was a new game.

"L.A. is a big place," he said. "And we're looking for one guy."

"Our boy Spackler has a bent," she said. "He likes his sex in a special way. You do have dogs on this planet, right?"

Silk stared at her. Jesus. This was getting weirder all the time.

King fought a growing sense of rage, mixed rather too liberally with foreboding. He had lost them. He'd paused at the beach long enough to get the name of the boater who had unwillingly supplied the escapees with their means of exit. The man would report the theft and King would be able to gain some information from the local authorities via his police net when they found the vessel, although he was almost certain such knowledge would be too little too late. Doubtless the pair would continue their flight much farther than the island's powercast would take their tiny craft. They would be departing soon, had they not done so already.

As King headed toward the last of his fallback rooms for his final disguise in Hana, he allowed his disgust and anger to rise, hissing up to fill his soul like superheated steam.

Dammit! He had nearly had his hands on the keys to the kingdom and he had fumbled them away. Had all the advantages and, not to put too fine a point on it, almost literally pissed them away.

A bearing in the battered cart squeaked as he turned toward the hotel. Well. There was little point in recrimination now. The past was history and he had to move forward or be left with the dross of time. He would put his AI program to work on outgoing passenger lists. They would hardly use their own names, but he was looking for a couple, of that he was certain. The spy wanted something from the local spindoc, he must know something, as King had suspected, and did he find the one, he would find the other.

The hotel loomed. The wind carried in it the promise of a rain shower fast approaching, the heavy scent of moisture gathering to discharge itself upon the semitropical haven.

A pity he had not been able to enjoy the locale. Perhaps another time.

He parked the cart and alighted. For a moment King considered an option. While he did not have his goal in hand, there still existed another choice. He *did* have enough information from which he could still make a more-than-tidy profit. He could demonstrate the existence of the prize and with careful negotiation could certainly convince old connections in The Scat to bring it to the attention of those who could—and who would—pay him well for what he did have. It would not be the fortune he envisioned, nor would it have the attendant benefits, but it would allow him to live quite well and comfortably for the rest of his life, was it managed properly.

The moment passed. No. He had spent too much of himself on this to settle for the lesser reward. It was personal, he had certain debts to balance, else he would not be able to sleep well ever after. He would always have that nagging wonder about his resolve, his competence, his very manhood. Such worries were supposed to be passé in this age, but King had never been one of the lilies, content to lie back and live on the dole with no more ambition than to get through the day. No, he was intelligent, mayhaps even brilliant, and trained in these matters. His skills had suffered some from disuse but they could be honed and made sharp once again, at least enough for this one final task. He would find the spy and the local and he would extract from them the secrets he sought and then eliminate them. True, he had erred, but no one knew it save himself, the errors had been embarrassing but not fatal, and he was still in the game.

It was not over yet.

NINETEEN _____

HAWAII WAS JUST far enough from Seattle to justify cranking up a suborbital arc ship. Anything under about three thousand kilometers wasn't worth the effort, you had to travel via commercial low-altitude jetliner and it took a lot longer, but from Hana to the northwest port of SeaTac they could justify it.

It had been a while since Silk had visited the mainland, and as the acceleration of the lifting ship pressed him deep into the hardfoam of his seat, he tried to gear himself up for it. You tended to forget, living in a place like Hana, how awful the rest of the world could be.

"You're infected, right?"

Silk turned to look at the woman sitting next to him. Danner. He wondered if that was her real name. No, probably not. "Excuse me?"

"You carry the birth control retrovirus."

Silk nodded. "Of course. Every native-born terran does. Otherwise the planet would be crawling with children." It took a second for him to get it. Then, "You aren't terran?"

She smiled. "Nah. I just work here. I'm an E2er, that's why they hired me, I can get stuff done on the outworlds with a whole lot less suspicion that way. So, does it feel weird to be sterile?"

"Doesn't feel like anything at all," Silk said. "I was born with it, so what would I compare it to anyway? If anything, it frees you from a certain amount of worry—you have sex with somebody, you don't have to fret about any little accidents.

If you get to the point where you want a child, you and your partner go in to your neighborhood clinic and have your sperm and ova put back on line. Takes about an hour and is covered under basic medical, doesn't even cost anything."

She shook her head. "I would have thought the Genetic Convention would have prevented such tampering."

"Everything else," he said. "Not that I'm an expert or anything, but it's pretty simple. A medic is allowed to fix any part of the human genomic makeup that is flawed, so there aren't any less-than-perfect children born, but no improvements on the basic model."

"So what were they afraid of? Two-headed guys with big dicks?"

He laughed. "I dunno. Maybe. My guess would be more along the lines of genetic supermen who would take over. Or maybe they were worried about crossing the wrong chain and creating another killer retrovirus like the old AIDS or the Sushi Plague." He shrugged. "It's not my field."

"So you got this nice stable population of—what?—seven billion?"

"Six and a half."

"And enough to go around for everybody."

"It's a little crowded in places, but basically, yeah."

"Kind of a dull utopia. Everything regulated up the ass, plastcrete stretching for hundreds of kilometers at a clip, healthy vegetables for a bland and boring diet."

"You don't like it, go back to the wilds where you can have ten kids and live in a house made of wood and burn dung for fuel."

It was her turn to laugh. "Never been offworld, have you?"

"No."

"It's not quite that bad. We have running water and everything on New Earth. And I hear the folks on York are thinking about replacing their animal fat lamps with hydroelectricity." Her voice was thick with sarcasm.

The arc ship's engines cut out and it coasted, still rising upward toward the outer edges of the atmospheric envelope. The silence was almost a tangible thing.

Danner peeled her cro-straps apart and slid the seatbelt off. She stood. "Even though you're a homebody, I like you, M. Silk. I'm going to the fresher."

She turned to start down the aisle, one of three on the

wide-body craft. She stopped and looked back at him. "You a member of the Twenty Klick Club yet?"

Silk's throat seemed to close up. He shook his head.

She smiled. "Want to join?"

Zia felt better. They'd gotten clear of the island without any further problems falling on them, were well on their way toward the mainland and laying a false trail. The land corridor from Seattle to Los Angeles was a busy place, tens of thousands of people traveling it every day. Once they touched down and she changed her identity again, they would blend into the herd and become invisible. Buy separate tickets, travel on a maglev train, maybe, and leave any pursuit scratching its head in Seattle.

As she walked toward the freshers in the rear of the aircraft, she could feel Silk's gaze on her from behind. A fresher wasn't the best place in the galaxy to fuck, but one could make do. She would give him a ride he wouldn't forget and bind him to her tighter because of it. It wouldn't be so awful. He wasn't bad-looking, seemed to be pretty bright if maybe a little more naive than he pretended to be, and he would have been without any sex since his woman died. Would have probably built up a nice charge by now, and she didn't care if he was shooting live ammo or blanks; her hormones weren't going to let her get pregnant if he spurted in her like a whale. Of course, that was just temporary, a one-year implant, and she could take it out whenever she wished. Not that she wanted any parasitic little versions of herself or a lover running around, but she sure wanted to have the *option*. How the people on this world—lilies, dole-ees, whatever—could allow themselves to be herded like sheep amazed her. Somebody tried to pass a law like the short-circuited reproduction system they had here on E2 and they'd be stuffed in barrels of molten construction plastic and thrown into the deepest gulch in the ocean. The terrans didn't mind because they obviously didn't need their balls anyhow.

The fresher door was just ahead. Silk back there was gonna need his testicles, though. For a little while, at least.

Ah, Zia, you're such a cynic.

King's AI program came up with nine possibilities, given the parameters of the search he instigated. Nine couples who

left the Port of Hana without any record of them ever having
arrived there. Of course, some could have come from other
islands via local air or sea traffic, and some might be locals
who lived here going elsewhere. Alas, none of the nine had
bought one-way tickets. That would have been too easy, not
to mention fairly stupid for an agent with any skill. King had
traced more than one person fleeing his company who had
made that mistake. Might as well have left a flashing neon
pointer for him. He didn't expect it here.

Of the possibilities, two couples were eliminated because
their destinations were offworld. He should have thought to
tell the AI that, but it hadn't occurred to him. The spy wouldn't
be going home just yet.

Of the seven remaining pairs, all were of about the right con-
figuration, insofar as King was able to determine. A man and a
woman traveling together, not too young or too old, according
to what ID his program could rascal from the travelcomp's
memory. Unfortunately, the local system was not set up to display visuals of the ticket buyers—too much memory required
for that—so all he had were the names, rudimentary biographs,
and destinations. The spy's documentation would be false, of
course, but likely deep enough to pass what inspection King
could bring to bear on it with his present hardware.

Four of the couples were traveling to the American mainland. One had as its destination Central Europe; one pair was
bound for Australia; the remaining duo had been booked on
a flight to Southeast Asia, an island in the Indian Ocean.

Now was where his experience must come into play. He
had not the means to follow or trace all seven couples. Given
time, he could hire agents of his own to establish surveillance
upon them, of course, but the flight times of the departed craft
would not allow enough leeway.

Staring at the color monitor's image floating over his computer, King made his choices.

Eliminate the pair going to Southeast Asia and the ones
journeying to Australia. If for no other reason than those
flights *would* be easy to trace because of their uniqueness.
A good spy would not flee to a place where she would be
traced so easily, and she would have to know something of
local geography even were she an *ausvelter*.

The European couple was a possibility, civilization was
especially dense on the continent and it would be easy to

get lost once they arrived, but King didn't think he would
do that in her shoes. Too far, the flight was the longest in
duration of the possibilities, thus offering the most chance of
being intercepted on arrival.

That left the four couples heading for the states. Two pairs
to L.A., one pair to Seattle, one pair to Chicago. They could
be any of them, but once more, the less time in transit idea
seemed reasonable to King. The closest destination and the
largest of the three metroplexes was Los Angeles. That's where
they were going. He couldn't be certain, of course, but it was a
calculated guess.

He had his computer book him a seat on the next flight
leaving, paying the exorbitant premium for the suddenness of
the reservation. He knew people he could use in Chicago and
Seattle to cover his less likely but still possible choices. Once
down in L.A., tracing the landees would be difficult, but not
impossible. It was likely the spy would use the same ID to
leave the port and he would only be an hour or so behind
her. The good thing about public transportation was that they
kept excellent records, records that Depard King knew how
to access. If his prey took a bus or cabriolet or even rented
a vehicle at LAX, he would be able to trace them. He'd have
to hurry, and he would need help on the ground there, too, but
it was still doable.

King left the hotel to go and do it.

Silk sat in his seat and stared at nothing. That this woman
had invited him to the fresher for fun and games was too easy.
Sure, she was gorgeous, and yes, he wanted to pound her, but
something about it wasn't right. Probably better if he sat right
here and waited for her to return.

Then again, he was still sure she knew something about
Mac's death. Given all the shit that had come down in the last
few days, he needed answers. So maybe it wouldn't be such
a bad idea to go and talk to her a little more . . . intimately.
Whatever her agenda, he was a spider, he could spin his own
scenario. He missed Mac, he wasn't over her death, despite
any hormonal urges he might be having; still, pillow talk could
be useful.

He stood. Found that his legs were a little shaky, but managed to amble his way down the aisle toward the fresher he'd
seen her enter.

• • •

Silk leaned back against the tiny sink and let his breath out in a ragged sigh. Danner squatted in front of him, her mouth on him, moving her head down almost to his base, her hands under his shirt to claw at his back. Oh, man! "Better quit that," he managed. Capacitorlike, he felt himself gathering voltage for a major spark.

She shook her head without moving her mouth away and began to suck him faster.

He held off as long as he could, then gave himself up to it.

"Oh!"

She swallowed, once, twice, three times, and when he had finished throbbing, she pulled away and grinned up at him.

"Your turn," he said.

She slid up his body, kissed him on the lips and thrust her tongue into his mouth. He tasted himself in the kiss, salty and slightly bitter. He broke the kiss, slid down, got to her nipple and sucked on it. She moaned, turning the sound into something almost like a purr. He continued his descent, moved and tugged at her clothes until he found that she was a natural blonde. Put his lips and tongue to work in the middle of the pale forest of downy hair.

"Mmm!"

He sucked and nibbled and used his tongue for long, lapping strokes and when she came, it was almost an ejaculation—her own salty, musky fluid ran down his chin. Her spasms were the most powerful he had ever experienced and they weren't stopping.

He had to feel that another way.

While she was climaxing he stood, fast, almost a lunge, and guided his still-erect penis toward her. She knew what he wanted, spread wide for him, and he buried himself in a single thrust.

The velvety clamp and release was exquisite, his passion roared hotter and he began to pound himself against her.

He was amazed at how fast he came again, at the shuddery, knee-buckling force of it.

He leaned against her, exhausted. It had never been this way with Mac. This was more exciting, more passionate, more . . . primal. Maybe that's how it happened with somebody you'd nearly been killed with only an hour or so earlier.

Silk was overwhelmed. He couldn't even speak. All he wanted to do was to lean against this woman, still stiff inside her, forever.

Zia was stunned.

Sex was her most powerful weapon, a tool, one she had always controlled, always.

Not this time. This time, the act crashed down on her like a wall shattered in an earthquake, it fell and buried her. She had *lost* it when he knelt in front of her, her brain had cut out, she'd gone stupid when his lips touched her mons.

She had *surrendered* to him.

That had never happened before, not *ever*, not since the age of fourteen and the first time she had discovered just what her power over men was.

It scared the hell out of her.

This guy was nothing, a civilian, not a player. There was nothing special about him, he was okay looking, that was all, but—

But *nobody* had ever touched her like this before.

Christ, what did it mean? Had her hormones gone crazy, was there some imbalance in her system? It had to be something like that, but even as she thought it, she felt herself shrugging mentally. So? It felt pretty good, didn't it? The best you ever had?

Yeah, that was true. And she wanted more of it.

And *that* was too scary to even *think* about.

She pushed him away, gently, but striving for control again.

"Better get back to our seats," she said. "We don't want any exploding bladders out there."

He managed a tired grin. "Let 'em pop," he said. "I could stay here forever."

She almost nodded, but caught herself. "Come on."

Reluctantly, he began collecting himself into his clothes. She cleaned up using wet paper towels, found her own underwear, struggled into it. It was cramped, and they kept bumping into each other. And it was *funny*. She had to work to keep from *giggling*. Jesus, she felt like a teener on a first date. Where was the ice bitch the other ops called her behind her back? How could this be?

Chemical, it had to be chemical, that was all.

But she found she was already wondering how it might be if they had a private room and a bed and plenty of time to play.

Jesus. What just happened here?

TWENTY

IT WAS LIKE a dream, Silk thought. Here he was on an arc ship dropping into SeaTac, a place four million people called home, sitting next to a spy who ten minutes ago had fucked him absolutely stupid. And the two of them were chasing another spy, one who had killed Mac. He had been shot, shot at again, and *none* of this felt remotely real. How could it be? He was a spindoc, a mid-level staffer for a major quasi whose only remotely esoteric skill was that he was pretty good with a crossbow—hardly something a terran secret agent would need to know.

"Masks and fems, please fasten your safety harnesses, we are entering SeaTac airspace in preparation for our landing glide." The femvox computer repeated the command in Japanese, Spanish, Mandarin and Bengali.

Silk locked his belts into place over his chest. It was a gesture, nothing more. It might make some people feel safer but he'd been spinning the results of dropbox and aircraft crashes for too long to be comforted by a seat harness. If this vessel plowed into the ground at speed, the passengers were all going to be stacked against whatever was left of the forward bulkhead like so many bloody pancakes.

Given what he had been through in the last few days, the idea of crashing didn't scare Silk a whole bunch.

Next to him, Danner was quiet as she snapped her own harness into place. She hadn't said much since they'd returned from the fresher. He would have sworn the sex had been as good for her as it had been for him, given her reactions in the tiny room, but she didn't act like it now.

Silk shook his head. Of all the things he didn't understand, women were at the top of the list.

Because he had been remiss earlier and all too aware of his inefficiency, King's level of awareness was heightened as he walked toward the somewhat-battered rental cart in the hotel's parking area. Thus it was that he saw the two men set to ambush him.

Normally he would have parked the vehicle in the busiest section of the lot, but because he had treated the cart ill, he did not wish to draw attention to it, so he had left it in a far corner with most of the damage facing away from the main traffic stream. That section of the plastcrete was nearly deserted.

King put his hand in his pocket, as though fishing for a keycard. He gripped instead the butt of his pistol. Another time he would have given the pair the benefit of the doubt, assumed they were what they purported to be, tourists exchanging a few words and smoking illegal tobacco cigarettes where no one would trouble them. Given the last few days, however, King's trust in his fellow men was nonexistent. Better to be paranoid and alive than naive and dead.

When he was within range, King pulled the pistol out and shot the nearer man.

Before the other man could pull a weapon of his own, King swung the pistol around to cover him. "Don't," he said.

The man spread his fingers and moved his arms away from his body. He had been under the gun before.

He hustled the second man toward the rental cart, forced him inside. "All right," he said, once he was also in the cart. "Who are you?" As he spoke, King relieved him of the sidearm he wore under the baggy shirt. The gun was an airpowered pistol, it would shoot lead or bismuth pellets, fatal if carefully placed at close range.

The man, tall and lean and almost hollow-cheeked, gave him a tight smile but said nothing.

"I can put darts in your eyes easily," King said. "You could spend months in the dark while they try to match them for a transplant. Or I could perhaps remove your manhood while you are unconscious. You could wake up blind and dickless. It is worth it?"

The thin man's grin only increased. Obviously he considered himself a hardcase. Mere threats of physical violence were not going to frighten him. And King did not have time to engage in any kind of extended torture. He could dart him and shove the unconscious form out of the cart, leave, and by the time whoever sent them recovered the pair, he would be well on his way to Los Angeles. Then again, such an act would leave him no more enlightened than he had been, regarding these new players. Information as to their identity could well prove necessary, even critical, later. No, he must know who they represented.

He had considered several possibilities since the shooting at Silk's. And he had eliminated some of these. The most likely possibility was that these two were in league with the offworld spy. A week earlier King would have been certain of this and would not have sought to explore other venues.

The two *could* be terran agents, part of the faceless new crop with whom King had never worked, but he did not think so. He had been out of the serious side of the business for some time, one might excuse his less-than-adept moves for lack of practice, but unless The Scat had gone completely rank, these two and the others at Silk's were even more inept than he; that did not seem likely. Aside from that, they did not move correctly. Scat operatives had a certain feel about them and his years in the business had, so he thought, given him the ability to recognize them. They did not seem good enough.

Which left the possibility, however remote, that this thin man was either a freelance who had happened across the same information as had King, or that he represented some player as yet unidentified.

It was best that King know which it was, and he had scant time in which to make the determination. If they were with the *ausvelter* spy as he suspected, that was not good but he could deal with it. If they were other, he must find out now.

Every man had something of which he was afraid, some terror that would cause him to do anything to avoid it. In his own case, it was not physical disability but mental malfunction that gave King shivers. To have one's mind fail was his worst fear.

"Go ahead, shoot," the thin man said. "Cut off anything you damn well please while I'm out, kill me. I'm ready to die. You don't scare me, you fucking polluter!"

Polluter!

King blinked. Polluter. Could it be? King's mind hummed and made the connection.

Well, indeed, it would make a certain kind of sense. There was an easy way to test the theory. The man had given him the lever he needed with that single word.

King smiled, kept the pistol pointed at the man's face. Reached into his pocket and pulled out a demistad coin.

The thin man looked at the coin. "Gonna buy me with that tenth?"

"Hardly. This only looks like a coin. Appearances can be so deceiving, don't you think? You look like a tourist, but you are not. I look like a civilized man, and that is not true, either. This is actually a highly sophisticated medical device. If I squeeze it, just so, and then scrape the milled edge against human skin, I can transmit a certain . . . infection to the person beneath that skin."

The man affected a shrug. "Poison. So what? Dead is dead."

"Oh, dear, perhaps I have given you a wrong impression. Forgive me. I don't plan to kill you. This isn't poison. It is a mutagenic retrovirus, an offworld bug tailored by the savages on Shinto. You won't feel a thing, won't notice the difference. But your DNA won't quite be the same. You won't ever be able to have normal children, and of course, anybody who comes into close contact with you will stand an excellent chance of catching the genetic disease—"

That was as far as he got before the thin man lunged at him, eyes wild, fear contorting his features, hands extended.

King shot him, twice, and still had to block the grab before the man collapsed.

He stared at the man. He hadn't even needed to come up with some horrible illness. The word "genetic" had done it. And that confirmed his newest suspicion. He had been wrong. These two were not the spy's confederates after all. A new set of players were in the game.

The Keep Humans Pure group had somehow stumbled into his discovery.

How very interesting.

When he was sure he was not being observed, King shoved the unconscious man out of the cart. He searched the other downed man and found his weapon, a match with the pellet

gun the thin man carried. They were willing to kill, given their
weaponry. So be it.

Using the second gun, he shot the thin man in the left eye.
He killed the other one with the thin man's gun. He placed
the guns into their hands and hurriedly departed. It might or
might not fool anybody but it would give them something to
think about for a time. And KHP would have to trot out a
new team.

Without appearing to do so, Zia watched Silk as the ship
finished its freefall segment and powered into a shallow glide.
They would be on the ground in a few minutes and she had
to get them out of the port without leaving a trail—even
though she was pretty sure they'd slipped pursuit, "pretty
sure" could get you killed. There was an old method, simple but almost infallible, and unless somebody with a gun
jumped them when they left the ship, Zia planned to use
it.

Next to her, Silk seemed calm. She'd certainly taken his
edge off, but she was also maybe a little more mellow than
she'd like to be herself, and that wasn't good. You wanted
to be a steppin' laserblade when you were in enemy territory,
able to slice your way out of trouble if need be, and right
now, fighting didn't interest her in the least. Not a good place,
she knew that with her brain, but her body liked it just fine. It
was the difference between being wired on speed or stoned on
hemp; while the latter felt better it wasn't where you wanted to
be, you had to move in a hurry. She didn't want to think about
it, what had happened with Silk, better to stick to business.
Maybe she'd better find herself a local doc-in-a-box and get
her hormone levels adjusted.

The engines of the craft rumbled louder as they banked to
the left and straightened, sinking fast. She looked through the
triple-plate windows, past the faint scratches caused by dust
brushing past at hypersonic speeds, and saw the ground rising
to meet them. The buses and cabs and trucks on the ten-lane
street below looked like toys, shining brightly in the late
afternoon sunlight. The air had a faint dirty tinge to it, a
brownish haze that hung low over green hills and what looked
to be remnants of an evergreen forest.

"Smog," Silk said. "Industrial pollutants mixed with natural
ones."

Zia said, "Hmm." She knew what smog was—there were cities on E2 where you couldn't see a hundred meters at noon on bad days. This was nothing compared to that.

"It used to be worse during the petrochemical days," Silk said. "Gasoline, lead, assorted oxides—looked bad and was worse for you. This stuff'll wash out in a good rain; it does that a lot here, rain."

The wheels of the heavy flier touched the runway with a rubbery *chonk!* The higher nose of the craft pivoted down and there was a second, quieter wheel-meeting-plastcrete sound.

"Masks and fems, we have arrived at our final destination of Seattle-Tacoma. Those of you continuing on other flights check departure times and locations with the gatecomp as you alight. Please remain in your seats until we have come to a complete stop at the terminal rampmobile."

Silk chuckled.

"Something funny?"

"Yeah. 'Complete stop.' What other kind is there?"

Zia nodded at him. "Is kinda redundant, isn't it."

Because they weren't carrying luggage, they were able to hurry past many of the passengers to the exit. The rampmobile had already arrived and Zia led Silk to the belt and onto it, continuing to walk and adding their speed to the conveyor.

"What now?"

She said, "We leave. After we stop at a bank first."

There was a row of ATMs just inside the terminal, gray blocks with keypads and holoprojic displays. Zia stopped at the first one and punched in a code. She held her latest fake ID where the reader could scan it. When the machine asked her what kind of transaction she wished, she tapped in a withdrawal for a thousand stads. That was enough money to be useful, not so much that the robot would take any particular note of it.

The drawer opened and Zia scooped out the crisp new bills. They liked multicolor folding money on this world—green, red, blue for different denominations. Normally she would have been content to use her credit cube but for the next part of this, she needed cash.

"Must be nice to be rich," Silk said.

"I wouldn't know, it isn't my money, it belongs to the taxpayers." She raised one hand and drew a short line on his chest with her forefinger. "That'd be you, sweetmeat."

She felt a quick surge of desire when she touched him, but she suppressed it and turned away. No, this was not good, this feeling. "Come on."

The terminal was huge, dwarfing anything on E2 or York, bigger even than the main ship's port on Paradise. And this was one of the smaller metroplexes. How could they live like this?

At the exit onto the surface streets, Zia walked along the line of cabs and buses and the few private cars, looking for what she wanted.

Ah. There. A delivery truck, a small electric van with faded lettering on the side that identified it as belonging to a flower shop.

The driver of the van was a young man with upswept hair that looked like a chopped-off cone. Like a miniature volcano had been stuck on his head. He sat in the no-park zone, drumming his fingers on the steering wheel, staring into space. The window was rolled up against the chilly afternoon. Zia tapped on the plastic.

Volcano-head looked at her blankly. She motioned for him to lower the window. He did.

"Yeah, what?"

"You want to make two hundred stads?"

His eyes got wide at that. He looked at Silk. "You want me to stomp him for you?"

"No, we just need a ride."

He looked at the row of empty cabs and buses waiting to be loaded in the line ahead of him and smiled. "Ah, gotcha. Where to, fem?"

Zia had the driver take them to the nearest large hotel, paid him, and after he departed, she repeated the routine with a kid working his way through college as a messenger.

After he dropped them off at a restaurant ten klicks away, they caught a cab to the maglev train terminal.

Silk shook his head. "Very nice," he said as they left the cab. "It would be almost impossible to track us, no logs anywhere close to the airport."

"That's the idea," she said.

"Of course, if somebody had been following us, keeping us directly in sight."

"Nobody was. Trust me here. I looked."

Silk nodded. He believed her.

"So now we catch an express train to L.A.," she said. "A nice three-hour trip down the valley. We pay cash for the tickets, unusual but not so much as to get us tagged by the ticketcomp."

"And we buy them separately under different names, right?"

She looked at him carefully. "That's pretty good. You sure you haven't done this kind of thing before?"

"Not at this level, but I get the idea. You want people looking where you point, not at your finger."

"You got it."

They went to buy their tickets.

TWENTY-ONE _____

HAD DEPARD KING been religious, had he the slightest real belief in any kind of higher powers, be they swart and hairy gods from human mythology or alien intelligences sitting in some cosmic control room, he would have thought surely he was being singled out by some such being for sport.

He paced in the L.A. port's VIP rest area, heedless of the soft chairs set artfully in the big room, too irritated to sit. His departure had been flawless, once he had disposed of the KHP agents at the hotel. He had gone to the port, sealed his weapons into an express mail tube that would be in Los Angeles waiting for him when he arrived, and boarded the flight without further incidence. The trip had been uneventful, he had allowed himself one drink, and slept for thirty minutes. Upon landing, he was met by the contract private investigator he sometimes utilized and shown the holographs of the couples arriving from Hana ahead of him. The small rat-faced man who could blend easily into any gathering larger than a handful had arranged to capture the likenesses of all the arrivees from Hana.

Unfortunately, none of them were the pair King sought.

Damnation!

Quickly he eliminated those names and had Ratso seek to determine if his subagents had been able to track the other couples, in Seattle and in Chicago. Now, all he could do was wait—

The agent interrupted his pacing, carrying a set of fax holos.

"Here are the two in Chicago," Ratso said.

King snatched the still-warm holographs.

"Not them."

"And a woman using this name withdrew a thousand stads from an ATM at the Port of SeaTac—"

The holo was blurry, a bad transmission, the resolution not nearly enough pixels for real clarity. Nine people of ten on the street would fail to make the match but King saw it. There she was. The fact she'd taken that much cash was also significant.

"That's her," King said.

"I'll get my people to check the rentals and buses—"

"It will be a waste of time," King said, "but go ahead and make certain—" He stopped.

Ratso stared at him. "Something?"

"Yes. Hold a moment."

So far, this entire affair had been an exercise in botchery, one ill-timed or insufficiently thought out move following another. While he certainly would have denied this to another, trying to pretend otherwise to himself was foolish. But in that instant, King had a flash of insight. As the old skills were recalled, as the days when he was at his sharpest fought free of the intellectual cobwebs and were allowed the light, it dawned upon him. It was not intuition, but rather a sub- or even unconscious collecting of information so subtle and gradual that it had to gather enough substance to be noticed:

The spy and Silk *were* coming here to L.A.

Such an assertion would only make sense to someone with an intensive background in espionage, one experienced in moving among the shadows under the rose and as in all things, one could not be certain of it; still, King knew it was so. If the spy had booked a flight directly to SeaTac, then she was too good to have gone there for the purpose of staying there.

And how could he know that L.A. was her real destination? Well, he could not, there was no reasonable explanation for that belief, none. But he was certain of it. He had, for the wrong reasons, arrived at the right place; more, he had done so before his quarry.

He smiled. If there be gods, certainly it was time they offered him some advantage. He had underestimated his opposition for the last time. He would assume—if he must assume anything—that the spy from offworld was as adept as he, better, perhaps. A good agent would hardly run in a straight line, he or she would expect the opposition to be sufficiently resourceful to eventually run down the thinnest thread if there was any way it could be done. If you expected to be followed no matter how convoluted your trail, you would take some care to leave at least a few red herrings pointing elsewhere, to delay if not altogether halt a tracker. Yes, they had gone to SeaTac but if the woman was as adept as King now realized she was, that would *have* to be a ruse. Anything else would be stupid and thus far she had not demonstrated such a thing. It was as if his personal gloom had been parted by a ray of sunlight, revealing a path in the wilderness. He was, finally, coming up to speed. He felt a sense of pride mingled with power.

"Check on transportation from Seattle-Tacoma to Los Angeles," he said. "Your parameters are limited to anyone who bought passage on a maglev train, local aircraft carrier or rental carriage using *cash*. Look for a single woman or a fem and mask couple leaving within the last two hours."

The investigator nodded, tapping the information into a small flatscreen he pulled from his belt. "That ought to narrow it down," he said.

"Indeed it should," King said. "Indeed it should."

Zia didn't have a lot of respect for the opposition. Yeah, they were fast on the trigger, but quick didn't matter if you couldn't hit your target. She had skated past them so far, and while that could be some kind of trick, she didn't think they were that smart. The game had been born on Earth, they had thousands of years more experience in the biz than the outworlds did, but it maybe had gotten a little senile on the home planet, too. If nobody makes a serious run at you for a long time, you might get to thinking you were invincible, that nobody could touch you. She had met people like that back on E2, guys who'd been in the field and been pretty hot twenty years ago, but who were past it. They sat in offices now, they bragged about the old days when things had been really tough, you ops today don't know shit, but they'd lost the moves. Lost the moves.

Zia leaned back against the hardfoam cushion of the train's seat. More comfortable than the aircraft had been. She glanced at Silk. He had his eyes closed but his breathing said he was awake. Something called the Willamette Valley zipped past the thick window at speed, they were moving at nearly four hundred and fifty klicks an hour. The track was elevated, a good thirty meters off the ground, and unless you looked way off in the distance, everything was a blur.

Yeah, so far, it had been a little tougher stroll in the park on a fine spring day, but not all that much. She had things well in hand, except for this hormone thing, and that was no big deal. She was a pro. Just because she found an itch didn't mean she had to scratch it.

Yeah?

Yeah.

Once they got to L.A. she would use another of her IDs, change her appearance yet again, and begin her search for Spackler. Between now and then, she could maybe dig something useful out of Silk to help on the hunt. Whatever.

Hell, maybe she could get a nap in, too.

Silk kept his eyes closed, pretending to be asleep. Truth was, the vibrations of the train had rocked him into a daydreamy state that wasn't too far away from nodding off . . .

The kid who had been running up and down the aisle just to trip the motion sensor that opened the door between this car and the one ahead of it thudded past for the tenth time. The double doors hissed as the pneumatics slid them open again. Just enough noise to be irritating, coming at odd intervals you couldn't get used to.

Silk slitted his eyes and looked at the girl, about six or seven, he guessed. Little rat. If she barreled past one more time, he was going to stick his foot out and trip the little monster. Where were her parents? Why didn't they put a leash on her?

Abruptly the thought made Silk grin. His father used to tell him that when he was young. Gonna put a leash on you, you little turd. Gonna nail one of your feet to the floor . . .

"Vennie? You in there, sharp?"

Vennie Silk laughed at Poncie. "Where else would I be, dumbo?"

Like him, Poncie was pushing twelve, and they had the day off from edcom 'cause of the storm.

"Yeah, well, open the window for a minute. I can't stay."

Vennie cranked the window to his room open, the handle squeaking as the mechanical arm shoved the plastic plate outward. He didn't bother to pull the mosquito net off, but let the casement frame stretch it like a sheet of rubber.

Poncie Williams stood on the wet ground just outside. The rain had stopped—supposed to be a hurricane the weather guys couldn't short out in time making it rain so much—but the wind was still gusting pretty good out there. The people on the coast only a few klicks south of here had been told to take off and glue down everything that could move before they left, too. The Mississippi Gulf Coast was gonna get pasted tonight, that's what the ClimateCom guys said. His dad said they would be okay here, though, prefab was too crappy for the wind to bother with.

"How come you can't stay?"

Poncie glanced over toward his cube, identical to Vennie's except Poncie's mother had painted it yellow instead of the usual green. Looked like baby puke, too. A stray wind gust picked up a piece of trash and twirled it past.

"My gramma kicked," he said.

"Tough."

"Yeah, well, she was old. Like sixty. Heart attack or something. She'd been in the hospital for like a month or something with the broken hip. Got an em—emboll something and it killed her. We gotta go do a funeral thing, my ma says."

"Sorry you're gonna miss the storm, sharp."

"Yeah, me, too. You ever wonder about what it's like?"

"What what's like?"

"Being dead?"

Vennie shrugged. "Not much. You get old or you get smashed up by a bus, you die. End of story. Can't do nothing about it." That's what his father said. *We get born, we live, we die, kid. End of story.*

"Yeah, I guess."

So Poncie left and Vennie went back to watch the entcom channel. And when the news of how a tree fell on a bus came on a couple of hours later, killing nine local residents, it didn't mean anything to Vennie.

Until he found out that one of the nine was Poncie Williams, age eleven.

He'd known Poncie since they'd been seven, more than four years, and he just couldn't believe he was *gone.* It didn't make any sense. How could something like that happen? It wasn't *fair.* It wasn't *right.*

Vennie lay on the bed and stared at the dull gray textured paint of the ceiling, all spiderwebbed with cracks that showed the prefab underneath. Outside the wind blew hard, making the casement edges howl, *woo-woooo*, like something from an entcom monster vid. No more rag-tag, no more sneaking into old man Jersey's store and stealing lik-a-sticks, no more trying to download the NC porno files from Online, at least not with Poncie. It didn't seem real. It was like a dream. In the morning he'd wake up and Poncie would be waiting at the bus stop, wearing that stupid purple shirt his auntie gave him, ready to razz the edcom teachers, just like always.

But the wind moaned and slapped at Vennie's house, threw recycle bins down the street and knocked trees over and when it was done and the morning lit things up, Poncie was still dead.

Poncie was always going to be dead, from now on.

The little twat triggered the door again and the sound woke Silk from his half sleep, half daydream. He didn't really mind it this time.

If you were a Christer or a Moham or into some other religious crap, if you bought into the fairy tales, then dead didn't matter. It was better, in some cases, to be dead—you won the big prize. But Silk had never spent much energy on mysticism. If there was a god in charge somewhere, he either had a fucking warped sense of humor or was pretty damned inept, given what went on in the galaxy. You had to be real lucky to get through life with any kind of joy at all; about the time you thought you were doing okay, the cosmic finger would ram itself up your ass, like it had with Poncie, like it had with Mac. Fuck that, and fuck God if He existed and did it on purpose or even let stuff like that happen if He could stop it. Silk didn't know what the wahees who were into religion thought mercy was, but he knew rat shit when he heard it.

Next to him, Danner apparently dozed. He looked at her.

She was almost beautiful, even with the crappy haircut and dye job and when it came to, well, coming, she was the best he'd ever had. There was a time when he would have been holding onto her like a clamp, trying to suck what energy he could from the experience, wanting to continue what he had discovered, but not now. No, now he didn't want to let himself get too close because he knew it wasn't going to last. Good stuff never lasted. Change would come and wipe it away, and what was the point? It hurt too much every time it was ripped away and he was getting tired of losing pieces of himself. Pretty soon there wouldn't be much left, just scraps of gristle and bone without feeling. He didn't need that.

She sighed in her sleep and her mouth gaped a little. She was a spy and from what he'd seen so far, a cool tool, hard and sharp and not giving anything away, but while she slept, she looked innocent, pure, sweet.

He looked away and shook his head. Don't get attached, Silk. That way lies pain.

TWENTY-TWO _____

As ALWAYS WHENEVER there was anybody else around, Zia's sleep was light, her automatic control on-line. Some noise on the speeding maglev train worked its way into her subconscious and triggered an alarm. She awoke instantly but the noise, whatever it had been, was past, no danger she could sense attached to it.

Next to her, Silk watched her come awake.

"I'm going to the fresher," he said. "And I'll stop by the snack bar on the way back. You want anything?"

"Something cool to drink."

He stood, stretched, and ambled off down the wide aisle.

Zia stared through the window at the countryside hurtling past. She hadn't offered to go to the fresher with him. The idea had flitted across her mind and because she wanted to go and see what variations might come up, she held herself back. She knew addicts, people who had to have something to the point where they would do anything to get it. People who craved drugs, exercise, even sex, though she'd never understood how that one worked before.

She understood it now. It wasn't going to happen to her.

Thinking about the terrain outside was safer. It was getting near dark, lights starting to kick on here and there, trailing phosphor lines if they were close enough to the track for the speed to stretch them out. She liked riding trains, did a lot of that when she'd been growing up. Trains showed you the back sides of places, spots you'd never see if you were in a plane or a flitter or even a car. Even on a young world like New Earth,

most trains still went to the industrial sections of cities, into
the factories and foundries and agroplexes. The big passenger
trains skipped a lot of that, but not everybody used the express
line. Short runs often tacked a passenger car onto the back of
a lumbering, rocking freighter and you got to see the places
they didn't dress pretty for the tourists. She'd always liked
that, being able to see the truth behind the facade.

Not that you could always separate those two in your own
life.

As she sat staring, the two men in the seats behind her
cranked up their conversation again. They'd been gone for
a while, to where you could buy liquor or smoke, and obviously they'd spent more than their share of time and money
at the place.

"Ah, fuckin' Mexico," one of them said. The younger one,
maybe twenty-two or -three, she guessed. "I hate that place.
Cops are always trying to get you for something."

"I hear you," the older one said. " 'Cept for Tijuana. Great
pussy in Tijuana."

"Yeah, that's right, I forgot about that. But them cops, man,
they're all crooks. You gotta keep a hold on to your ID, you
know? They'll steal it, sell it to somebody, just like that." He
snapped his fingers.

Zia shook her head. Drunks seemed to be the same all over
the galaxy.

"Yeah, you right. One time I was down there, trying to find
a friend of mine, we was supposed to go see the guy and the
donkey show, you know the one, when these two cops stopped
me . . ."

Zia remained aware of the sound but tuned the words out.
She had places to go and things to do, she wasn't so foolish
as to think her job was all gonna be like a class drill, she
was, after all, hunting one man who could be anywhere on
the planet. But she really wasn't worried about it. Spackler's
bent was severe enough so that he had run away from home
to indulge in it and even here on perverse old Earth the market
wasn't all that big for what he liked. She had been told you
could get anything you wanted here on the homeworld, you
had the stads and connections, but sometimes you had to go
a ways to find it.

E2ers were pretty liberal about how you pleasured yourself,
as long as consenting adults were involved. They took a dim

view of adults messing with children or animals, however. The children thing was easy enough to see, and nobody much argued with that; the animal relationship question was a bit harder. So what if a farmer out in the middle of nowhere valley wanted to play games with a sheep or whatever? His business, wasn't it? New Earth wasn't like the old planet, was it? Did everything that everybody did have to be regulated to the last dotted "i" or comma?

No, the answer came, but when it involved the health of the race, maybe it needed a look. Yeah, the terrans were bugfuck about quarantine after they lost people to an *ausvelter* plague, but at the time it made sense, even if it didn't later.

So, the animal lovers said, what's that got to do with anything?

So, animals carry certain diseases that constantly mutate. Some of which even the E2 tackdrivers can't nail down and cure. Remember the original AIDS retrovirus?

Yeah, so? Like Black Plague, right? They cured that a long time ago, right?

Right. Except, the prevailing theory is that people would never have caught it in the first place if some wetwick wadjii out in the backcountry hadn't held down a monkey and stuck his dick in it just to see how good it was—then went home and gave what he picked up to his human lover.

Oh.

Yeah. Oh.

"Here you are," Silk said.

She took the paper cup from him and sipped at it. Some sweet and fizzy concoction, not bad. "Mm. What's this?"

"Coke," he said. "You don't have this on E2?"

She sipped at the drink again. "Not yet."

"There's a reason to stay home right there."

That got a smile from her. Damned if she didn't like this guy. She wished she could understand why.

King knew that patience was a virtue in his business but he was nonetheless impatient. Ratso had come up with more than thirty possibilities, people traveling from the Seattle plex to the SoCal area, via air, maglev, even by boat. The last didn't make sense and would take days to arrive in any event; the others were more pressing. Ratso had half a dozen people at the air terminals for the dozen couples or so who would arrive by air; fortunately, several of them would be on the same flights. King himself sat in the Delta-United waiting area at LAX anticipating the arrival of the next flight, only moments away from landing. He had altered his appearance yet again, this time in a way he thought sufficiently clever to fool even a wary spy: he was now in the guise of Larry Mkono, South African. He'd thickened his nose and lips with an injection of pseudocollagen his body would absorb and excrete harmlessly via his kidneys in a few days; he'd darkened his skin to a deep chocolate and now sported a pair of brown contact lenses and a black, curly wig. At this juncture, his intent was merely to find the quarry and follow them. The passage of time had cooled his anger somewhat so that vengeance, while still a part of his intent, was not uppermost in his consideration. He would attend to that later, of course, but for now, his efforts must be made to pay in other coin.

"Delta-United flight 1088 is now arriving at gate 77," the PA system chipvox said in English. It went on to repeat the announcement in several other terran languages, most of which King was able to understand. In Japanese, the sentence ended with the verb; in Bengali, it could have been one plane or more, depending on the context; in Spanish, the dictionary program used the old style word "avion," which could be either an aircraft or a certain bird, depending once again on the context . . .

The passengers filed off and into the terminal. Many had friends or relatives waiting, and the embraces, smiles and genuine bonhomie grated on King. No one had been waiting for him with smiles at a terminal thus for a long long time. None of his family still lived, save a sister who didn't know if he were alive or dead; no wife, no lover, no one of any permanence in his life. True, he was not an unattractive man and certainly he could have such relationships, did he really desire them, but always his work had been his mistress. As a teacher it had been history who first sang seductive songs to him; as a spy, the thrill of the hunt, the chase, those had been sufficient. Lovers, of course, he had indulged himself aplenty, and once, a brief affair with a British agent had shown promise, had seemed about to bud into full flower, but she had died in a ferry explosion in Hong Kong, another of the senseless accidents that had no meaning, no explanation. It had been twelve years ago and he had not thought very much about her for a long time. Lately, however, such scenes as this airport greeting sometimes brought her to mind. Reflections on his personal history, the days of his youth, he supposed. Some early mid-life ruminations on the road not taken. Pointless, a waste of time.

The happy-to-see-and-be-seen travelers and receptionists thinned and departed and while he waited for half an hour to be certain his prey had not hung back to confound pursuers, he knew they had not been on this aircraft.

He tapped the control on his inside-the-ear phone and subvocalized Ratso's number into the button mike crowed to his shirt collar. Despite the earplug's tiny size, the voice was clear and sharp when Ratso answered, the bass register giving him an almost normal tone.

"Yeah?"

"Nothing here," King said.

"Here, either. There's one more in about fifteen minutes, a crop duster flight that picks up and drops people in every burg on the way here, from Portland to San Luis Obispo."

"I'll meet you at the gate," King said. "Discom."

King stood, flicked the phone on standby, and started for the exit. He would not have to leave the building complex, but he passed several tall, sealed windows on his way to the other jetline terminal. Outside, night fought once again its electrical nemesis and lost, the lights of the port easily holding back the darkness. Once, night had been supreme, cloaking the Earth more or less unchallenged. Oh, certainly there were stars and the moon, and pale flickery generated by the planet herself: glowing volcanoes and stormy lightnings, phosphorescent St. Elmo dancing on the seas; there were the lures generated by creatures of the deeps and insects of the air, foxfire in rotted tree stumps, stray wisps of swamp gas combusting spontaneously, sparks from quartz under pressure . . . but those lights were faint, those were ancient history. King had been to places like Hana where the city glow glimmered faintly enough to reveal even the minor constellations, but those places grew fewer each year. A popular nightclub outlined in blue neon sat atop K2; Antarctica sported an internationally acceptable city called Cold Town of more than forty thousand permanent residents. A resort in the Gobi was home to a fifty-klick man-made lake, a disneyland and sixty-nine hotels. Time's bright arrow flew onward, and the dark past could not keep up. That had always been the way of it.

They still had an hour or so until the first of the maglevs arrived. Ratso had people two stations on either side of the L.A. stop and he and King would be at the main terminal when the train got in. He knew he had no choice but to set his snares and await results, but he did not like it.

Patience, he told himself. Patience.

"We'll be arriving in Los Angeles in about forty-five minutes," Silk said.

Danner nodded.

Despite the fact he had been sated only a few hours before, he felt a strong sexual urge gripping him. He fought it—not too hard—then told himself, what the hell: "I don't suppose you'd like to take a walk with me down to the fresher?"

She looked at him. Stared at him. "I don't think—" she began.

He nodded, started to turn away, brushed her leg with his. The energy was electric, gooseflesh arose, the hair on his neck tingled. Jesus!

She felt it, too, for she gasped.

Time stretched thin and long.

"Oh, hell," she said. "Oh, hell. Let's go."

She led the way, and Silk hurried to keep up with her.

TWENTY-THREE _____

THE TECHNOLOGY OF fake ID manufacture being what it was, King could have easily convinced the rail authorities he was a police official, but there had been no need. He stood on the platform playing a citizen awaiting a beloved one, as he had seen others do at the air terminal only a few minutes earlier. He was not alone and no one begrudged him his nearness to the incoming train. Unlike the worry about air hijackings that had never entirely gone away, even in these relatively weaponless and civilized times, stealing a maglev train was unlikely in the extreme. King supposed there were people that stupid, but the obvious question of where one would *take* a pilfered train had thus far kept the speeding bullets relatively safe from interference. A train was mated to the magnetic repellors of its track and it would travel nowhere else, certainly not under its own power. The weapon scanners still standard at air- and spaceports were not to be found at train stations, though bomb sniffers were used on luggage, whether carried on or checked through. Some new terrorist organization was always a worry, albeit not a major one.

King, in his South African disguise, smiled. He hardly thought the spy or her consort would be carrying any explosive devices.

The approaching train sent a shudder through the vibrating platform. The aerodynamic nose of the engine glinted under the station lights, the titanium cap scratched but still brilliantly shiny. The train itself was quiet, and the pulsedampers mounted along the sides of the rail bed kept the powerful magnetic flux from stealing any stray bits of steel or iron from standersby or ruining delicate computer circuitry. The trains themselves were shielded, of course, but in the early experimental days the track beds had become littered with metallic detritus that fell or was tossed toward the tracks. There were stories of bicycles being jerked into the rails, of chronometers stopping blocks away, of superconducting industrial motors shattering when a train passed by half a kilometer distant. Infant technologies usually had problems. The first nuclear power plants produced massive amounts of radioactive waste, the first starships sometimes logged into Empty Space and were never seen or heard from again. The price of civilization. As an historian, King found such things fascinating. Truth was so much more interesting and stranger than fiction.

He allowed his mind to wander as the train slowed. He recalled the last words of the Union general, John Sedgwick, uttered some seven or eight hundred meters from the Confederate firing line at the Battle of Spotsylvania, during the Civil War: "Why are you men dodging so? They couldn't hit an elephant at this distance—"

The trained rolled silently to a stop and people immediately began streaming from the exits. King had taken a position by which departing passengers would have to pass him to reach the interior of the station. Ratso was posted on the opposite side of the train just in case someone tried to slip past that way.

The stream of people flowed past, some being met, others not, a shifting, many-footed creature ambling along like a somewhat disjointed centipede—

There they were!

King fought to keep from moving suddenly, and to maintain his neutral expression. He wanted to smile broadly, to proclaim victory, but this was only the first step, and he had been thwarted too many times during this entire episode to allow overconfidence to claim him again. Remember your training, do this by the numbers. Somebody might well be able to hit an elephant at this distance.

He could not risk that the spy might see through his disguise, even though he was fairly certain she was not expecting him here. He turned and moved toward the terminal's interior, joining the flow of traffic as if he were one of them, his quarry thirty meters behind him.

When he was inside the entrance, King moved to his right, to the side of the door. The crowd pooled somewhat as more of the passengers were met. Thus impeded, the press of bodies thickened, and when the spy and Silk worked their way through the mass, the density was enough so that another light touch would be unnoticed.

As Silk passed by him, King moved in close and fired the spring-powered piston of the responder tube; at the same time, he shoved a little girl, using his hip, so that she stumbled into Silk, hitting him solidly and nearly falling herself.

"Hey!" Silk said.

The tiny sting of the smaller-than-a-pinhead responder burying itself in the thick and not particularly sensitive skin and muscle of Silk's upper back would, King hoped, be lost in the sensation of the child bumping him.

"Jesus, watch where you're going!"

When the little girl turned to see who had pushed her, King was already lost in the crowd.

King worked to keep the pair in sight, but the pressure to do so was greatly lessened. The problem with tailing a trained operative who would certainly be alert for any signs of surveillance was that it was almost impossible to do without four or five operatives of one's own. There were a dozen ways to reveal a shadow, were there the slightest suspicion such existed, and King expected the *ausvelter* to utilize them. Maintaining contact with a subject was easy enough, but doing so without the subject becoming aware of it, did they bother to look properly, was another matter entirely. If you could see them, it was likely they could see you, and since secrecy was paramount here, King could not risk it. Even if his disguise worked now, it would not continue to do so. If the spy spotted him more than a time or two, he would be burned. Ratso was good, but King did not trust his sub-ops. Therefore, the responder.

As the couple exited the terminal and searched for a taxi, King tapped his phone and called Ratso. "Bring the car," he said. "I have them."

They carried no luggage, King noted as he hung back, pretending interest in a wall-mounted holoproj ad for the latest in high-tech running shoes. He pulled his transmitter from his tunic pocket and touched a small pressure pad. The tiny LCD screen lit and a map and coordinates flowered colorfully. A dot blinked on, gave a small *ping!*, and blinked off.

King grinned. The technology was hardly the state of the art, it was thirty years out-of-date, but sufficient here for his needs. The tiny pellet buried under Silk's skin contained a flashchip memory module around which was built a microtransceiver. Unlike bugs of earlier stripe, the responder did not broadcast unless it was asked, and then only if by a very specific command on a minuscule frequency bandwidth. Thus provoked, it gave out a fiftieth of a second compressed pulse and no more. Someone scanning for a hidden bug would therefore be most unlikely to find the responder. Since it gave off no signal until queried, a scanner would have to be operating when that happened, and while there were rooms where monitoring took place constantly, a spy on the move would probably not have access to such a place. Even so, a single compressed pulse could easily be missed or dismissed as background noise. The pellet itself was muoplastic, more or less transparent to common medical X-ray or ordinary fluroproj scans, and coated with hypoallogenic polymers that would offer a normal immune system little about which to worry itself. The power source was electrochemical, using an AAHO differential designed to run from contact with mammalian flesh and would normally last for nearly a month.

Push the button on his transceiver and it would *ping*. And with that tiny cry, Silk's little parasite would tell King exactly where it—and Silk—were.

He had them now.

In the taxi, Zia watched Silk rubbing his back against the seat. "Something?"

"Yeah, got a little itchy spot."

"I'll scratch it for you later."

"You already took care of that just fine," he said. He smiled.

Zia nodded and returned the grin. Yeah, she sure had. And it had been every bit as good as the first time. She could get used to that kind of lovemaking in a hurry. And at the moment, she was less resistant to the idea than she had been. Consider Silk: Here was a guy who suddenly had a load of crap dropped into his lap—partner killed, assassins running around, spies and undercover stuff—and yet he was functioning. It was easy enough for her to shrug stuff like this off, it was her job, she had been in training or doing it for so long it seemed normal to her. But to a civilian, it must be a big bump in the road to hit at speed all of a sudden. Give him points for that.

Then again, he was naive. That he'd drank the story she'd poured didn't speak real well for him. Yeah, she was good, but she wouldn't have swallowed it when she'd been sixteen. She'd already learned by that age that most, if not all, men said whatever they thought would get them what they wanted. And women, too.

No, she wanted smart in a man, somebody who wouldn't let somebody like her come in and dance him around like a trained *doub* at the kiddie petting zoo.

Interesting conflict, isn't it?

Yeah. On the one hand, she liked 'em sharp and ready. On the other hand, she didn't trust those she knew in the biz who *were* S&R. You want a player, you have to expect him to play. Nature of the beast. You have to grind off some rough spots to get slick enough to slide good, but sometimes along the way you lose too much. A thin layer there between just perfect and ruined, isn't it? And trust was never part of the equation.

Not, she thought, that she was looking for any long-term connections anyhow. This was biz, she'd get it done and go home. Later was later. Now was what counted.

One of the reasons Silk was such a good liar was that he had a feel for the truth. He'd learned that the best stories always have plenty of that in them, otherwise they don't scan—not for very long or for very many listeners, anyway.

As he sat next to Danner in the taxi, going to God only knew where, that piece of him that was somehow always connected to the truth, the part that knew gold from iron pyrites stood shaking its head at him. *She's a great fuck, the best you ever had—*

Yeah, *that* was true—

Shut up and listen. But you know what I'm going to say anyhow, don't you?

Yeah. Danner—if that was her name—wasn't exactly painting him the whole pix.

Ratshit, pal. She's a liar. First class, big time, mondo mucho primo.

Yeah.

So, what are you doing here?

Silk thought about that.

The taxi driver muttered, "Fuckin' traffic controllers!"

Around them, the flow of cars and buses and assorted smaller vehicles—cycles, bikes, trikes—had slowed to almost a crawl. The street leading from the train terminal was sixteen lanes wide, not counting the pedestrian walks on the sides, which were virtually empty of walkers but which had cyclists apparently willing to risk an expensive citation for illegally using the walk.

"This ain't supposed to happen," he said. "Fuckin' property taxes went up, sales tax went up, income tax, everything, to pay for the most expensive piece of hardware and software in the world to regulate the fuckin' traffic. And look."

Silk glanced out the window. It was night but the lights of the vehicles and the post lamps sprouting from the sides of the street made it look like a soccer stadium. *Jesus, it doesn't even get dark here. Definitely not Hana.*

How would he spin this, it was his job? *Be tough.* If this was what it looked like in L.A. any substantial part of the time— and it was—coming up with clever stories would get old real quick. Assuming the government didn't want the equipment or its operators blamed, traffic terrorists, major sabotage, or acts of God would only go so far before the lilies started shaking their heads and not buying it.

L.A. had always had too many vehicles in too small a space—Silk remembered reading in some history com there was a time when there were more private automobiles in the area than there were people to operate them—but the computer system the driver was talking about was supposed to guarantee a steady forty klicks per hour anywhere in SoCal. Looked like they blew that one.

Getting off the subject here, aren't we?

Silk stared at the creeping traffic. People were lighting their phone number signs and flashing them through bus and car windows, can't move, might as well talk. Silk knew a couple who had met that way, during a jam, and wound up contracted—

Silk—

Hey, fuck you, okay? I'm here because whatever else she is, Danner is some kind of spooklet. She knows stuff she couldn't know otherwise, she knows about Mac. Maybe that part of her story is true, okay? She couldn't have just pulled that out of the air, she *has* to know something about all this crap and even if she's lying about most of it, some of it has to be real. I would know if it wasn't.

That much I'll stipulate. But is it the real reason?

Silk looked at a busty woman with purple hair and a too-tight shirt stretched across her chest framed in the lighted window of a bus looming to the right. She had her name and phone number flashing in pink next to her face as she smiled down at the stream of traffic. "Kandi," the name was, and the number had a toll-code in front of it. A professional talker of some kind, he realized, pornocon, probably, but maybe a psycher—looks could fool you. Was she just taking advantage of a rare jam? Or did this happen often enough that she did this regularly? Climbed onto a bus, flashed her number, sold talk to bored drivers or riders who spent too much time turtling along the streets?

Silk?

Yeah, yeah. Mac is part of it. And maybe if we hadn't screwed our brains out in the freshers I'd be catching the next arc ship home, I don't know, okay? It's an interesting ride, I don't have anything else I have to do, I want answers—what do you want from me?

Why, nothing but the truth, That's all I ever want.

You're asking for a whole fuck of a lot, pal.

Kandi slipped on a headset, smiled, and dimmed her number. She had a customer.

Silk's back itched and he rubbed it against the seat.

TWENTY-FOUR

WHEN THE TRAFFIC finally allowed freer movement, Zia had the taxi drop them at a large hotel near the train depot. They caught a second conveyance and went back past the terminal in the opposite direction. As far as she could tell, they were clean, hadn't picked up a tail. Not that she'd expected one, but you always checked.

After a short discussion with the driver of the third cab, a much longer ride took them to a small, somewhat run-down hotel in a rather seedy section of the metroplex called Woodland Hills. Zia saw traces of what had been a nice town once upon a time, but whatever it had been was mostly gone. The shops jammed together along the streets wore faded and peeled storefronts, the neon and fauxholo signs flickery or partially burned out, the metal or cheap fullerene-woundwire bars over the scratched plastic windows scaled with rust or gone buckyball gray. In among the food markets and clothing shops were a thick sprinkling of pornoproj palaces, skinstores, tattoo parlors, alcohol and smoke shops. Apparently prostate massage was a big seller here, too. On stucco walls and storefronts where there had once been blank spaces, pulse-paint graffiti gleamed dully in overlays that had to be ten layers deep in places. People made their marks, expressed their art, only to see it covered over by someone else who wanted a piece of the passing audience, probably before the colors had a chance to set and dry properly. There were more pedestrians here than she'd seen before, but not the kind of folk you wanted to stop and chat up. Here swaggered a troop of muscle boys and girls in white spandex that covered them from hair to feet but showed everything down to their pores; there, two chemheads shuffled along in some thick mindfog, unconnected to their surroundings. Whores of both sexes stood or walked, raising flaps or opening pop seams at the street traffic, showing off the goods underneath their clothes, trolling with live bait for paying customers. Three children, pre-teen boys from their looks, sprinted suddenly out of a small market. A fat man dressed in orange robes and a turban and waving a knife followed them but gave up the chase within a few meters.

Zia had been in worse neighborhoods, though not recently.

She'd have to see about getting some kind of weapon pretty quick. You wanted to swim with these lamprey, you'd better have teeth to show them.

"You take me to the nicest places," Silk said.

She turned away from the diorama of urban underclass and looked at him. "It's not *my* planet, Terry."

"You don't have slums on E2?"

"Not like this."

"Well. You're a young world. A good slum takes a long time to build."

"I thought the birth control laws were supposed to eliminate stuff like this. To save enough resources for all."

" 'The poor have always been with us.' And the lazy. Nobody starves on Earth, the dole sees to that. If you don't have to work to live, some people take that as a sign they shouldn't."

"So you're saying it's their own fault they live like this?" She waved at the street.

"Not all of them, but some of them . . . yeah. Everybody gets meals and medical and shelter, a clothing chit, plus basic edcom. Anybody who wants to go further can get more assistance to do it, they want to. Some people like the easy route."

"You think being a street whore is easy?" As if to underscore her words, a heavyset woman with bright red hair lifted a loinclothlike patch of her tight pants to show a thick nest of pubic hair dyed the same hot shade as her head. The hair had been trimmed into the shape of a cartoon heart. She had a tattoo or maybe a drawing on her pooched-out belly of an androgynous face with mouth open and tongue outthrust so that the end of it disappeared under the hairy heart. She thrust her mons at the cab and yelled something that didn't penetrate the interior save as a vague question.

Silk shook his head. "I didn't say that. But there is a choice. What that whore does requires no special skill and if she can avoid the regulators, she won't even have to pay the tax or license fees. There are jobs going begging even here, but she would have to stand on an assembly line or smile at surly customers all day to make the same money she can make spreading her legs for twenty minutes. That's her choice."

"And whose fault is it she can make more selling sex than working honestly?" It wasn't until after she had spoken that Zia realized how angry she was, and that her voice had climbed into that anger. And being a professional whore took more skill than he thought.

Silk stared at her. "Not mine."

She turned away from him and looked back at the street. "Unless you're born rich, you have to sell some piece of yourself if you want to get ahead."

"There's always the dole," he said.

She didn't speak to that.

The cab wound its way up a hill, past buildings that had once been large houses before they'd been subdivided into rental rooms. Here the streetlights allowed more of night's dark to enshroud the city, there were patches where little if any light went. No private cars parked on the street, no bicycles that weren't chained to something solid. Not a neighborhood in which you would be taking an evening stroll alone, not if you had any brains.

"You sure about this?" Silk finally asked.

Danner turned away from the window, glanced at the cabbie, then at Silk. "Yeah. I'm sure."

When he started to say more, she cut her gaze to the driver and shook her head slightly, warning him not to speak further.

He shut up.

The cab reached the top of the rise. Ahead lay a small hotel, a squarish block of prefab that went several levels down the side of the hill. A green neon sign protected by a thick wire mesh identified the building as the Outside Inn. As Silk watched, an insect flew into the sign's mesh and was zapped by a charge of electricity, sparkling once as it burst into flame and then fell trailing a thin line of green-tinged smoke. If there were warnings that the mesh was dangerous, he didn't spot them. Here as on the streets below, the windows and door were protected by bars.

The cabdriver took his payment, slammed the door and snicked the locks into battery, gunned the electric motor and sped away.

As Silk and Danner moved up the walkway toward the hotel's door, two men stepped out of the shadows into their path.

Silk's gut twisted and his bowels went loose and tight at the same time. Fear laid icy hands on his shoulders and throat and he wanted to turn and run. Violence was supposed to be under control on Earth. He had believed that, until lately. On a world where owning a gun was worth major locktime, it seemed that every other person he'd met lately was carrying a weapon and dangerous. These men weren't terribly huge, nor did they seem to be armed—he could see their hands and they were empty—but the sense of threat was as thick in the air as his fear was in him. One of the men wore a blue lamé jacket that had seen better days; the other had on a black shirt with the sleeves cut out, showing flabby bare arms that wore monochrome blue tattoos up and down their lengths: snakes, spiders, what looked like a rat.

"Hey," Tattoo said, "you got change for a fiver?"

Before Silk could speak, Danner said, "No—and I'd be real surprised if you had a fiver." Her voice was flat, hard, and as cold as Silk's bowels felt.

Lamé snickered. "No need to be shitty about it, twatso."

"You are between us and the door," Danner said.

Jesus, was she crazy? Why didn't she just give these guys a couple of stads and let them go about their business? She was stepping on their balls.

Silk gathered himself, found his hands had already clenched into fists. He hadn't been in a fight since he was fifteen, these guys could have guns or knives in their pockets, was Danner trying to get them killed?

Tattoo stepped forward, toward Danner, and raised his hand, as if to push her or grab her shirtfront.

Oh, fuck—! Silk started to take a step to meet him, so nervous he was shaking.

Time stalled, stopped, then restarted—but at maybe one-eighth normal speed. Maybe a tenth.

Silk thought something had happened to his eyes, it was as if all he could see was a cone right in front of him. Sound went away, the buzzing of the neon light's transformer shut off as if the power had been cut, and all his attention became riveted on Tattoo's arm as it moved toward Danner, moved as if they had all suddenly become mired in sludge, the arm drifted up and in, oh . . . so . . . slowly . . .

Danner reached up with her right hand and caught Tattoo's hand, reached across the back of it and clasped his palm with her fingertips. She turned her entire body, a sharp pivot to her right.

Tattoo's arm straightened as his wrist twisted, levered by her turn, and he lurched to the side; his body dropped under the level of his shoulder.

His face lit with surprise, his eyes went wide, his mouth gaped. He may have yelled, but Silk didn't hear it if he did.

Danner finished her turn, still pivoting on the balls of her feet, and now her left arm came across her body, elbow bent so that her forearm was at a ninety-degree angle to Tattoo's now straight arm, her fist clenched.

Her forearm smashed into Tattoo's upper arm, just above his elbow.

The joint popped—Silk heard that—a wet *crack!* that seemed terribly loud in the otherwise dead silence.

Oh, man—!

Danner's fist slid up Tattoo's arm, past the snakes, past the spiders, and the big knuckles of her fore- and middle fingers slammed into his temple.

All of it was so slow, a special effect on some entcom show.

Tattoo's head snapped back and spittle flew in an S-shaped string from his open mouth. The spit glittered in the light of the sign, a slimy worm, serpentine—

Danner pulled her forearm back from the strike, relaid it on the upper arm just above the elbow—that was definitely a rat inked into the pale skin, right there—and dropped her body into a crouch. She still held on to Tattoo's hand and with her weight against his joint, Silk saw there was no way he could resist her.

Tattoo went down, sprawled face onto the plastcrete walk, hard. Very hard—

And Lamé came in then, lunging with his arms spread wide to grab, only Danner pivoted on her left foot so that she was nearly facing away from Lamé and thrust her right foot out, heel leading. Lamé more or less impaled himself on the foot, catching it just under his breastbone. It stopped him, cold. He wheezed, clutched at his abdomen, and doubled over, unable to breathe. She pulled her foot back.

Danner still held onto Tattoo's hand. She let it fall. Came up and turned to face Lamé.

Time resumed its normal speed.

Silk had been prepared to fight, his nails had bitten into his palms where he still had his fists clenched, but it was all over now.

Tattoo lay on his side, trying to cradle his damaged arm. Blood streamed from his nose where he had smacked it into the walk.

Lamé moved around in a little circle, taking tiny steps, trying to draw a breath, both hands holding his solar plexus.

Danner's face was alive, eyes bright and clear, a tiny smile in place, her hands held up in a fighting pose. She allowed her hands to settle slightly, straightened from her semicrouch. "Let's go inside," she said.

Mouth dry, Silk could only nod. Jesus. How could she do that? Beat the crap out of two thugs in like three seconds and then act like it was no big deal?

"Silk?"

They went to the door.

King and Ratso drove past the little hotel where the responder told them it now was. They were no more than a minute or two behind the spy and Silk, he judged, they had passed the cab coming down the hill and since it was the only other vehicle on the road save their own, King knew it was the same one they'd just missed catching the registration numbers on when his quarry had boarded.

It was highly doubtful that the *ausvelter* they all sought was at this decrepit lodging house, but he would have Ratso check it out discretely as soon as possible.

Two men who had apparently been in an altercation of some kind made their way down the walk just below the hotel and King wondered if they had been so stupid as to brace his quarry. Probably so, cutpurses and footpads not being well known for their intellectual capabilities.

"Looks like those two musta bumped into our subjects," Ratso said, echoing King's own belief.

"Possibly. I believe I mentioned the pair is rather adept."

Ratso nodded. King had told him no more than he needed to know, which was precious little; still, Ratso was no fool and doubtless he suspected that he had not been given full details. That hardly mattered. He would do his job and accept his pay and by the time he realized there was so much more to this caper than he'd been led to believe, it would be too late for him to try to extort any additional money from King. Or maybe he would be generous with the man later, if he felt so moved. He would be able to indulge himself in any way he wished, or very nearly so. It might be amusing to make Ratso here a moderately rich man, simply for the look on his face when he realized it.

King smiled at the thought. Finally, things were going his way. He intended to keep it just so.

TWENTY-FIVE _____

THE CLERK AT the hotel didn't ask if they wanted separate rooms and that was fine with Zia. Even though she was tired from all the travel, she wasn't *that* tired. She was going to be with this guy for a while—no way to know how long— she might as well live in the moment, right? Maybe it would fizzle here and now, and maybe she could get past this sudden unexplainable attraction she felt. It would be a relief. But now that there was time and a place, she had to know.

Three hours later, as Zia fell into an exhausted and sated sleep next to Silk, who was already out, she knew it wasn't going to be quite so easy to get past the attraction. So far, it just kept getting better. It wasn't just that he was a pretty skilled lover and would do anything she wanted, it was what she *wanted* that bothered her so. This was unreal, not who she was. She had lost control and that was scary, terribly frightening, and yet, and yet—

She *liked* it.

Damn.

When Silk woke just before dawn with a full bladder, he could hardly make himself get out of the bed to walk to the fresher he was so tired.

He rolled out of the bed and looked at the woman sleeping lightly there. She could sense him moving, he could see that in the dim lights that spilled from under the warped door to the hallway and from the tritium strips that ran along the baseboards—these latter probably designed to keep sleep-fogged people like himself from walking into the closet to pee. Naked, gorgeous, only partially under the thin sheet, one leg out in the too-warm room, she was unlike anybody he'd ever been with. She wasn't telling him all about this business, he knew that, and there was also something at her core she held back. Even bucking under him in a wet, throbbing white-heat or moaning as he used his lips and tongue on her, there was a part of herself she protected, he could feel it.

He didn't really understand that; in his own lovemaking he almost always cut loose, gave his own passions free rein and swatted them into a full gallop. When it was the best for him was when he surrendered to the moment, became mindlessly sensual and lost himself in the fury of it all. Mac had always said she enjoyed it the best that way, too.

Sure, he could be a measured lover. He could slow himself and improvise a lot of variations, keep himself and his partner on the edge for a long time, and he took a certain pride in making sure his partner got all the attention she wanted and needed. Once as an experiment on a mutual day off, he and Mac had lain in bed reading, joined together at the crotch, bodies nearly at a right angle, legs entwined in a giant X. He had remained hard inside her for almost two hours, barely moving, until neither of them could stand it. Still, the best times were those in which he and his lover crashed together and rushed toward their climaxes in a frantic, breathless flat-out sprint. And damned if this woman couldn't run with him—or even ahead of him. But she was holding back. And he wanted that from her, that piece she kept protected. Her passion, all of it.

In the fresher Silk peed, then rinsed his mouth out with water from the squeaky tap, splashed a little on his face and wiped it dry with the threadbare towel. Looked at himself in the small chromed steel mirror over the cheap plastic sink. He needed a depil or a shave and there were bags under his eyes and maybe a couple more gray hairs he hadn't noticed before. This was all crazy, running around with a fucking spy—and fucking was surely the right word—in Los Angeles, looking for an offworld pervert supposedly involved in a devious plot. And Mac's death was connected to it, but he was not at all sure just how. He was going to have to do some serious thinking about all this, very soon. He knew he wasn't along just for the ride, he couldn't pretend everything was okay, and he'd have to deal with it.

But not now. Now he needed to get some sleep.

When he got back to the bed, he climbed in very carefully to keep from waking her, allowing his weight to settle slowly. She put a hand on his leg, slid it up, cupped him, her eyes closed, her breathing even. She didn't sleep very deep, but he was sure she was not altogether awake, either.

Jesus.

"What do we have?" King asked Ratso.

The two of them sat in a coffee shop down the hill from the Outside Inn. It was the kind of establishment that made you want to spray everything with disinfectant before you touched it, and even then to use gloves or mayhaps a stick. He had no intention of drinking the dark swill the waiter put in front of him, even had the porcelain cup not been stained with purplish lip paint on the edge. Even so, King felt good. The situation was under control once again and he was in command of it.

Ratso took a gulp of the coffee, apparently not the least worried about being poisoned. Said, "There are nineteen guests in the place, including our two. Four are permanent, the other thirteen registered for periods of a day to a week, none of them even close to the description you gave me."

"Very good."

"The woman called a rental agency this morning and they are going to deliver a car to her in about twenty minutes."

"I assume you have collected the information on the rental unit?"

"Yeah. I was too late to bug it, but I got the plate and ID."

"That should be sufficient, our responder is still in place."

Ratso took another drink of the dark and oily brew. "I don't suppose you want to let me know what's going on?"

"In a word, no."

Ratso shrugged, finished the coffee, waved the empty cup at the waiter. "Got any fresh pastries back there? Prune Danish or pie?"

Destined to die young, King thought. Risking his life this way. He smiled. It was good to be in control.

• • •

Zia stood under the trickle that passed for a shower and tried to wash away the worry, along with the juices of her latest sexual session with Silk. Steppin' laserblade? Right. Uh huh. She felt more like a lettuce leaf left out in the hot sunshine too long. What she wanted to do was lay in bed all day, snoozing and cuddling with Silk. Maybe read a zine, that was about the limit of her ambition.

For just a moment she let the fantasy run: She'd quit the service, change her name, she and Silk would disappear, maybe to another tropical island like the one he lived on. Pick fruit from the trees, spend all of the nights and most of the days in bed . . .

Right. And then one day while she and Silk were screwing each other senseless, some young hot spark looking to make a major flame of herself would step through the door and delete them. Nessie had rules about retiring, and running off with some terry because he was magic in a sleepsack wasn't one of them.

She shut the water off, squeezed as much as she could from her hair, stepped out, and looked into the mirror at the new color. Mouse brown, it was called, the hotel had sent a runner to buy it for her. And her hair was shorter still, almost a crew cut, the brows dyed to match. She'd pick up some new clothes while they were out, makeup, too, and adjust the image even more.

Another day, another face, another name.

Silk had already showered. He sat on the edge of the bed, waiting for her. He looked tired. Should be, given the wake-up exercises they'd done. God.

As she fluffed her short hair dry, she watched him, using the mirror. She didn't really need him here, she knew. They had talked enough for her to know he didn't know anything helpful. He'd been good cover for her escape from the island and when she'd picked him up, she'd thought maybe his woman—Mac, he'd said—had told him something she could use, but she was pretty sure that hadn't happened.

She used a second towel on her body, moving the wetness around as much as blotting it. As she bent to dry her legs, she saw him glance up and watch her. He wanted her again, she could feel the pressure of his gaze on her. He couldn't possibly have anything left right now, least not as far as penetration went, but he was more than willing to use his lips and fingers and tongue on her . . .

Stop that.

She should ditch him, she knew. Cut him loose with some kind of explanation that would keep him satisfied long enough for her to finish her job and leave. Send him home in one piece with a few good memories, tell him she'd be along to see him later. He'd go on about his life eventually, and if he wouldn't forget about her, he would survive. She thought they were okay, had gotten away clean, but you couldn't ever be positive. The opposition—whoever the hell they were—could come roaring out of the stone jungle here and attack at any time, in theory, and they both could wind up warm meat on the cool plastcrete. That was part of the risk she took every time she went on a caper, part of the job. Risk brought the adrenaline high, and the game was more interesting when you outshined the other side with your neck on the line. It was like chess or *go* or *tandimi*, you moved and countermoved and played for a win with big stakes.

She finished drying herself and reached for her undergarments.

Yeah, that was fine for her, but Silk over there hadn't signed on knowing the truth. She'd conned him, roped him easy, using the noose she was an expert with, her sex and her ability to spin a story. She'd bound him to her, and somehow in the doing of it, damned if she hadn't bound herself to him, too. Ordinarily she wouldn't have worried about him in the least. She'd used a lot of people in the last few years, some of them badly. It was part of the biz, something you had to get used to or quit. You were a player or you got played. But this time, she was feeling sorry for one of the playees. If sorry was the right term.

She didn't want to think too much about that.

Damn.

She finished dressing. A few minutes in a public print shop would allow her to become another woman with another background, yet one more color in her chameleon's palette. Then they could go look for Spackler. It wouldn't hurt to keep Silk around another day or two, not while they were still searching. She could always cut him loose, that was an option, right?

Right.

She frowned at herself in the mirror. Who did she think she was fooling?

"Ready?"

"Yeah," he said.

"Let's go find the bad guy."

She drove the rental car expertly, better than he would have, Silk saw. Another skill they taught secret agents. He had taken the classes in secondary ed as a kid more for credit and the experience than the expectation he'd own his own vehicle anytime soon. Even fifteen or twenty years ago buying a private car was expensive and a hassle. Of course he had driven Mac's more than a few times, but this was a different model, different controls, and this sure as shit wasn't Hana. Here the traffic was so thick you could walk across almost any street on the rooftops of cars without ever having to touch the ground. Even with safety devices, doppler and warning sirens and automatic cutouts, people still thumped into each other fairly frequently in L.A. Hundreds of times a *day*, according to the unspun version he'd heard. Imagine.

He would have yelled at the driver of a van that cut them off, racing to beat the change on a traffic signal, but she was calm, like an underground pool deep in a cave. Cool, calm, quiet, Danner was. No, not Danner, he reminded himself. She had changed her name, given herself a new ID in a few minutes with a rented holoproj in a print place. "Call me Zia," she'd said. "Zia Rélanj."

"Zia," he'd said. "Pretty name. Where'd you get that one?"

"It's not uncommon on New Earth. My cover is thickest when I can fall back on E2 camouflage."

He nodded. "Zia."

She smiled when he said it.

"You drive well. The traffic doesn't bother you?"

She chuckled. "No. Almost everybody on the outworlds has some kind of personal transportation. On Mchanga they have contests to see who can come up with the most colorful expression to throw at bad drivers. On Ujvaros you're allowed to beat the crap out of anybody who puts you at risk in an automobile. Not legally, but the law looks the other way. Makes for more polite operators, it does."

"Hmm. According to history, people in this town used to shoot at each other with guns when they thought they were ill-used on the roads."

"Really? I hadn't heard that. That's crazy."

"That's us terries. Mad as a wirehead on two-twenty. Where, by the way, are we going?"

"Fong's Pet Store," she said.

"A pet store?"

"Yeah. They specialize in large dogs. To a select group of buyers."

"Damn, she's dangerous at the controls of a car," Ratso said.

"Just attempt to keep her in view," King said.

"Way she's driving, I might have to kill people to do that."

"You tend to hyperbole. Do whatever is necessary."

King watched the car weave in and out of the traffic as if it were some maddened tropical fish: darting, hovering, drifting sideways, speeding up and slowing down to take advantage of any empty space large enough to occupy. She was actually quite skillful, he saw, recognizing a talent close, if not equal to, his own abilities. King could also fly a light plane or copter, pilot a hovercraft, and operate several varieties of heavy machinery—tractors, earth-movers, and the like. All necessary talents for an operative who might be called upon to pass for something at a far remove from what he really was, or, failing that, to escape from pursuit. He had not had much direct experience with *ausvelter* operatives so he was not clear as to what models they utilized in their training, but The Scat liked to think of itself as latter-day ninjas. Able to blend into virtually any scenario undetected and, in the rare event notice was taken, able to do whatever was necessary to get the job done and escape relatively unscathed.

King himself thought the historical aspects of ninjitsu were entirely appropriate. He trained his body so that it was never very far from peak fitness—one could not maintain a peak physical tone for long, but one could certainly hold a plateau a week or two shy of it. He was strong, knew sufficient martial arts to defend himself and kill if need be, and though some of his sub rosa talents had been admittedly a bit loggy from disuse, they were coming back with practice. Of course, many of the old ninjitsu skills were pointless in today's society—one did not need to worry about moats and singing floors—these had been replaced with knowledge of electronics and weaponry that ancient ninja would have cheerfully killed hundreds to possess had it existed during their era.

"There she goes again. Look at that turn!"

King did not speak. The mice were leading him to the particular mouse he wanted and he was the cat. He did not as yet know where they were going, but it seemed apparent that they knew. Then all that had passed before, the errors about which none knew save himself and these two, would be, like all of the mice, deleted. With much pleasure accompanying it, too. And unless he was mistaken, soon, too.

TWENTY-SIX _____

"YOU FONG?" ZIA said.

"Yep. What do you want?"

Silk stared at the man behind the counter. He was tall, lean to the point of anorexia, with blond hair, blue eyes, and no trace of the Orient in his features. Maybe forty years old, but he could have been younger, the thinness made him look hard and worn. He had bad skin, pocked and flaking.

There were a couple of colorful red and yellowish birds in cages, plus a big green and blue one out and sitting on a perch. A square glass container on the counter held a snake, and another had in it several white mice. The place smelled like rancid piss; the barred windows were thick with grime, allowing little of the morning to filter inside. Dust motes swirled in the stray sunbeams. Of other animals there were no signs. Except for the three of them, no one else was in the place. If the area of Woodland Hill they'd seen the night before was bad, this strip made it look like the astro-rent district of downtown Maui City. You could probably catch twenty diseases just breathing the air in here.

"We're looking for a . . . pet," Zia said. She glanced at Silk, and he would have sworn her look was an equal mix of guilt, shame and desire. Jesus, she was good. That thought took the time to worry him a little.

"This is a pet store, femmie. You want to be a little more specific?"

"A dog. We, ah, want a large dog."

"Male or female."

"Male, definitely male."

Fong's grin was too knowing, it gave Silk a chill.

"Fixed or potent?"

"Potent."

"Trained?"

"Of course. Why else would we come here?"

Fong nodded, but he was leery. "How *did* you manage to come here? Ain't no doggies in the window."

"A . . . friend sent us."

"Uh huh."

"I don't think he'd want us to use his name, but you sold him a bitch recently. He's about thirty-five, short, got an *ausvelt* accent?"

Fong nodded again. "Maybe I remember him. We're talking cash here, femmie, eight hundred and fifty stads."

"That's high. My friend didn't pay that much."

"Like you said, he bought a bitch. All they gotta do is receive. Easier to train, cheaper than a male, he's got to give *and* get. And dogs, they're particular about where they stick certain things." Fong looked at Silk and inclined his head a little.

Silk felt dirty. He wanted to grab this guy and shake him, maybe slam him against a wall or two.

"Seven-fifty," Zia said.

"This ain't the shelter, femmie. Eight-fifty or take a walk."

"You deliver him?"

Fong snickered.

One of the birds made a sound that was a pretty good imitation of the laugh.

"Of course we deliver. You don't see any dogs *here*, do you? Do I look stupid?"

Zia grinned. "Watch the door," she said to Silk.

He wasn't slow, but Zia leapt over the counter before he could reach the weapon under it. She shoved him with the heels of her hands and he flew back against the wall and hit hard.

The bird on the perch squawked and flapped its wings.

Silk glanced at the door but quickly back at Zia.

She reached under the counter. Pulled out a chunky gun.

"Well, well. What have we here? Looks like a small bore sawed-off shotgun. This is a real antique, Fong, gunpowder and metal BBs."

Fong shook his head, still leaning against the wall.

"I don't keep any money here."

"Single shot, but with the barrel chopped down like this, you could clear half the room with one round. Probably sprain your wrist from the recoil, though."

"Listen, cunt, I said you're wasting your time—"

Zia grabbed the front of the weapon with her left hand and jammed it into Fong's stomach.

He yelled, "Hey! You're fuckin' crazy!"

"That's right, larbo, I am, and I would just as soon blast your guts all over the wall as not."

"Wh-what do you want?"

"The dog you sold to the *ausvelter*. You delivered it."

"Yeah, yeah!"

"I want to know where."

Fong swallowed dryly. Silk could hear it from where he stood.

"You're not police," he said.

"Nope. We're the bad guys, Fong. We kill people. You don't give me an address right now, you get to be dead, how's that?"

Silk flicked a look at the door. Nobody there. Jesus, she sounded convincing. *He* believed her.

So did Fong. "I'll get it."

He moved to his computer console, gave it a code, and ordered it to display the address that went with the code. The computer responded mutely.

Zia looked at the projection for a moment. "Okay."

"Computer off," Fong said.

"We're leaving now, and we're taking your little toy here with us. I hope you don't have any foolish loyalty to your customers, Fong. If the guy we want has cleared out when we get there, we come back and shove this thing up your ass and pull the trigger, you understand? And if not us, one of our *kyodai*. We have a big family."

"Christ, why didn't you say who you were before? Fuck him, I don't owe him nothin'. I don't want any trouble with you guys."

"Go," Zia said.

Silk walked outside, Zia right behind him. She made a small effort to cover the gun with her windcheater, but not much. Not likely anybody in this neighborhood was going to stop them and complain. Amazing.

"What's a *key-yo-die*?"

"Yak lingo for 'brother,'" she said as they reached the car. "If Fong thinks we're *yakuza* he won't do anything stupid. At least no more stupid than what he does for a living."

Silk sighed. He realized his pulse was hammering along pretty fast, there was a pit-of-the-stomach feeling like needles of ice forming in his belly. But it didn't feel altogether bad. When Zia had shoved that slime against the wall, Silk had wanted to cheer. In a society where violence was frowned on, he was finding out that he saw uses for it. Not good. But true, nevertheless.

"Damn, you see that?" Ratso said.

King lowered the binoculars. The shop window was smeared and filthy but good electroptics made up for a lot. They had not been able to discern all that went on inside the pet store, but they had seen the woman assault the man behind the counter and then point a gun at him, one she had not had when she went into the store.

The question was: Why?

"Are you certain as to the nature of this business?"

Ratso watched the pair who were just entering their own vehicle. "Yeah, I checked it out. Guy sells animals to perverts. Some people get spasms from doing it to a dog, or watching a dog do it to somebody, or even themselves. Sickies."

It was disgusting, but King did not bother to voice the sentiments. Obviously they had come to see this fellow for information and while he did not seem particularly cooperative, surely he had supplied them with what they wished, else they would still be convincing him of the wisdom of so doing.

But—what?

"So, do we follow 'em, or go talk to the gummy in the store?"

"Stay with them. Whatever they learned in there might not be sufficient in itself to tell us what we wish to know."

"We're rolling."

The professional part of Zia felt pretty damn good. She had Spackler's address, she was sure of that. This might be over sooner than she thought.

She glanced over at Silk, who was a little pale and nervous. Twice in two days she had used her fighting skills, first with the two idiots at the hotel and now with Fong. It had turned Silk on, excited him, she could tell, and even though he didn't like it, he *felt* it. If she pulled over and offered, he'd probably take her right here in the middle of the street.

Well. She understood about risks and danger. Christ, hadn't she given him her real name? That was stupid, you never did that on a caper, not ever, but there it was.

Why had she done it?

She thought about that as they drove through the ugly streets of L.A. toward Spackler's hiding place. She'd asked the car's map for general directions, without giving it the street and building number, she wasn't that far gone. But why her real name? Even though he thought it was another phony one?

What it came down to was, she wanted to hear him say it. Wanted to see how she liked the sound of it in his mouth when he called her "Zia."

And had it been worth it?

Too early to tell. But she liked it so far. It wasn't exactly honest, but it was closer to the truth than she usually got. A whole lot closer. This whole business was getting sticky. When an op started telling the truth, she might as well pack it in, that way lay real danger.

"Zia?"

"Yeah?"

"What are we going to do when we find Spackler?"

"Don't worry about that yet. First we have to find him."

Zia. She liked having him say it. Definitely.

TWENTY-SEVEN

"ECHO PARK DISTRICT," Silk said. "According to the sign."

Compared to the rest of the traffic-impaired and dirty plastcrete village they'd been moving through, this area looked nice. There was a small lake surrounded by a grassy lawn and palm trees off to one side of the street, probably the park in the name, and neat, clean houses and apartment cubes that climbed the hill across from that, colorful stucco blocks in pastel pinks, blues, tans and oranges.

Zia nodded. "We're close."

She'd explained her idea as they drove: they would make one pass by Spackler's address and look the situation over, then devise a plan once they knew the terrain.

They came to a T-intersection. Just beyond it, a tall mesh fence topped with razor wire bounded a freeway, twenty-eight lanes of slow-moving vehicles, mostly trucks and buses. One of the reasons Silk hated to come here. Los Angeles had the best surface road and freeway system on the planet, including the state-of-the-art traffic computer supposed to stitch it into whole cloth. But on a good day it could take three hours to travel fifteen kilometers. On a bad day, you might as well walk: you'd get there faster and probably less irritated. There were people in this city rich enough to afford fifty cars and their operating fees who chose to ride bikes or to walk because they hated the traffic snarls that much.

Zia turned left, eased the car into a short line of people riding scooters and bicycles, and climbed a short hill. Near the top of the hill, she turned left again. Because there was a woman having trouble climbing with her small child on a multigeared bike ahead of them, they crept along. Just what they wanted, actually.

"You see the house numbers?"

"Yeah."

She rattled off the one she'd memorized.

"It'll be on your side," he said.

"How do you know that?"

"All even numbers are on one side, all odd ones on the other."

Funny, you'd think a spy would know that kind of stuff. Even one from E2, she'd spent any kind of time on Earth. *One more crack in the facade, eh, Silk?*

Yeah, but she's such a great lover . . .

"There it is," she said. "Tan place, just ahead. Looks like it runs down the side of the hill, maybe three flights."

Silk nodded.

"I bet we can see the back side of it from down by the lake," she said.

"Looks like three units in the building," Silk offered. "From the address you got, Spackler's would be the one on the bottom."

"Yeah. Okay, let's circle back down and stop at the park."

They did just that.

The day was warm for a November afternoon, even here in L.A. Parents and children dressed in shorts threw food to the ducks swimming in the lake. Small rental boats powered by pedal-driven paddlewheels churned around in lazy arcs. An idyllic scene, out of place in the vastness of the sprawling city.

"I need to use the fresher," Zia said.

"Go ahead."

She ambled off toward the concession stand and boat rental kiosk.

Silk stretched, walked around on the sidewalk. Saw a spot crusted with white and looked up to see a dozen pigeons perched on a satellite dish mounted in a palm tree next to the walk. He smiled at the birds and avoided walking under them. It all still felt like a dream.

There was a post phone not far from where he was and of a moment, Silk had a desire to use it. He went to the phone, tapped his ID number into the unit, and waited. They were—

what?—three hours ahead of the islands here? It was almost ten o'clock here, it should be okay.

Xong answered eventually. The unit didn't have a video so Silk couldn't see him, but from his voice, he was still mostly asleep.

"Silk?"

"Yo, Xong-dong. *Que pasa?*"

"Silk, Jesus, where *are* you?"

"Los Angeles."

"What the fuck are you doing in L.A.?"

"Practicing my driving. Listen, Xong, I want to ask you something—"

"I want an exclusive, Silk. This is a story that could shove me right up into perpetual byline country—"

"What are you talking about?"

"You don't know? Christ, man, half the police on the planet are here looking for you. Not just local heat, but SuePack and Scat-cats, too. What'd you do, Silk? Howcum Terran fucking Security is nosing around asking questions about you? Is it something to do with Mac? Don't spin me here, Silk, whatsza deal?"

Silk stared at the phone as if it had suddenly turned into a big spider. Jesus.

"Hey, Silk? Are you—? Oh, shit!"

"Xong? Bryce, what?"

"My biopath has detected a tap. Somebody's in the pipe with us."

Silk started to ask who it might be, but a cold flash shocked him into slamming the transceiver into its slot, breaking the connection. He'd seen enough entcoms to know phone conversations could be traced in a hurry—especially if the listeners were some official government agency.

Who wanted him? Why?

He turned away from the phone suddenly. He was going to have to have that conversation with Zia—Danner—whatever her real name was, and right now—

A private car rolled past, two men inside. For some reason, Silk found himself staring right at them as the car moved by. The passenger was black, the driver a smallish man with sharp features that gave him a ratlike appearance. Silk didn't know either of them, had never seen them before, but in that moment with his paranoia flying full speed, he was suddenly sure they were watching him. Neither man even glanced in his direction, but he could not shake the gut-twisting certainty. He fought to keep from turning and staring at the departing car. A dark green Mitsubishi four-seater, he didn't get the plate number, but the colors were local—

"Silk?"

He spun and jumped at the same time.

"Fuck, don't do that!"

"Hey, hey, relax. Sorry, I didn't mean to—"

"Who are you? What is really going on here?"

She blinked at him. "What?"

"I just talked to a friend of mine back on the island. He says the place is thick with cops, local, regional, planetary, looking for me. Which means they are really looking for you. What is going on?"

"You talked to him? On the phone?"

"No, lady, I telepathed him direct. Yes, on the goddamned phone—"

"Get in the car!"

"Not until you fucking stop this fairy tale and tell me what the truth is."

"I don't have time to argue with you, Silk. If they are looking for you, then your friend's comline is compromised and they already know where you are. They can have a flier dropping on that phone in five minutes, maybe less. We have to collect Spackler and get the hell out of this area or they'll collect us!"

"I'm not going anywhere."

She glared at him, shook her head. "All right. I'll say this once and fast, so listen close. I am an undercover agent, and I work for Internal Security, the headhunters. We have traitors in the organization, like I said, and Spackler knows the names. If we don't get him before the opposition does, he dies and we got nothing. That's who's looking for you, the flippers, the rogue agents inside Terran Security. Without the names, everybody in this operation is at risk. Me, you, everybody."

Silk stared at her. She sounded sincere. Of course, that didn't mean shit, he could sound sincere while lying through his smiling teeth, had spent much of his working life doing just that.

"Look, I promise I'll explain it all later. Please, get in the car."

Silk blew out a breath. Fuck. Could he trust her?

"Please?"

He nodded.

They moved toward the car. Fast.

"Sorry I couldn't get the scanner working in time," Ratso said.

Seated next to him in the car, King shrugged. It might have been helpful to know the text of the telephone conversation Silk had just terminated. Perhaps not. He could have been calling to check the weather. "It does not matter. I believe we are near our quarry. I would hazard a guess that he is somewhere on the loop they made before they parked for the woman to use the fresher."

"What's the drill?"

"Park about midway along the block up the hill where we can see them arrive. You do have the weapons?"

"Yeah, under the seat."

King bent to reach under the seat. He removed two hinged plastic cases each about half a meter long. Each of the cases held a 6mm CO_2 pellet rifle. The weapons fired lead bullets with hard plastic nose caps filled with poison, an artificial variant of that found in certain South American frogs. A solid hit would be fatal to a human within seconds.

While his original intentions included a long session with his antagonists in which he taught them the error of their ways in a most painful manner, the nature of the prize required a willingness to give up such pleasures did such become necessary. The spy and her consort would still die and he could comfort himself in his new French villa while drinking vintage champagne and eating whatever he wished, did that death have to be quick and merciful. After all, victory went to the player still standing after the game. The losers would take whatever embarrassments he had suffered with to their internments, telling no tales.

King opened the case and removed the two parts of the rifle. He assembled it, checked the electronic dot scope for functioning, and slid the gas canister into place. He loaded the five-round stripper clip of ammunition into the rotary magazine. The plastic nose cones on the bullets were sufficiently hard to allow the penetration of flesh before the spinning motion of the projectile would tear the protective caps free, thus exposing the poison thereunder.   -

Any solid hit would do it, better still should the bullet strike bone.

Ratso parked the car. He looked nervous.

"Something?"

"Pretty heavy-duty hardware," he said. "I mean, we're not supposed to leave any witnesses around if things go to hell, right?"

"Correct. Save for the man our subjects have gone to fetch, no witnesses. He is not to be injured if possible, certainly not fatally. Any passersby who see us . . ."

Ratso swallowed. He had dealt in error deletion before, he knew the routine. If it were somebody's misfortune to see them, they were to be taken out, be they little old grannies or a troop of Cub Scouts.

"Here they come," Ratso said.

"Best you assemble your weapon," King said.

Zia knew there was a risk here of barreling into a bad situation, but she had no choice. Loverboy there had blown it, there were probably copchoppers heading for the phone at the park by now and when they didn't see anybody there, they would toss a net over the neighborhood and stop everything that moved. Before that happened, she had to have Spackler in hand. It wasn't how she wanted to do it, but it was what she had to work with.

She pulled the car to a stop directly in front of the triplex unit.

"Okay, here's how it goes," she said. "We haul it down the stairs, you kick the door and stand back and I go in first." She pulled the sawed-off from under the seat, broke the action and checked the load. If she had to shoot she'd only get one shot.

"We grab Spackler and hustle him to the car. You drive, I'll keep him under control. You stay within the limits, don't break any regs, and head for the Silverlake Airport. It's a private strip not far from here, we can rent a hopper and get out of town. Stay on the surface streets, don't get us jammed into a traffic lock."

Silk nodded. His face was bright with fear.

"Let's go."

She stepped out of the car, the gun held down by her leg to break up the silhouette.

The building was in good condition, but refurbished and not new. The stairs weren't plast- but actual concrete, the tread plate edges worn and smooth. She took them carefully—it wouldn't do to fall and blow her own head off with the shotgun.

At the bottom of the steps was a small porch protected by an overhanging roof. A fruit tree of some kind stood in a small yard that was mostly dirt. Dog turds littered the ground, big ones.

This is the place, kid.

They hurried to the door, a thing of pressed fiber, no glass. The windows to both sides were curtained, covered entirely from within.

Silk moved to kick the door.

She waved him off, a short choppy motion. Reached down and tried the door's handle. It clicked and the door swung inward. Not even locked.

As she shoved the door open, however, a dog started to bark. The sound turned into a snarl as she stepped into the room.

Spackler stood in a small kitchen off to her left, drinking something. When he saw her burst in through his door, he dropped the cup. White splashed as the cup hit the countertop in front of him.

Zia started to bring the shotgun around to cover him.

"Anna! Attack! Attack!"

The barking, snarling dog was to her right, and it was big. Some kind of shepherd mix, probably went fifty kilos. As soon as Spackler spoke the dog moved. It took three or four quick steps and leapt for her, jaws opened wide to tear her throat out.

There did not seem to be any pedestrians about, a thing that would greatly simplify their task, King thought. A vehicle went past now and then, mostly fuel-cell electric scooters or bicycles, but at the moment the street was clear.

When the spy and Silk had gone down the stairs, King had Ratso move the car so that they were twenty meters away and facing the building, on the same side of the street. He had merely to step out and lay the short rifle across the top of the car's open door to be in perfect position to cover the top of the stairs. At this range, with this equipment, it would take one shot each to drop them. They could then fetch Spackler and be off, the game all but over.

King did so wish to extract painful payment from the spy and Silk, especially the latter. His wound from the crossbow was healing well, but there was enough damage remaining to remind him it was there and how it had been incurred. Still, he was a professional and this was not the time, nor was it the place for sophomoric indulgence. Once his original anger had abated, as it always did, reason once again held sway. Kill them, take the prize, depart, that was the logical thing to do. And as for Ratso, his earlier bonhomie toward the little man had also abated. Once the operative had served his purpose, it would be best to eliminate him, too. Even though money could buy much silence, the old canard about honor among thieves held in it more than a bit of truth. And while dead men might tell tales to a forensic pathologist, they would do so only if one had occasion to examine the body.

King smiled. Tying up loose ends was usually part of every operation and once these were knotted neatly, he would never have to concern himself with such things again.

A helicopter went by overhead, low and dropping lower. King spared it a glance. A police aircraft.

He frowned. Something happening at the park. He hoped it had no connection to their business.

Silk saw the dog—big fucking dog—go for Zia. Before he could do more than take a step toward it, it jumped at her.

As it had before when the two men had attacked them at the hotel, time went into a slomo fugue. The dog drifted through the air, pink and gray gums pulled back to reveal long yellow teeth. Zia stood frozen, a holograph, eyes wide, watching the dog. But wait. Her hand moved, the hand holding the blockish gun in it. And now she shifted to her left, turned, pivoted . . .

The dog could not alter its flight. It arrived at where Zia had been a quarter second before, in time to have her smash the gun into its skull. That didn't stop its leap, but its head was knocked askew by the power of Zia's hastily swung club.

The dog flew past, trying to turn, twisting its body. It slammed into the wall behind Zia. Slid down and lay sprawled, unmoving.

Zia was turned and if she saw the man who ran past her, she couldn't get around in time to stop him. He headed for the door.

Silk moved. Blocked the man's path. Was this Spackler—?

The man was smaller than he, but moving. He hit Silk, hard. They both went down . . .

"Hold it!" Zia yelled.

The man and Silk came to their feet in normal time. Hard as he had been hit, Silk didn't feel any pain.

"That's a scattergun," the man said. "You shoot, you'll hit us both!"

"That would be too bad," she said. "You try to run, you're past tense, Spackler."

Silk felt a coldness stab him. Would she shoot and risk hitting him? Or was it a bluff?

Spackler evidently believed her. He spread his arms and opened his fingers. "Don't shoot. I don't want to die."

Behind her, the dog whimpered. It lay on the floor on its side, not moving much but obviously still alive.

"Anna! Let me help her!"

"Should of thought about that before you sicced her on me. Somebody else will take care of her. We're going for a trip."

"You bitch! You stinking cunt!"

"Nice to see you, too. Turn around."

She moved to stand behind Spackler. Grabbed his collar and put the gun against his lower spine. "Move stupid and they'll be able to drive a truck through the hole this thing'll make in you. Be a real shame to die so young. Up the stairs."

As an afterthought, she turned and looked at Silk. "You okay?"

"Would you have shot us both?"

She laughed, a release of her tension, he saw. "Nah. He's too valuable alive. But he didn't know that."

Silk watched her start to march Spackler up the stairs. He wasn't sure he believed her. Not at all.

"I don't want to go home," Spackler said, his voice a whine. "Please, why don't you just leave me alone? I won't tell anybody, I swear!"

"Shut up," Zia said.

Tell anybody what? Silk wondered. That didn't make sense. They wanted to know the names of the sellouts, right? Why would he say he wouldn't tell? Did he think they were the other side? And he was pretty sure she would have shot the man had he tried to run. That didn't make sense, either. Not if her story was true.

Well. The time to stop being a passenger and start being a driver had come. He'd ridden along as far as he was going to, he either got answers or he was going to step off this ride. If whatever story she spun didn't scan, he was done here, great sex or not. He wasn't as stupid as she apparently thought and it was time to let her know it.

TWENTY-EIGHT _____

IT WAS ODD, how a man's mind and perceptions worked. As he followed Zia and the captured Spackler to the top of the stairs, Silk noticed how the concrete steps and the stucco walls clashed. The building was a pale brown, more of a cream or a tan, while the steps had been painted or stained a dark, ugly green. The color had worn off in spots, revealing the dull gray of the cast cement under it and the effect of it all was somewhat mottled. A vacant lot next to the building full of assorted kinds of trash scattered down the side of the hill added to the effect. Given how nice the rest of the neighborhood seemed to be, the junk on the lot seemed out of place.

Zia and Spackler had almost reached the top landing at the street level. Silk's head had barely cleared the top when the color of the steps jogged his memory as he glanced down the street and saw the Mitsubishi parked nearby.

The *green* Mitsubishi with two men in it.

After his phone conversation with Xong and with Zia doing a fast dance to get him into their car, he had forgotten all about his flash of paranoia when he'd seen the green car go by. Now it came back.

The passenger door on the Mitsubishi started to gull open. Zia was looking in the opposite direction, one hand still gripping Spackler's shirt, the other holding the gun pressed against his spine.

The black man alighting from the Mitsubishi was big.

He hadn't seen him before today, at least not looking like that, but Silk remembered other times when a big man had threatened him.

The guy could be a salesman or a guy come to visit and if so, Silk was gonna feel real stupid, but in that moment, panic grabbed him.

"Get down!" he yelled. He lunged up the stairs and hit Zia's back with his shoulder. The force of it took them all up onto the sidewalk, but also knocked both Zia and Spackler flat—

The black man had a gun. He swung it up and over the partially open door—

Jesus, they were going to die—

The door to the Mitsubishi had a low-lock position and King's intent had been to step briskly from the vehicle, press the door into the proper attitude and lay his weapon across the top of it. He had briefly considered simply calling to the spy and Silk to surrender, but rejected it. Too risky. Best to simply shoot them and be done with it.

He was aware of Ratso sliding out on the opposite side of the car, and all too aware that something had gone wrong. The trio ascending the stairs reached the top but then dived to the ground.

Damn!

The door was out of his way, if not in position to use for a support. At this range, he could shoot offhand easily enough. He snapped the rifle to his shoulder, put the tiny red dot cast by the laser sight onto the woman's head, and squeezed the weapon's trigger—

Spackler chose that precise instant to scramble to his feet.

Between King and the spy.

Spackler did not make it all the way up. The shot caught him in the chest and he fell backward toward the spy, blocking most of her from view as he collapsed.

Oh, no—!

Zia felt the impact of the bullet as it hit Spackler. He collapsed onto her and she instinctively put her hands up to stop him. Lost her grip on the shotgun. Saw and heard the weapon hit the sidewalk and skitter away. Spackler was between her and the shooters and effectively blocking them at the moment but without the gun, they were in big trouble. She shoved at Spackler, trying to hold him up enough to use him for cover while she tried for the gun—

Silk saw the shotgun bounce and slide toward where he lay. Only a few centimeters away.

The men at the car kept shooting. The sound was a compressed gas *whump!* repeated two, three, four times. Spackler's bones had disappeared, he was like a sack of rice, limp, filling himself. And absorbing the bullets.

Zia lunged from behind Spackler on her right side, stretching for the gun—

Too far—

"Ah!" she yelled, and rolled.

It wasn't possible, some part of him knew, but Silk saw the bullet punch a hole in her back, just under her left arm. Her shirt flew away from the front of her body. *Went right through her*, he thought.

He was almost getting used to this kind of slow time. He looked at the two men shooting, saw the smaller one coming around the car, the bigger one moving along the side. In another second or two they would be here and he knew in the pit of his soul that when they got here they would kill him.

In that instant, he stopped being a passenger on Zia's train.

Silk grabbed the fallen shotgun.

He had never fired such a weapon, never even touched a real gun before, but he was a fucking expert with a crossbow. The principle was the same: Aim, pull the trigger.

He thrust the gun toward the little man coming at him.

The man saw him. His eyes went wide and he pointed his own weapon at Silk and tried to fire it.

Some bored god must have decided that Silk's lot hadn't been good lately. He took pity on Silk and the little man's gun went *click!* Maybe it was empty or maybe it jammed— Silk didn't care why.

The little man was in front of the bigger one, blocking his view.

"Move!" the black man yelled.

But the little man was backpedaling, trying to get away from Silk. He was twelve, maybe fifteen meters from Silk, no more.

The black man stuck one hand out to shove the little man aside so he could shoot—

There weren't any sights on the gun Silk held. He gripped it tightly with both hands, pointed it like a fat steel finger and pulled the trigger. It was rough, the trigger, had a lot of creep—

A bomb went off. Silk's ears rang and an acrid, burning smell washed over him as the gun bucked and nearly tore itself from his hands. Jesus—!

The little man's face sprouted red splotches. Silk saw one of his eyes explode. The little man's arms went wide, the gun flew high into the air and he spasmed into a backward leap. He hit the big black man and they both fell. The sidewalk didn't have any kind of railing next to the drop down the hill and the two men tumbled down, rolling.

Fuck! He had killed them!

"Get the car!" Zia yelled.

Silk scooted around on the sidewalk to stare at her. She had her right hand pressed under her left arm where the bullet had hit her and was on one knee, trying to stand.

"Silk, the car!"

Silk came to his feet. Started toward the car. His feet felt as if they had been turned to blocks of wood.

"Wait, you'll need the key." She fished the plastic card from her pants pocket. There didn't seem to be very much blood from her wound, a stad-coin-sized spot, no more. She sailed the card toward Silk.

He snatched the spinning plastic rectangle from the air.

"Hurry!"

By the time he got the vehicle turned around and moving toward them, Zia was up and trying to drag Spackler's body toward it. Silk pulled the car to a stop and opened the door.

"Help me get him inside."

"He's dead, Zia."

"I know that. Come on."

He'd never really appreciated the term "dead weight" before. No matter how he gripped the body, some part of it wanted to stick to the ground as if it were glued there. But they finally managed to drag and stuff Spackler into the rear compartment. It seemed as if it took a long time but it was maybe four or five seconds.

"We should get you to a medic," he said. He glanced at the slope. From here, he couldn't see the two men he'd shot.

"I'll be okay. The bullet went through the lat, didn't have time to expand." She sniffed loudly, repeated it.

What—?

"Good thing, too. Smell that?"

Silk inhaled. It smelled like something . . . burned toast? No, not quite, but like that—

"Poison," she said. "From the bullets in Spackler."

Jesus! "What about them?" He looked back over his shoulder at the downed men.

"The heat is going to come down here any minute. Do you want to be here when it does?"

Silk drove.

Because he was in good shape and knew how to fall, King's roll down the side of the hill did not do him any great damage. He banged one elbow against something and tore his shirt, but all in all, it could have been much worse. He fetched up against the rusted-out shell of a clothes washer almost at the bottom of the incline and the impact did stun him for a second, but when he got to his feet, he knew he had not broken or sprained anything, nor had the blast from the shotgun reached him.

Lying somewhat closer to the top of the incline, Ratso did not appear to be quite so fortunate. He lay facedown, unmoving.

King scrabbled up the slope.

He reached Ratso and turned him onto his back.

Dead. The shotgun's pellets had turned his face, neck and upper chest into fleshy ruins. One of the projectiles had apparently entered the man's eye and sped into his brain, doubtless the killing vector.

Damn.

He had to get out of here and he had to do it quickly. In such a neighborhood as this one someone would have reported the gunfire. That police copter could not be far from here.

He glanced down at the body. Ratso would have nothing on him to lead an investigator to King's doorstep. And since he had always used a code name when dealing with the dead man, even a thorough search of his files would avail the authorities little.

Assuming they did not capture him here.

King ran toward the rental car. He did not bother to pick up the rifle Ratso had dropped. Let the police try to sort it all out, the more they had to contend with here, the better. Silk still had the responder planted in his back. He could be relocated, did he not get out of range. Spackler and the woman were likely dead by now, King was certain he had seen them both struck by his or Ratso's missiles. That Silk had the presence of mind to load them into his vehicle was irksome in the extreme, but could he catch the man before he dumped the bodies, the game was not yet over.

As he drove away, the sound of a furiously barking dog followed him.

Zia's side had begun to ache where the bullet had punched through. She knew she needed to clean the wound out—bullets moving at high speed weren't too bad, they tended to heat-sterilize themselves from friction in the barrel, but they carried fibers from clothing into a human target. She'd been lucky the hit was shallow and the poison hadn't gotten her.

But that was later. Right now, they had to get away from here.

"How did they follow us?" Silk asked.

"What?"

"That black man, I'm pretty sure he's the same guy who broke into my cube and who later chased us when we left Hana. How did he find us?"

Zia shook here head. "I dunno."

Traffic was not as thick as usual. They managed to leave the vicinity of the shooting quickly. Silk had the car's computer map giving him directions to the airport.

"So, even if they followed us to L.A. from Hawaii, which I'm sure they didn't, how did they keep up with us? I've been looking for them and until I spotted them down the hill—I saw the Mitsubishi by the park, I should have said something then—I'm sure they weren't behind us or anything."

It was a good question, Zia realized. How *had* they managed that?

"Some kind of electronic tracker," she said. "They must have tagged one of us along the way somehow."

"How? I mean, we're wearing different clothes, we don't have any luggage, nothing to tag—"

"Damn, Silk, I don't know. I've just been shot, give me a little slack here, okay?" Which was true, but no excuse. He was thinking better than she was at the moment, a nonplayer. That was not good.

He blinked and looked at the computer map. "Oh, sorry."

They drove in silence for a few minutes. The thin traffic clotted a little and they slowed.

"Silk? You okay?"

He shook his head. "Not really. I shot those men. Killed them."

"It was them or us. You didn't have any choice."

"I can still see them falling, the little one's face all blown apart. Makes me sick to think about it."

"At least you're alive to think about it. If you hadn't shot, they would have killed us. It's the law of the jungle, you do what you have to do to survive."

Silk shook his head again.

She understood. The first time she'd killed somebody had not been nearly so messy but she remembered it as if it were yesterday and not six years past. He'd been a custom's agent on Shinto, a fair-skinned, blue-eyed man with curly brown hair who'd done his job too well. He had discovered her hiding in the freight container and grabbed her. They had struggled. She panicked, hit him hard, and he'd fallen from the stacked containers, forty meters to the hard plastcrete below. She hadn't seen him hit, but she'd heard it. The sound came back to her in a hundred dreams, there was nothing quite like the noise a human body made impacting that way. She had not seen the body, but later reports confirmed the man's death. He had just been doing his job, but then, so had she. Too bad. She could say that now, and even then she had pretended to be offhand, as if it hadn't affected her, so the other ops wouldn't know, always the cool facade. But six years later she still remembered the smallest details too well. He'd had blue eyes.

Poor Silk. He was in the middle of something he didn't know anything about and now he was a killer. She felt sorry for him.

Well. If they got clear, she would make it up to him. Enough pleasure could erase a whole lot of pain.

TWENTY-NINE _____

SILK WASN'T SURE what he expected when they got to the airport but whatever it was, it wasn't what happened. Zia shook off the effect of the bullet wound in her side, somehow tucked and folded the bloody shirt so it didn't show. She spoke to the woman in charge of renting aircraft, showed identification, made arrangements and there seemed to be no problem at all.

When she came back to where Silk stood nervously waiting, she said, "Okay, we got a plane."

"What did you say to manage that?"

"I have a license, I have a thick credit line, that's basically all you need for domestic rentals. We'll have to disable part of the computer once we log in a flight plan so it doesn't tell on us, and we'll have to do some low-level stuff at a couple of borders, but we're basically in the clear once we lift."

"Are you going to tell me the truth about what is going on?"

"Silk, I already—"

"—Because if you aren't, I'm staying right here. I'll take my chances with the local law. I *killed* two men fifteen minutes ago, Zia."

She sighed, stared at him. "Okay. Let's get airborne, and I promise I will fill in all the gaps, okay? I—" Her eyes fluttered and she swayed.

"Zia?" Silk reached for her, concerned.

"It's—I'm okay, just felt a little faint for a second. Come on, we have to find a way to cover Spackler so we can load him on the plane."

"Why?"

"We have to dump the body at sea, somewhere it won't be found."

"Why?"

"Look, I'll tell you once we get away from here. I promise." She put one hand on his chest. It felt warm through his shirt.

"That isn't going to work this time," he said. "I've been fucked stupid and it was a whole lot of fun, but it isn't enough now. We start playing by my rules or we don't play anymore."

She laughed. "You know, I could get to really like you. All right. If the opposition finds Spackler dead or alive, they'll get something we aren't ready to let them know yet. If you don't believe anything else, trust me on this one thing. I wanted him alive, but now that he's dead, he's no less dangerous."

Silk didn't understand what the hell she was talking about. Truth was, the idea of turning himself in to the local police and trying to explain all of this—spies, killing, dog-fuckers— didn't appeal much either.

"All right. But if you start feeding me another plate of monkey mud, I am done with this mess."

"Fair enough."

Zia felt—not to put too fine a point on it—like shit. The bullet wound ached, she expected that, but she felt weak, feverish, light-headed. She'd been battered worse and hadn't gone into shock, which was what worried her at first. Then another idea seeped into her mind: Maybe some of the poison in the bullet had gotten into her system. Not much, or she'd already be dead, but the stuff they used in killing rounds was pretty potent. Even a trace could cause problems.

As they walked back to the car where the dead Spackler waited patiently for them, Zia thought about her options. This assignment had turned to goo around her and she was wading in it up to her neck. Sneaking offworld in the usual manner was not going to be real likely, she couldn't risk it. Of course, once Spackler was disposed of, her getting away might not be all that important, except if they caught her, none of the blocks she had against chem or mindwash would hold. Terrans knew more about torture than anybody, they were the masters, and if she fell into their hands they would peel her like an onion, layer by layer, until there was nothing left. They wouldn't have as much as they would if they got Spackler's corpse, but they would pretty much know what they only suspected now.

So, the last-ditch, lottery-chance option was her best bet, bad as it might be. If it didn't work then it wouldn't matter, she'd erase herself before she let them collect her. If it did work, she could justify using it to the boys back home. Sure, sooner or later the terries were going to find out, but as long as it didn't happen because of *her*, that was the important thing—

She almost stumbled as they reached the car. Could Silk fly a plane? She could program the flight line, put in the glide path codes for the landing strips they'd have to use to refuel along the way—it was thousands of kilometers, too far for a single hop in the craft she had just rented. But she would have to trust him if she got worse, and she was going to have to tell him *some*thing or she was going to lose him. She knew enough about men to recognize a back-to-the-wall pose; Silk was in one, and she needed him. Maybe even *wanted* him.

Shit.

"Which way?"

"Hangar Thirty," she said.

Silk drove. She had him stop next to a recycle bin before they reached a guarded gate to the hangar row. Zia found enough trash to cover Spackler's body where it lay on the floor in the rear compartment. It might look strange, a mound of used paper, but at least it wouldn't look like a corpse. If the guard took too much interest, Zia would deal with that.

The guard, a bored woman watching a holoproj in the kiosk, glanced at Zia's receipt for the plane and waved them through without taking much of her attention away from her vid.

Zia wanted to laugh. Given how slack everything on this world seemed to be, least regarding her biz, how come she was in such a mess here?

They reached the plane. The craft was a six-passenger business jet, the single engine mounted as part of the tail assembly. Even without the full automatics it carried it would be an easy machine to pilot and with her training she could almost do so with her eyes closed.

Inside, they found blankets. They used two of them to wrap Spackler's body, waiting until nobody seemed to be looking their way, and hustled him into the jet. There was a luggage compartment big enough to hold him and accessible from the interior floor. Once he was stowed out of sight, Zia felt better.

There was an aid kit, and Zia asked Silk to help her clean
the bullet wound and put a bandage on it.

"I don't have a current passport validation," he said.

"We aren't flying the tourist hop. We wouldn't want to use
your ID anyway."

He finished sticking the bandage into place. Best they were
going to be able to do until she got to friendly medical hands.

"Okay. Let's get this beast out of here."

Silk followed her into the pilot's cabin.

Zia slid into the seat on the port side and began to go through
a preflight check.

"We're supposed to be taking a two-week vacation," she
said. "We fly from here to Denver, there to St. Louis, there to
New Orleans, there to Miami. This thing has enough range for
each of those hops without refueling. Very efficient bird."

"But we aren't going to Miami," he said. It was not a
question.

"No. We are going to—push that button there on your right,
the green diode, yeah, good—we are going to Içá."

"Eeka? Never heard of such a place."

"Understandable. Içá is a flyspeck on the map, a tiny town
on a river of the same name in Brazil, about a hundred klicks
east of the old border with Colombia." She was still that much
of a pro, able to rattle that off when a native like Silk didn't
know where it was. "Right in the middle of what's left of the
Amazon rain forest."

"Sounds like a great vacation spot. A nowhere river in the
steamy jungle. Why are we going there?"

"Because we can get help there, help we can trust."

"Why—?"

"After we get off the ground, Silk. I've got to rig this
computer so it will take us where we want to go while telling
the plane's owners we're going somewhere else."

"You can do that?"

"Sure. Can't everybody?"

King could not find the signal.

The responder's range was not great at best, plus this was
a city whose air was filled with electronic dross that interfered
with reception generally, and the only method that would work
for a ground search once the device was lost was both old and
slow. One quartered an area driving north-south or east-west,

hoping to hear the response. He had his computer locked into the signal so that if the responder gave forth its cry he would be able to locate the source quickly, but first it had to be heard.

If they escaped from the city before he could find them, the amplitude of his problem would be greatly magnified.

King sighed. Once more he had thought himself in control and once more, when the moment had arrived for judicious action, he had found himself embroiled in disaster by misfortune's laughing hag. It truly did give one pause. By all rights, the assassination should have succeeded. Yet it had not. Luck favored some while it frowned on others, it had certainly done so in this event.

Spackler certainly was dead, unless the spy happened to have an antidote to a poison for which none was known on Earth. He was certain he had seen the spy herself take a round, so she should also be nothing but a brief historical footnote, if that. Silk must be the only one left ambulatory. In a city not his own, without resources, pursued by others with much more backing than King himself had access to—how long could he fumble along before he was collected? Even luck as wondrous as his must eventually falter, must it not? Surely so. And King had to find him before the other players in this game did so.

He must know how valuable Spackler was. He had taken the bodies with him, had departed in what seemed an impossibly rapid manner. When King achieved the crest of the hill, the man had already vanished. And while his own flight had been likewise quick, to avoid the authorities he knew must be about to converge upon him, King had not thought Silk could have gotten out of responder range so fast. His fervent hope was that the device had not been damaged during the shooting. Had it been rendered inoperable, he would be—not to put too fine a point on it—screwed.

As if the thought had triggered something in the cosmos, the responder's signal spoke suddenly.

King laughed aloud. If there be gods, then thank you for small favors, he thought. It was only just, given how they had treated him thus far.

The computer locked the coordinates into its map. Only a few kilometers from here. Good. It was not finished yet.

"That's got it," Zia said. "The course is programmed, the computer will tell them our cover story, and we are ninth in line for takeoff." She turned to Silk. "You know how to fly this thing by any chance?"

"Not really. I used to be pretty good at FlightSim."

"Which is . . . ?"

"Computer simulator. A game. I know what most of the main controls are and I've piloted various aircraft with computer mockups of them but I've never actually flown a real one."

She shrugged. "Well, if I've gotten my program right a chimp ought to be able to manage it, but you never know. Things happen you don't expect."

"Oh, really?"

She smiled, but she looked pale to him, she seemed to be drifting a little. "You okay?"

She blew out a short breath. "Yeah, basically. I think maybe the round I took might have leaked a little when it went through."

Silk felt a stab of worry. "Is there anything we can do?"

"Not given what we have to work with. It will either kill me or it won't. If it does, we'll be over water most of the way—wrap something heavy around Spackler and dump him the hell away from anybody. When you get to Içá, tell them what happened, they'll take care of everything from there."

He stared at her. "That's cold, Zia."

She listened to something over the ear button from the control tower. "We're two from takeoff," she said.

She turned to look at him. "You care, don't you? Damn, Silk, if I were in your shoes, I'd be pissed, really pissed. Here I am, risking your life, telling you stories you don't believe, and even if I might be a pretty good lay, you ought to feel like slapping my teeth out. Instead, you *are* worried about me, whoever I am." She stopped, frowned, as if realizing she had said more than she intended.

And in truth, she was right. All of the shit she had put him through, he should feel like knocking her silly, or at least screaming at her long and loud; and yet, what he felt was not so black and white. Yeah, she *was* the best fuck he had ever had and while that by itself wasn't enough to make up for everything, there was something else there with the sex, something . . . deeper.

What, exactly? It wasn't the same thing he'd felt for Mac, but it was more than just very pleasant friction. There was some kind of connection with this woman, something more complex than simple pleasure. She had certainly shaken his life up, no question there. He'd never in his dreams expected to be jetting away from Los Angeles with an undercover agent born on another world, carrying a corpse, pursued by killers.

By any sane standards, feeling any kind of affection for Zia—or whatever her real name was—ought to be the furthest thing from his mind. And yet, he *did* feel something.

"We're up for takeoff," she said. "Lock your safety harness."

Silk did as he was told.

She worked the controls expertly, as far as he could tell, and the little jet began to sprint along the runway. They left the ground so smoothly he could hardly tell it; one moment they were rolling, the next moment they were flying. She banked left in a long looping turn and continued to climb. In a few minutes the city haze was below and behind them as they arced out over the shining Pacific.

The computer had an address but not what place occupied that spot. As King drove, he tweaked the responder frequently and upped the transmission time, to make certain he did not lose the signal again.

He was no more than half a kilometer away from the coordinates when the responder abruptly changed locations. It did so impossibly fast, the computer could not lock it down. King stared at the screen. It could not be, the speed at which Silk moved had to be upward of three hundred kilometers an hour and increasing, nobody could drive that fast even if the streets were entirely empty—

The signal vanished, faded, even as he realized what was happening.

They were in the air.

Ahead, he saw the sign that identified the small airport.

King screamed, a wordless bellow of pure rage.

THIRTY _____

SILK WENT BACK to the jet's tiny fresher, basically a narrow stall with a chemical toilet, a small sink and not much else. When he was done, he ambled back to the control cabin. It was twenty minutes after they took off, well out to sea and eight thousand meters up. It was time to make good on his promise. He either got something from her he could recognize as the truth or he got off at the first stop and end of her scenario, period.

Zia's eyes were closed and she wasn't moving.

"Zia?"

Panic surged. He shook her. "Zia!"

She moaned and Silk's relief was immense. Alive!

He yelled, rubbed her hands—they were cold and clammy—slapped her cheeks lightly, but he couldn't rouse her.

The jet seemed to be doing fine on its own, so he unbuckled her safety harness and carried her to the passenger section. The seats were made so they would fully recline. He flattened one of them into a narrow bed with her on it. Found a blanket and covered her. He stood and stared at her, unsure of what to do. He remembered the aid kit, went and found it. There were five kinds of bandage, antiseptic, steroid cream, aspirin, decongestants, antihistamines, a small hypodermic injector of adrenaline, an inhaler for asthma, some other pills that were identified but that he didn't recognize. A printed sheet of tightly folded paper tried to give a viewer with good eyes a quick course in medicine, assuming he could read, quicker still if he just followed the simple pictures above each block of text.

No antidotes for poison bullets.

Silk had once taken a first aid class, but that had been ten years ago and he hadn't had any real use for it. Maybe the adrenaline would help, it was for anaphylactic shock. Yeah, and maybe it would make things worse, too.

He stared at the unconscious woman and knew he did not want her to die. He wanted to get this thing between them, whatever it was, worked out.

He undressed her under the blanket, pulled the adrenaline popper out, twisted off the needle covere and jabbed her on the front of the thigh, like the aid kit's instructions said. He pressed the plunger—shit, he forgot the part about aspiration—but it didn't make any difference. Zia grunted, but otherwise did not offer any response.

Silk raised from his crouch next to her and swallowed, trying to get rid of the sudden lump in his throat. He was in a jet without a human pilot in the middle of the ocean going to a jungle in South America. There were people looking for them and he had killed some of them not an hour ago. He'd had better days.

Then again, Zia was out and he was running the show, for however long it lasted. Maybe that was better than hanging on to an out-of-control bus. He could stop this if he wanted. The question was, did he want to stop it? At the moment, he found to his surprise that he did not. At least not until Zia was awake.

Did he have access to his former resources King could have located Silk via the responder anywhere on the planet. The Scat's spysat net enshrouded the globe like a fine mesh, crisscrossing it with electronic eyes and ears that could see or hear things most amazing. Want to know the title of that hard-copy book the subject is reading on the park bench in Washington Square? No problem. Interested in the phone conversation the subject's maid is having with her boyfriend? Easily done. Wish to find a responder implant in a subject aloft in a small jet somewhere unknown? Give us the frequency.

Alas, those resources were no longer at his beck.

Instead, King sat at a public access terminal in the small airport's lobby, staring at the flight plan filed by the woman now calling herself Zia Rélanj. There was his first information and a surprise it was, too. If the woman had rented the craft, then she had not been hit with one of the poison bullets or it had failed in its function. Perhaps she was immune, given all the other smiles she had gotten from Dame Fortune, that might be a possibility.

Enough idle speculation. Back to the flight plan.

It was public information or nearly enough so he got it with a minimum effort. The holoproj was a bit on the worn side, the resolution somewhat fuzzy but readable. There was a stale, waxy smell in the demi-booth, an odor King associated with the cheap CD drive of the bare-bones CPU. His first computer had a similar scent. It had been part of a shipment that had passed through the dock where his father worked as a dispatcher and his father had stolen it, not especially for him, but because it was available. His father had not been clever enough to discern the computer's operation and so it had fallen to Depard at twelve by default. His father had not considered himself a thief—everybody picked up odds and ends from work, everybody, he had said so more than once. It was no big fucking deal.

King stared at the flight plan as it scrolled. The jet's computer told a tale, but if it was anything less than a total prevarication, then he could achieve orbit by flapping his arms.

King's father had been a small-time thief, generally ignorant and proud of it, barely one step in front of the dole for most of his life. Even the dole caught up with him when his employers finally grew tired of his thievery and discharged him. King had been fourteen at the time and until he left on his seventeenth birthday, not a day went by without his father lamenting his lot and cursing those he blamed for it.

"Fucking pricks, it never cost them a fucking thing, the fucking insurance paid for it, everybody does it, so why the fuck did they piss on me for it? Bastards!"

King's father had a temper, and after a few drinks or a popper or two, he would usually start to kick things around. The furniture, the walls, King, if he happened to be available. King's mother—she had left when he was not yet two years old—was also the subject of his father's rage. Fucking-cunt-whore-bitch was his father's name for her, usually spoken as a single slurred word.

"That fuckingwhorecuntbitch! I'd kill her if I could find her!"

Not that there was any danger of that. His father was too ignorant to locate his ex-wife, even if she had been living in the same run-down multiplex, unless he perhaps happened to stumble over her. And even then, he was usually so drunk or stoned he probably would not recognize her, or remember her five minutes later if he had recognized her. In fact, she was not living in the multiplex or the city or even in the county under her maiden or his father's name, because King had checked.

Ignorant, stupid, brutish and a chemhead addict, that was King's father. On the morning of his seventeenth birthday, when his father flew into his usual rambling rage, King had lost his own temper. When the man reached for him to slam him against the nearest wall, King's reason fled and he fought back. A lucky punch knocked his father down and they were both so stunned by that that the fight stopped. His father sat on the floor in his addled state, staring at nothing. "I knew it would come to this," he said, his voice a whine. "I knew that even my own son would fuck me over."

King went to his room, packed what he could carry in two cases, and left. Other than that, all he took was his resolve: He was not going to be like his father. He would educate himself, he would never become a substance addict, he would control his temper, he would be very successful. Whatever it took, he would do those things.

King shook his head and tried to lose the memory. He had accomplished most of his resolutions. He was as educated as any man in his chosen field. He had enough standards banked even now to live his life without having to work or stoop to the dole. If he could but relocate his prey yet again and finish this operation, that modest wealth would be multiplied a thousand times. He was not addicted to any chemical substance. Most of the time he controlled his temper. He did not think his father would be proud of him— he was too stupid to not resent King's success—but certainly King felt he had proved himself. He had not seen his father since the day he left, nor did he wish to, save in the late-night fantasies he sometimes indulged himself in: *Look at me, old man. See how much more I am than you could ever hope to be.*

Then again, if he failed to recover Silk and the *ausvelter*, his triumph would not be quite so complete.

And how was he going to do that?

• • •

The guy had an enormous cock, Christ, it had to be a third of a meter long, big around as her arm, and yet Zia knew she could take it and drain it dry, no problem, this was what she did, she was good, she was the best at it. He moved to put it in her—she couldn't see his face, didn't know who he was, but knew she knew him—and she grabbed him and pulled him into herself, he sank all the way in one thrust. But all of a sudden it was small in her. and even though he was pumping away like a hamster, she couldn't even feel it. She stared at the ceiling, sad, bored, waiting for him to finish, but then he was gone and she was walking into the library where the old woman who sat at the front desk waved her over and gave her the reader and the tapes about Hansom, the famous spy who had lived on Ujvaros during the Trade War and messed up the enemy so bad they'd put out a million-stad reward for him. But they never caught Hansom and when he got back to New Earth after the war was over, he was famous, he wrote a book, they made a vid about him, she had seen him once when he gave a talk at the concert hall when she'd been only twelve, two years ago, Jesus, now she was a kid, not a woman. But when she sat at the table to look at the tape, Silk came in and sat down next to her, only he was a kid like her, no more than fourteen, and he smiled at her and she was in love, just like in the romance vids. He held her hand and it felt electric, a thrill ran through her that was much, much better than when Uncle Lou had put his finger in her pussy and moved it in and out—

Only then she was running, but slow, like her feet were stuck in mud or something and the thing behind her, it was a monster, she couldn't exactly see it but she knew it was bad, it was getting closer and when it caught her it would kill her and eat her and all she could hear was the pounding of her heart, thump, thump, thump—

Silk sat in the pilot's seat and tried to figure out how to fly the jet. It wasn't the same as the FlightSim he used to play, but it wasn't too far off. The general controls were pretty much alike, the computer, though doctored by Zia, was something he could operate if he had to, and probably he wouldn't have to. Everything was automatic. The plane could land, take off, almost by itself. All he really had to do was tell it when, after any refueling stop.

He looked at the map and realized they were going to land on the southern tip of the Baja Peninsula in about three more hours, at a spot unnamed but thirty klicks south of some place called Todos Santos. Silk searched his memory, rummaging through unused and ill-remembered Spanish: All Saints?

The jet could land itself with no help from him, but he suspected he was going to have to talk to somebody about refueling. He could use her ID for that, Zia had programmed the stop and maybe it would be okay, but he wasn't sure. Between there and here, he decided he was going to dump Spackler's body. Not a pleasant thought, but if when he crossed into Lower California, a state with ties to both the States and Mexico, he didn't want to have to answer any questions about a fucking body in the luggage compartment. Explaining Zia would be easy enough, could surely spin a story to cover her being sick or something, but even an idiot would have trouble with a we're-going-to-bury-poor-old-Tom story when the corpse wasn't in a casket and was full of poisoned bullets.

It turned out to be fairly easy, though it took a while. There were spare tanks of oxygen mounted in the luggage compartment and one of them must have weighed fifty kilos. He tied Spackler to the full tank using the man's clothes and several wire coat hangers. That done, he positioned the body over the exterior door to the compartment and went back up onto the jet and sealed the floor opening shut. There was a safety to keep the luggage compartment's exterior door from opening in flight, but Silk was able to disable it.

When Spackler dropped, the jet lurched a little, it got noisier, but that was all. Silk was able to see the corpse and green oxygen bottle fall using the jet's belly cam. He didn't see it hit the ocean, but unless the laws of physics had gone crazy, the *ausvelter* would splash down and sink pretty damned fast.

Silk closed the outer door. The sound level dropped.

According to the map, they were past the continental shelf and the ocean depth below the jet was just over four thousand meters. Spackler the *ausvelt* pervert was going to the bottom of the sea, four klicks down, to feed whatever lived there and in a week or two, there probably wouldn't be a hell of a lot of him to find. Silk remembered the parrot fish back home who liked to nibble. No, probably not much left at all. Give my regards to Davy Jones, Spackler.

Okay, that was one thing done. He still had almost two hours before he was supposed to land. Maybe he better try to figure out what he could about all this shit. He went back and checked on Zia. Still out, still breathing okay. He returned to the pilot's chair and sat.

All right. *When did it all start? When the big guy broke into your cube?*

No. Before that. What was it Mac said, that night when you were going to the party?

She'd been talking about an *ausvelter*, Spackler, he now knew, and he'd had something wrong with his blood. Something called a . . . prorasia? Decrasia? Something, figure it out later, you'll know it when you see it. Mac found something unusual about him, that's the thing, something that intrigued her. Okay. Then Mac got killed and all this other crap started raining down.

Assume nobody is telling the truth, or at least they are spinning the hell out of it. There was something wrong with Spackler, not plague or anything or Mac would have been worried about it and not just interested. Something that Mac was killed for—if that part is true—and something that everybody and his fucking kid sister want bad enough to kill anybody who gets between them and it.

What?

What could be that important? And did it have something to do with the medical thing Mac noticed about him? Or was it something else, something he knew?

Silk sighed, stared at the vast blueness ahead of him, sky and ocean. The air was broken by a thunderstorm off in the distance to his right—starboard on a plane or ship—and a few patchy clouds. The air in the jet was cool, stale, smelled faintly of lube.

Okay, Spackler was from E2, he knew that much, assuming Hans the sausage-disguised-as-a-doctor wasn't a better spider than Silk thought, and he wasn't. Spackler had left his own planet, was in quarantine on Earth, broke out and ran. He liked dogs too much, but that he was bent wasn't worth all this hassle, was it?

Silk recalled what he'd heard the man say as they marched him up the stairs just before somebody shot him dead. *I don't want to go home*, he said. *Please, why don't you just leave me alone? I won't tell anybody, I swear!*

If home was E2, then Spackler thought Zia was going to take him there. She had mentioned a little trip, but that didn't mean she was who Spackler thought she was.

Who did he think she was, Silk?

Hmm. There was the question of the day. She said she was from New Earth and Spackler sure thought she was. But she also said she worked for Terran Security. Assume for a second that Spackler had been right about where Zia wanted to take him—why would a terran agent want to take an E2er to New Earth? That didn't make sense, if Spackler had something of great value, wouldn't they want it themselves? Relations between Earth and the outworlds were not the best, the vac war, it was called, for the vast emptiness between the stellar systems. There existed between Earth and the outworlds an armed peace, a certain amount of fear and xenophobia, distrust, no love lost . . .

Here's a thought: Zia sure as hell is some *kind of secret agent, but what if she is working for her homeworld? Wouldn't that make more sense, given what you've seen?*

Silk felt a cold flash envelope him. That made a lot more sense. She did escape from quarantine, she'd told him that, and while her story was that she'd been a plant, what if that part was a lie? The best spins had plenty of truth in them, so they rang at almost the right tone if you tapped them, you'd have to have perfect pitch to catch the difference.

What if the bad guys you shot turn out to be Terran *Security agents, Silk?*

Oh, boy.

THIRTY-ONE

HOW TALL EXACTLY were the trees? Silk wondered. He couldn't see them because it was dark, but the jet's sensors knew they were there. The computer gave him a less-than-exact height figure, rounding it off to the nearest five meters and that number came up too high. Shit.

Zia was still out. She had groaned a couple of times and broken into a sweat, but otherwise had been unresponsive. The first refueling stop in Baja had gone smoothly—after the jet taxied to a stop, the only part that hadn't been done by the autopilot—two men had driven a small truck to the side, pumped in fuel, and departed, never speaking to him. One of the men gave him a thumbs-up sign, that was all.

Silk had been scared dry after he lined up the jet at the end of the runway and ordered the computer to run program, but there hadn't been anything to worry about. The takeoff had been smooth and flawless.

The second landing had been in Quepos, Costa Rica, and the procedure with refueling and takeoff had been almost identical. Whoever ran the airstrips had obviously been told to mind their own business and mind it they had. Eerie.

Now, however, they were almost on the equator, about to pass over the coast of Colombia, and the jet had dropped to within a dozen meters of the ocean's surface. They skimmed along above the wavetops like a seabird seeking fish, close enough for him to see the whitecaps under the starlight. Ahead of them on the land were trees, a hundred klicks past that, mountains, and twelve hundred kilometers past that, Içá.

Unless the jet's program gave them some altitude, the trees would get them; if they didn't, the mountains surely would. Even if the jet clipped a few branches and escaped, they would splatter like a balloon full of ink against one of the foothills of the Andes unless they ascended.

However bad a pilot Silk might be, he couldn't do any worse than that and he was sweating as he reached for the override to try—

Suddenly but smoothly the jet climbed. It cleared the tops of the tallest trees by maybe fifteen meters. Silk saw the doppler read on the screen and realized that the jet's sensor input must be part of the flight program. He realized that Zia had done this on purpose, to avoid detection by local radars. If she'd done it right, the jet would hug the ground, but ascend or descend as necessary to do it safely.

If she'd done it right—

"How's it going?"

If he hadn't been strapped into the seat, Silk would have jumped a lot farther. "Jesus!"

Zia leaned against the control cabin's back wall, staring at him.

He unbuckled himself and stood. "You okay?"

"I've felt better but I'll live. How long have I been out?"

"About seven hours. I gave you an injection of adrenaline."

"Probably helped. Where are we?"

"Colombia. Just crossed the coastline."

"Good."

"Yeah, well, I'm glad you think so. I want some answers."

She put a hand on his shoulder, moved past, and slid into the pilot's seat. "Okay, give me a minute to check things out here. You didn't mess with the settings, did you?"

"No."

"What about Spackler?"

"He's fish food."

"Half a victory is better than none."

She touched buttons, looked at readouts, nodded. "No problems with the refueling stops?"

"No. Nobody even spoke to me, just pumped in the fuel and left. No more than ten minutes on the ground each time."

She finished her scan of the controls, pivoted the chair on

its base, and looked up at where he still stood. "Okay. You want to sit down?" She gestured at the second chair.

"Not really."

"Maybe you'd better."

"Oh, shit."

"Yeah. Afraid so."

He sat.

Having exhausted his resources, King found himself once again wishing for those he had once been able to command as an official agent of The Scat. Assuming Silk still had the implant, the spysat net could locate him were he still onplanet.

So it was that he sat outside a small apartment complex in Sunset Beach, south and east of Seal Beach, which was south and east of Long Beach. The apartments overlooked the bay and a thin stretch of sand dotted even in the dwindling November daylight with those courting skin cancer, since from their color, many of them seemed to disdain the use of sunblock. The apartments were old and weather-worn, but well maintained, and boasted a security system normally found only in much more modern buildings. This was the kind of place that agents of The Scat chose to reside in for the lack of external ostentation.

King sat in his rental car, still wearing the black man guise, watching the building. Unless he was very much mistaken, Martini Pearce still maintained his residence here. Not under that name and whatever alias he now sported was not discernible via simple channels, such as the public phone or reverse directories, but it was King's belief that Pearce was too much a creature of habit to have left, were he still among the living. And if *that* were so, then Pearce would still be working for Terran Security. Pearce had been a plodder, uninspired and unambitious, content in his status as an information handler. He hadn't been in the field in fifteen years when King had known him and had never espoused the slightest desire to leave the safety of his computers.

King sighed. Pearce was a man who had risen to a station he desired and was thereafter content to coast until the end of his tenure. He would be about fifty now and unless he had developed a penchant for plastic surgery and exercise, he would still be fat, bald and—to be euphemistic about it—

plain. King had not seen him in a dozen years but he was sure he would recognize the man on sight.

Pearce would be able to access the spysat net, he did so as part of his normal routine. Right there from his home.

A short-haired young woman wearing nothing save a bright green thong bikini bottom and springskates rolled along the walk. King watched her as she zoomed toward him, then flexed and leapt a meter and a half into the air, spread her darkly tanned legs wide in a Russian high jump, then dropped down gracefully onto the resilient skates. Her breasts were small, but they bobbed from the springy impact. She smiled at him as she zipped past.

King watched the woman's bare ass as she skated away from him. Young, firm, going to live forever, never going to fall and get scraped, all of that shined from the athlete as she moved away.

He sighed. Life had its beauty, but also its ugly side. He hadn't wished this course, would rather have accomplished his task without having to stoop to somebody like Pearce. A misstep here would surely be fatal—if The Scat suspected he was meddling in this affair and his reason before it was completed and he had his bargaining chip in hand, he would be deleted like yesterday's news file. A threat would suffice to force the stolid Pearce to do his bidding, but then the man would have to be disposed of so that he would not carry tales. Too bad, but what else was he to do? The matter had escalated beyond easy solutions. Risk was necessary. Already he had lost too much. Spackler was certainly dead, the *ausvelt* spy and her consort had stolen away via air and probably disposed of the body by now. That's what he would have done in her place. She'd been sent to fetch him, he supposed, and failing that, deletion would be the second choice. With Spackler dead and gone, King's information was no less valuable but would fetch much less without some concrete proof. He had to collect the spy and Silk. They could be made to confirm King's story and from the ruins there could be a profitable salvage. He had to find them and a part of him wished it so as much for the victory as for the money. They had beaten him at every turn, hardly from brilliance, no, simply from dumb luck, but even so, it rankled. They must be made to pay.

A short, fat, bald man emerged from the front of the complex and walked toward the bus stop on the corner. Pearce.

Smiling, King alighted from his vehicle.

"You must have thought about it," Zia said.

The jet climbed again. A late thundershower to the north spewed enough lighting so that Silk could see the jagged claws of the mountains looming ahead.

"Yeah, I have. I also thought about dropping you into the ocean with Spackler."

"Why didn't you?"

He shrugged.

"So, tell me what you think."

"So you can figure out how much to let out? Fuck that. I'm done playing your game. You're a liar, lady, I know, because I'm a liar. How about the truth?"

"Not much fun being on the other side, is it?"

He glared at her. "No." But even now, because he didn't want her to think he was entirely stupid, he said, "All right, I'll tell you what I think.

"I think Spackler wasn't supposed to be here—on Earth. Somehow he got off his homeworld, *your* homeworld, E2 and got away. He knew somebody would be coming after him and he broke quarantine as soon as he could."

He stopped and looked at her. Another lightning flash strobed through the windshield, revealing her face. Her expression was neutral. "Go on."

"Who they sent to bring Spackler back was you. You don't work for Terran Security, you work for E2's version of it."

She nodded. "You're smarter than I figured. What else?"

Silk felt his gut twist. Fuck. She *was* an offworld agent.

"There's something weird about Spackler. Mac came across it. It isn't plague and it isn't obvious—Mac was good at her job—but it's so important she died because of it." He took a deep breath, let it out.

"I have to know. Did you have anything to do with her death?"

Zia shook her head. "No. I don't think Spackler did, either. The big man, I don't know who he was, but he wasn't operating like Terran Security. He's some kind of X-factor. He knew what Spackler was, I don't know how. Maybe he got it from Mac, maybe he killed her to get it, I can't say. It wasn't our people."

Silk let out a sigh, realized he was holding his hands clenched into tight fists. He relaxed them. He hadn't wanted her to be involved in Mac's death.

"It's got to be something genetic," he went on. "Something illegal according to the Genetic Convention." He remembered the conversation they'd had on the flight from Hawaii to the mainland, just before going to the fresher together. What had she called Earth? A dull utopia? "Hard to believe, but I think Spackler was some kind of improvement on the basic model," he said. He stared at her.

Another strobe of lightning. They were closer to the storm, thunder followed the flash in a couple of seconds. Rain slashed against the windshield.

"I better route us around that," she said.

She fiddled with controls. When she was done, the jet veered away from the storm.

She looked back at him. "I'm not supposed to do this, you know. You never tell anybody any more than you have to."

"I understand," he said, "that's my job, too. But I've got most of it, haven't I? We're in shit up to our eyebrows and I've earned all of it."

She nodded. "Yeah, I guess. You could have dumped me with Spackler."

But she didn't speak for a few seconds.

He waited.

"You're right about most of it. I work for New Earth, I was sent to bring Spackler back. He was a medium-level scientist in the genome improvement lab in the Badlands Research Center. As long as he was where nobody paid attention, as long as the project was tooling along without results, Spackler's off-hours diversions got by. But when the project came up a winner, big eyes turned their way. We have politicians on New Earth, too. Spackler and his dogs didn't fit the new image. He had nine of them, a whole harem. Light as bright as got shined on him is hard to hide from. So he cut and ran as far as he could."

She was still holding back, but Silk nodded, waiting.

"The guys in charge aren't ready to let the old planeteers know what they've come up with. I can't tell you exactly what it is or how it works, I don't have the chemistry. I did some snooping and found out some terms: telomeres and telomerase, senstatins, retroviral neurochromatics, anemone distillation, dehydroepiandrosterone, a whole raft of other

tongue-twisters I can pronounce but don't have any idea what
the hell they are or what they do. Bottom line is, it works."

Now Silk did speak. "What, Zia? *What* works?"

She stared at him. "The genetic infection. You get it, and
unless you get hit by a train or fall on a wet fresher floor and
smack your head on the bidet or something, you don't die. It
stops aging, Silk. They call it the Forever Hormone."

He stared at her. Oh, man! No wonder everybody and his
sister were after them! Jesus. If this was true, it was the most
valuable thing in the galaxy. A cure for aging. To live forever?
Talking big magic here, the biggest!

*And what do you think the terran authorities are going to
do to anybody who knows about this until they get their hands
on it? Maybe even after they get it?*

"Oh, man," Silk said, shaking his head. "We're fucked."

THIRTY-TWO

PEARCE—STOLID, PLODDING, dull-as-unsalted-rice-pudding Pearce—went for a gun hidden under a couch cushion. He jerked the cushion up with his left hand and snatched the weapon with his right, moving smoothly and with enough speed and skill so the action had to have been practiced more than a few times.

King was more startled and amazed than frightened, but not so much that any of his own reflexes failed him. He shot Pearce twice with his own small pistol. The charges in King's weapon were still of the nonfatal variety but no less effective for that.

Pearce collapsed sideways on the couch, the little weapon in his hand almost brought to battery but not quite. "Almost" was insufficient.

He stared at the unconscious man for a moment, feeling the somewhat laggard rush of adrenaline surge through his body.

Pearce with a gun. Rather amazing.

Had he not gone through the convoluted adventures of the last few weeks, King might well be the one lying sprawled now instead of the surprising Pearce. The experiences had stoned his edge to a sharpness he had not had for some years, enough so that even though his conscious mind had not expected Pearce to put up any resistance, his subconscious warrior-self had not lowered his sword. Interesting.

King took three steps across the expensive Persian rug and squatted. He pried the tiny handgun from the man's fingers and looked at it. It was an antique, well maintained, of dark blued

steel with some sort of mottled brown and pale yellow bone
or antler grips. On the right side of the slide was an engraving
of a rampant horse, and the designation: COLT AUTOMATIC,
CALIBER .25.

He turned the weapon over, saw a safety lever on the frame
and a crosshatched button on the left grip. He pressed the latter.
A magazine popped partially out of the butt. He stripped the
cartridges from the magazine and examined them. These numbered six, constructions of yellow brass shells with copper-clad
bullets, each of which was tipped by a tiny blue hemisphere
inset into the coppery orange. As an historian, of course, he
knew about gunpowder firearms but he seldom got a chance to
examine one so closely, such things being highly illegal. This
particular weapon was hardly an example of a major killing
machine, having been designed to slip into a purse or pocket
and used as a last resort. It would have very little stopping
power, though the blue-tipped bullets probably represented
some improvement on the original solid version. And given
the rather rudimentary sights, accuracy past a short range would
have been possible, but likely only in the hands of an expert.

King reloaded the magazine, slipped it back into the gun until
it clicked into place, and pulled the slide back, chambering the
first round. Pearce would never have had time to perform that
act, he should have had the pistol in that condition under the
cushion. King supposed that Pearce had probably been worried
the weapon might have discharged accidentally had he kept
it thus, and that could have been painful and embarrassing,
if not actually fatal. The term "automatic" was a misnomer,
technically to be applied only to weapons that fired continu-
ously when the trigger was pulled. What this thing ought to
do is chamber a second round from the action of the first, and
so on, until the ammunition was expended.

He stood, pointed the gun at Pearce's temple, and squeezed
the trigger.

It was very loud in the enclosed space, the report, enough so
his ears rang. A small cloud of gray smoke belched from the barrel and the smell of it was sharp and acrid. The tiny gun bucked
in his hand, as if trying to leap free, at the same time throwing
the empty brass hull out to his right. How very interesting.

Blood seeped from the wound in Pearce's head. When King
squatted again to check for a pulse, the thready, rapid heartbeat
stopped suddenly a moment later.

Hmm.

King pivoted the safety lever up into position, leaving the rounded hammer cocked, and slipped the weapon into his pocket.

One never knew but that it might come in handy.

The rented jet sped through the night at a height to make an unseen watcher in the woods below likely to duck. Silk sat silent in the seat next to Zia, staring at the onrushing darkness.

Zia's emotions were mixed. Her feelings were more like a suspension than a true solution, she thought, if they were allowed to stand still for a while, they would settle out into their component parts and she'd be able to keep them separate. At the moment, though, the cocktail was a scary blend of worry and lust and anger and . . . something else she couldn't quite put her finger on. The problem of Spackler was gone, but replaced by Silk—what was she going to do with him? She had to get offworld, and pretty quick, given how things had gone so far. But she couldn't leave him here, not knowing what he now knew.

She could hardly take him with her. Yeah, she might be able to give the ups back home a dog and pony show so they wouldn't toss him in a cell or schedule a fast brainburn but only at the risk of losing her career. *He followed me home, can I keep him?* might sound cute on a five-year-old, but offworld agents who showed up with complications like Silk wouldn't be considered real trustworthy in the field after that.

Zia Rélanj? Oh, sure, she used to be a pretty hot op, before she dragged a boytoy back from an assignment. She's shuffling files at the Omega Station in the Laybeâh Desert these days, right?

Right, unless they can find someplace worse.

Shit.

But what option did that leave her?

She glanced over at Silk, who was lost in his own thoughts.

Can't bring him along, can't leave him behind to get peeled by whoever it is chasing us. What's the other choice?

You don't really have to ask, now do you?

Zia shook her head at her inner voice. No. I really don't want to do that.

*Right, so he's a good lover. So he opened a door that was
closed before, so what? There are swinging D's at home you
can play with, guys who can make this one seem like a boiled
noodle, now that your engine is on-line. They all look alike in
the dark, right?*

"No, I don't think so anymore."

"What?"

She blinked. She'd spoken the last part aloud without realizing it. Jesus, she really was off the broadcast, way off.

"Nothing."

"How much longer until we're there?"

She glanced at the controls. "Maybe an hour, seventy
minutes."

He said, "You know, I ought to hate you."

Her belly seemed filled with something alive trying to escape
and an intense cold flashed over her.

"—but I'll be goddamned if I don't want to tear your clothes
off and fuck your brains out, right here and right now." He
shook his head, as if amazed at himself.

The rush of joy she felt was only partially sexual, she knew
that. He was right, and she couldn't blame him even a little if
he never wanted to see her again, not after all she had done
to him. But the truth was, she wanted him to want her, wanted
him to feel desire, passion, even—

Don't say it, don't think it—!

—love for her.

What the fuck do you *know about love?*

"It's got to be hormones," he said. "It can't be anything else,
only . . ."

"Only what, Silk?"

He shook his head again. "I don't know."

Realization flooded her.

He felt it, too. It wasn't just the sex. It was more.

Oh, man! This was awful. What if he felt the same way
she did? What if the magic—whatever you wanted to call
it—was really there? Many paths up the mountain, she had
read, and what if one of them started with sex and wound
up somewhere else altogether? For no good reason other than
it did?

Shit. It wasn't fair. It couldn't be. You didn't fall off a cliff
and into love with somebody like that.

Not and have to kill him.

"We have an hour," she said. "The computer is doing fine on its own."

They reached for each other.

King caught a suborbital that would put him down in New Amsterdam, Brazil, a large coastal city on the Atlantic. From there, he could catch a local jet to Manaus, a large town on the Amazon over a thousand klicks inland to the southwest. While the spysats could not be certain where Silk's flight would terminate, the triangulation of his signal pointed in that direction. The jet would have to land within a certain range to refuel, King had the fuel capacity statistics. True, he would not be able to use the codes Pearce had reluctantly provided for more than a few days before The Scat scrambled them. Once they found Pearce's body, all the dead man's work would become suspect—death of an agent by violence was always cause for a sudden flurry of temporarily enhanced security operations.

No, he would have to find Silk before then, or at least pin down a general location. Brazil was a big country, but the interior was still sparsely populated compared to Los Angeles. One way or another, King felt as if he could track them down.

As the ship filled with passengers, King leaned back in his first-cabin seat and stared at nothing. All throughout this venture, he had concentrated either on the financial remuneration or the anger engendered by his frustration, but there was another piece of this puzzle he wished to collect. In fact, it was a prize more valuable than all the money, any vengeance he might extract from the spy or Silk.

To live forever.

It had always been his intent to demand that for himself as part of the transaction with those who would purchase the genetic jewel. His studies revealed to him that such longevity could not be immediately made widely available here on Earth, that the problems attendant would be legion. The social aspects would be a nightmare. Marriage would suffer, childbearing would be severely restricted, laws against violence of any kind would necessarily be passed—what use immortality if one was run over by a careless truck driver? Or buried under the collapse of a shoddy building? The early death of a man who might reach six score years with care was considered tragic; how awful it would seem that a man who might reach a thousand years was cut down at thirty, or fifty or two hundred. Tragedy, indeed.

On the frontier, where the numbers of mankind totaled in the millions, such longevity would not seem such a problem, not at first, and probably not for some lengthy period. Eventually it would grow to be difficult, of course, but men seldom worried about a future that was a century or five ahead of them.

The ship's engines came to life. King settled himself deeper into his seat, making certain his harness was securely fastened. Would people still use such craft were they practically immortal? Some would, certainly, but many would not. Statistically, chances of dying in a shuttle or dropbox or jet crash were very small. But how many people would risk forever against sudden death? If you had eternity to look forward to—or perhaps the expansion death of the sun in millions of years—wouldn't it be safer to travel by other means? An armored car, say? An unsinkable ship? Yes, it would take longer to cover substantial distances, but so what? Time would become a cheap commodity. Life would be too valuable to risk.

King thought about the weapons shipped to his destination in a security tube. Possession of such things whose function was nothing else save as possibly offering violent death had been long a crime, but in a future where people had radically extended lifespans, a sentence of a hundred or two hundred years for merely owning a gun might well be the norm. Actually using a weapon would be considered horrendous.

Not that he thought the authorities would offer the cure for death that Spackler represented to the public at large. No, they would certainly try to regulate it, perhaps even keep it secret save for a small elite. But such knowledge always outs. Some enterprising chemist or geneticist would eventually happen across someone equipped with the new and improved chromosomes and would lose no time of his own duplicating them. It might be years or decades before that happened, but when it did, an angry public would howl down the offenders in voices loud enough to be heard across the galaxy.

The ship taxied, began its takeoff. King closed his eyes.

Don't let this one crash, he prayed to any god who might be listening. Let me live long enough to see this through and collect my dues for it. Allow me that and I shall happily build you a temple—when I can look forward to living long enough to be considered a demigod myself . . .

THIRTY-THREE

IN THE DWINDLING night, the jet made a wide, slow turn, banking to the port side and actually climbing a little from the treetop height at which it had been cruising.

"We'll be back on the ground soon," Zia said.

Silk nodded but did not speak. And what then? She hadn't wanted to talk about that and during the just-finished passion storm, neither had he. One of the true joys of sex was, once it got going good, you didn't have to think anymore. But they would have to talk about it eventually.

"There's supposed to be a town," she said. "Where we want to go isn't actually there but maybe fifty klicks away. We'll be okay once we get to the safebase."

"Will we?"

She turned the pilot's seat to look at him.

The com came to life.

"Attention, Lear Rental P-one-six-nine," said a voice in clear but heavily accented English, "this is Iça Air Control responding to your compgen request for glide. We have modem lock, you are cleared on runway two."

"We're in the pipe," Zia said to Silk. She touched a tab on the board. "This is P-one-six-nine, copy your cast, Control, lock is green."

"ETA three minutes to final approach," Control said. "Welcome to Içá."

As the jet finished its circle, Silk said, "Where'd you learn to fly? Spy school?"

"Not really. My uncle was a bush pilot in the wide country, back on E2. He delivered odds and ends to people who wanted to get away from civilization but who didn't want to give up all their comforts. He taught me when I was a teener."

She kept her face neutral, but Silk heard something in her voice.

"What's the matter?"

"What do you mean?" She glanced at him, surprised.

"It's not a happy memory."

Now she stared at him. "How do you know that?"

He shrugged. "Am I wrong?"

She didn't say anything for a few seconds, then shook her head.

"No. Uncle Lou was a bush pilot in more ways than one. The flying lessons weren't free."

Silk let it drop. It didn't sound as if she'd had a great childhood. He sometimes wondered if anybody ever had.

King dared to use the codes he'd forced from Pearce twice more before he reached New Amsterdam. Once in midflight, just after the suborbital ship had begun its descent, again as the vessel swooped toward a landing. Both times his portable computer wended its way through the electronic shunts and shuttles and found the responder's signal. He was still in Brazil, but no longer moving toward Manaus. According to the computer's map, the signal now originated from a place called Içá, much farther into the interior of the country.

Hmm.

As the vessel thundered to its landing at the local port, King considered his next course of action. He had planned to take a local flight to Manaus, but his worry now was that whatever the spy and Silk intended might happen before he could reacquire intimate contact with them.

King spoke with an agent of the carrier immediately upon attaining the interior of the port. Yes, there was a charter service nearby where he could rent a plane, just down corridor D, that way.

Sí, there were pilots available, as well. You are most welcome, *señhor* . . .

Since King's skills as an aircraft pilot were out-of-date and ill-used for years, he would hire somebody to do that for him.

This venture had been expensive thus far, in money as well as time, but he expected to recoup the former *and* the latter, thank you very much, a millionfold each. At the least.

The air outside the sterile recycled atmosphere of the little jet was warm and damp but not too bad as the dawn splashed over them. Zia stood on the apron with Silk, their rental jet parked behind them. How had he known how she felt about her uncle? If he could see through the façade she always kept up in front of her past, her skill had gone to the Badlands, sure enough.

"Not as hot as I thought it would be here," Silk said.

"What?"

"We're not far from the equator," he said. "I figured it would be like a steam bath, even in winter. This is not bad, almost like Hana."

Zia shrugged.

"Now what?"

"Now we rent some kind of transportation and go for a little ride."

Silk yawned and nodded. He stretched, bent and touched his toes, straightened. "I don't suppose you'd want to rent a room first and sleep for a couple of hours? I'm grainy and stale, I could use a nap."

"We'll sleep after we get somewhere we can relax without worrying about our backs. Come on." It came out a little harsher than she wanted it to, but she was also edgy. And she needed to be back in control. This whole affair had blossomed like a weed in her otherwise clean garden and she didn't know what to do. Yeah, it was a weed but it was also not that ugly a plant . . .

Zia signed a hangar-fee document, presented her false passport ID, along with one she'd cobbled together for Silk, then rented an electric cart that had seen better years. The two of them headed out of the port toward the safebase to the north. They had to pass through the main section of town before they could leave it.

Içá was a sleepy village of maybe five thousand, clumps of warehouses and light industries sprinkled into the blocks of six-story prefab apartment cubicles. A smelter on the edge of the outskirts belched dark smoke into the humid air, but there didn't seem to be any other factories cranked up. The place smelled like burned alcohol fuel mixed with tropical pollen. The streets were coming to life with vehicles, mostly motorbikes and unpowered trikes, a few walkers dotting the sidewalks, heading for work or on some early morning personal errands. Zia remembered her own childhood, what it was like living in a small town, knowing your neighbors, going about your business in your own little world. Sometimes she wondered what it would have been like if she hadn't taken the path she took, if she'd stayed in End of the Road, married local, had kids, worked at the Fishhook Inn waiting tables. Would have been a hell of a different life. There was a time when the idea would have made her want to puke.

But now . . . ? Well, it didn't seem so awful, not really. She liked the game, liked being a player, but with Silk here messing up her well-made plans, the future suddenly seemed up for renewal. Was she ready to dump it all and walk away?

No, not really.

But was she ready to delete Silk and go home in at least semitriumph?

That was a tough question, too—

"Pull over," Silk said.

"What?"

"Right there. By the sports store."

Zia glanced over at where he was pointing. It was a small building in the middle of a row of similar places, diamond-mesh over the plastic windows. Automatically she slowed the cart. "Why?"

"I want to pick up a couple of things."

"Look, we're only going to be on the road for an hour or less—"

"Maybe so, but according to the map a big chunk of the fifty klicks is along a winding road bounded on both sides by rain forest. If somebody jumps out of the jungle, I want something to wave at him other than my dick."

"Oh, I dunno, Silk, that's pretty formidable, you ask me."

"Zia . . ."

"Nobody is gonna leap out of the woods—"

"No? How'd they find us before?"

She pulled the cart over to the curb. "Damn," she said. "I forgot to check us for bugs. I'm getting stupid here, Silk. It's your fault, all that sex. Damn."

• • •

Inside the store, the owner or manager yawned at them and fired off a rapid bleat of Portuguese. He was a short man, sad-eyed with thick black hair combed straight back and a mustache that covered most of his mouth. He reminded Silk of a walrus he had once seen in a zoo.

Silk said, "You speak English?"

The walrus shook his head. "No, no Englez. Español? Nihongo?"

Silk smiled. His Japanese was worse than his Spanish. He searched his memory. What was the term?

"*¿Ah . . . tengo . . . uh,   tiene . . . arbalesta?   Ballista?*" Shit—what was the word? "*¿Cruzarco?*"

Something got through. Walrus grinned and nodded. "*Sí, sí,*" he said, followed by another rapid blast of Spanish as fast as the earlier Portuguese that Silk also missed. What was the Spanish for "slow down"? *Retardo? Retarda?* Jesus, he was butchering the language, he was sure of that. An English speaker from Hawaii trying to do business with a Brazilian Portuguese speaker, using primary-ed Spanish. Christ.

It didn't matter. The man moved to a locked cabinet and opened it to reveal a display of three crossbows.

Silk looked at the weapons mounted on the inside of the cabinet doors. One was a practice weapon, probably had a twelve-kilo pull, the body of which was of cheap spun fiber stained to look like wood. A piece of junk. The second was a precision model, a little better made, for shooting sit-down matches, but also a light pull. The third was a hunting instrument. He'd seen such things before but never played with one. It was heavier than the others, probably a fifty-kilo draw with a built-in cocking lever, bearing a simple peep sight without any electronics. It was a little known but hardly secret fact that in some parts of the world there were still hunting preserves where—were you extremely rich—you could stalk with a bow or crossbow or even a gun certain live animals unaffected by the plague of long ago. Deer, impala, some kinds of goat or feral pigs. Supposedly here in the Amazon were several such preserves.

Silk nodded and smiled. "Yeah. That's the one." He pointed. "There. *Allá.*"

The shopkeeper removed the crossbow from the cabinet and placed it on the counter. Silk picked it up, put it to his shoulder, looked through the sight. Nodded and put it back on the counter.

"Quarrels? Arrows? Uh. *¿Flechas?*"

More liquid Spanish Silk couldn't keep up with. But Walrus reached under the counter and came out with three arrows. One was a blunt-tipped practice quarrel, the second a more precise aluminum target shaft, no head. The third was a spunglas hunting quarrel with a delta-shaped steel cutting head sharp on the edges. Looked a lot like the antique ones in his collection.

Silk tapped the hunting arrow. "Give me ten of these. *Diez flechas, por favor.*" Okay, what else did he need? "*¿Tiene chucillos?*"

The man nodded, smiling larger, and pointed to a glass case with knives displayed on a board. Silk squatted in front of the case, picked out a small tanto-style sheath knife of stainless steel with a black handle that looked like it was hard neoprene. He tapped the glass. "This one." He stood and faced the man over the counter. He waved the crossbow and darts, then the knife. "*¿Cuánto? En estándaros?*"

The shopkeeper pulled out a calculator and tapped in some numbers, then turned to show it to Silk.

Six hundred stads. In the United States, the bow and knife would probably cost half that much. But Silk couldn't be particular here. He nodded.

He turned to Zia, who had been watching with interest. "He wants six hundred stads."

"You think a crossbow and a knife are going to be much use?"

"I don't know. I hope I don't have to find out."

"Fine. I'll get my credit tab—"

"You have any cash?"

"Couple thousand, why?"

"We don't want to give him my license number and have it show up on a scan somewhere, do we?"

She nodded. "Probably won't matter, but you're thinking. Will he sell the weapon to you without a license?"

"Business looks a little slow. I offer him a couple hundred extra, I think so."

"Go ahead. It's all rascaled money, anyhow. Swiped here by the genius of E2 offworld accounting ops. Ask him if he's got a fresher."

Silk nodded. Turned back to the man. *"¿Dónde está el necesario?"*

Walrus pointed.

Zia handed Silk a pad of folded currency. "Pay him and meet me in the fresher."

He grinned.

"No, not for that. We have to check each other for bugs. Better get a pocket knife or some tweezers if he has them."

Walrus wasn't happy with the idea of selling the crossbow to Silk without a license, but when Silk started fanning hundred-stad bills onto the counter, the man swallowed, rubbed at his chin, and scooped the money into his hands. Probably report the damned thing stolen, but given what else had been going on, being accused of bribery or theft were pretty small concerns. Silk managed to convey that he wanted a penknife, and one with a tiny tool kit built in was produced. Silk had the man unbolt the bow from the stock and using more gestures than words indicated that he wanted it packed with the quarrels into an innocuous-looking plastic tube. He would reassemble and test it once they were out of the city. He tucked the sheath knife under his belt and pulled his shirt down over it, then went to find Zia in the fresher.

She was naked. Despite his exhaustion, he felt a surge of desire for her. He put one hand on her shoulder.

"None of that. I want you to examine me. I've checked myself as best I can, but go over my back and butt, my scalp."

"With pleasure. What am I looking for?"

"Anything that looks as if it doesn't belong on a naked woman. Funny mole, tick, puncture wound, anything unusual."

She turned around.

Silk did as he had been told, but the nearness of her and all that bare flesh aroused him. As he squatted and put his face close to her buttocks, he slid his hand between her legs from behind.

She clamped her legs together, hard.

"Dammit, Silk, this is serious."

"So was I."

"Later."

He smiled at the cleft of her beautiful ass. Leaned forward and kissed one cheek softly. "Okay."

He searched carefully, but didn't find anything.

"Okay. Your turn," she said when he was done.

He stripped, turned quickly to hide his erection, but not quickly enough. "Jesus, Silk, you part mink or something?" But she smiled as she said it.

After a few seconds, he felt her pinch his back. "Damn!"

"What?"

"You have a little spot here, a puncture wound. Like somebody stabbed you with a needle."

"I don't feel anything."

She rolled the skin around under her fingertips. "Got a little ball a few millimeters deep. That's how he found us, the big man. Looks as if he got close enough to shoot a transmitter or a responder into you. Hold still."

"What are you going to do?"

"Dig it out. Thing's got a short range, runs off bioelectric power, probably, old stuff, but if this guy was with Terran Security, they can footprint the whole planet with a watchsat. They might be able to pick up a signal."

Silk felt a sharp pain in his back.

"Hey, ow!"

"Sorry. Almost got it . . . there!"

He turned around, saw Zia looking at the tip of the penknife blade. There was a red speck on the end of it not much bigger than a pinhead. "Damn," he said. "It's so small."

"So's a virus but it can do a lot of damage." She put the speck onto the edge of the sink and pressed the flat of the knife blade against it. It made a tiny crunch Silk could hear, and there was a smell he couldn't quite identify for a second until he remembered pinching fire ants as a kid. Kind of a bitter, acid stench.

"Let's go," she said.

Silk hurried to dress.

The small jet King had rented zipped across the sky at several hundred kilometers an hour, rapidly devouring the distance from the coast to the Amazonias interior. A few hours and he would be there.

To reassure himself for the third time since this flight had begun, he unfolded his computer and triggered the responder transmitter. He turned the sound off, but left the visual running. He glanced at the pilot sitting in front of him, but the man was lost in his own thoughts, probably would not have thought anything of the responder's tiny beep had he heard it.

King frowned at the computer screen. Nothing.

He triggered the transmitter again.

No response.

He ground his teeth together. Damn. Had The Scat found Pearce so quickly? Was the system codes he'd garnered compromised? Certainly that could be. Regrettable but possible.

The other possibility was that the responder had malfunctioned.

Yet a third possibility could be that it had been discovered and rendered inert.

King sighed. It did not matter why, he had to accept and deal with it. The responder had been relatively stationary for the last few hours—relatively meaning it hadn't moved more than a hundred klicks in any direction. This Içá was not a large town and it was in an area that was still sparsely settled, no more than a few people per square kilometer. If they were there, he could find them. And it did not make sense that they would fly all the way to this remote area from Los Angeles just to take in the local sights. No, they were there, somewhere, probably hiding and planning their next move.

Why there?

He didn't know. But if he hurried, he hoped to find out.

"Can this thing go any faster?"

The pilot lurched awake. "Excuse me?" He had a flat, nasally Australian accent, probably some expatriate dope or rare animal smuggler when legitimate business wasn't sufficient. Given the smell of the plane's interior, animals had spent some time in it.

"Threaten the engine," King said. "I just recalled an earlier appointment."

"Your money, mate."

The jet increased speed as the pilot pushed the throttle forward.

THIRTY-FOUR _____

WHEN THEY WERE a few kilometers away from the town, on a stretch of road bounded by trees and thick underbrush laced together with vines, Silk assembled the crossbow.

Zia watched him peripherally as she drove.

When he was done, he said, "Why don't you pull over for a minute?"

"Why?"

He hefted the crossbow. "I want to see how this shoots."

She nodded. Of course. That was one of the first things they taught you in the biz. Learn your weapon, if you had one.

She found a clear spot and drove the cart completely off the road. A bus went past, and a couple of vans and trucks hauling logs, but the road wasn't real busy. The warming air held a jungle stink, a fecaloid odor of rot and waste overlaid by pollen and plants heating up. Nice place, the rain forest. Reminded her of a public fresher in Cat Town on a summer night.

Silk alighted from the cart. He examined the sights on the crossbow, fiddled with the back one, used the little lever to cock the string. He pushed one of the stubby arrows into place. It seated with a small *snick*. He aimed the weapon at a thick-boled tree about fifteen meters away. The thrum of the string was quiet, compared to a gas or chemical explosive gun. The arrow zipped away so fast she lost it, then hit the tree at chest-level with a meaty *twock!*

Silk nodded. Fiddled with the sights again, then loaded and fired a second arrow. This one struck about a handspan below the first one.

Silk nodded again. "It's dead on at this range," he said. "Want to try it?"

She shrugged. Ancient weapons hadn't been part of her training but the principle should be the same.

He handed the crossbow to her, showed her how to cock and load it. "There's a little ball on a post for the front sight," he said. "Center it in the circle of the rear peephole and put that where you want the arrow to land. The trigger is a little stiff but no creep. Keep the sights aligned until you see the quarrel strike the target."

Zia raised the weapon and aimed at the space between Silk's two arrows. Quarrels, he called them. She pressed the trigger crisply. The crossbow jumped a little, but she had a good grip on it and she held it as still as she could. The quarrel hit the tree a little high, almost touching the first of his darts, but still between the two. Acceptable accuracy for a defensive weapon at this range, though she'd rather have a plasma or caseless rifle with a laser scope. She didn't think they were going to need one of those or the crossbow. Once they were at the safebase, they should be, well, safe. The base was disguised as a botanical research camp, as she understood it, a small operation supposedly studying local flora. And assuming her briefing had been correct, there would be a way offworld waiting there for emergency use. Probably a one-shot riser disguised as a low-flight aircraft. It wouldn't take her home, but it would get her into orbit where a rendezvous with a freight ship whose ownership was disguised via a series of dummy corporations would be standing by.

As Silk pried the three darts from the tree, Zia thought about what she was going to tell him about the process.

What *was* she going to tell him? She hadn't decided yet what she was going to *do* about him. It was driving her to the edge of herself and she did not like the territory.

"Okay," he said. "We can go, I'm done."

King's rented craft danced forward at the limits of its ability, the little engines roaring themselves hoarse. He had made up some time with the increased pace, added to that which he had gained in the arc ship, a much faster way to travel long distances than an ordinary jetcraft. He shouldn't be more than a few minutes behind them when they landed at Içá. He had prevaricated a story that ought to get cooperation from the locals. If they were in the village, he would find them quickly enough. If they had left, he would determine how. If they flew, he had a plane. If they had departed overland, he would follow them. There were only two roads in or out of the town according to his computer's map, one ran along the river, the other north and south. He was getting close, he could feel it, and he was determined to make an end to this, here, as soon as possible.

"Be on the ground in fifteen minutes," the pilot said.

"Good."

The tropical growth in Hana was lush, but this place made it look tame. Silk watched the trees march past the cart, and it was a fecund green, a riot of shades, so dense, verdant, and thick that in places he could not see a meter into the forest. There had once been a danger of all this being destroyed and much of it had been cleared, but this patch loomed over the road as if it would overwhelm the cheap macadam if you took your attention off it for a moment. A cascade of kudzulike vines and creepers would wash over the cleared path and obliterate it were it not hacked or sprayed back and in a few years you wouldn't be able to tell man had ever been here. There were spots where the trees formed a canopy over the road and it was like moving through a tunnel.

"Amazing," he said.

"Yeah. We have a few places like this on E2. Kind of makes you feel insignificant, doesn't it?"

"Mm." He'd had much the same thought. You could easily imagine half-naked savages leaping from the brush, waving spears; or big spotted cats perched in the trees, ready to drop, all teeth and claws, to rend prey bloody and lifeless.

"So what happens when we get to this safebase?"

She was quiet for a moment. "Well. Let's get there first. We'll have—ah—a couple of options to discuss."

He looked away from her and back at the tangled growth. She didn't want to talk about it, that was clear enough, and something made him reluctant to push her. Maybe she didn't like the options she was considering.

Maybe he wouldn't like them either.

The road wound along, tight curves that serpentined back and forth, forcing Zia to keep the cart's speed to little more than a brisk walk. There were many streams and the bridges across these were narrow and ill-kept. When the rare vehicle approached from the opposite direction, Zia or they had to yield at the bridges, there was not room for two carts to pass each other upon the small spans, much less a bus or van. Even this dilapidated cart could have made a fifty-klick run in an hour or less, had the road been straight and level. On this path, the trip was apt to take three times that, Zia told Silk.

He nodded. Nobody had overtaken them from the rear, nor had they come upon anybody poking along any slower than their own pace. There didn't seem to be anything to worry about.

"Look at that," Silk said.

A man stood at the edge of a relatively clear spot a couple of dozen meters off the road. He appeared to be cutting a tree down with a small powered saw. He spared their cart a brief look, then continued his work. The man wore a T-shirt and shorts, with a colorful blue scarf wrapped around his head, covering his hair. He was swarthy and tanned and sweat stained his clothing.

"Local industry," Silk said.

"Maybe. And maybe he's a lookout posted for the safebase. I were running it, I'd have a guy with a com on either side of the approaching road to keep me informed of strangers heading my way. It's gonna take us another hour, maybe more to get there. Plenty of time to hide something you don't want seen."

The car negotiated a couple of hairpin curves before Silk spoke again. He said, "You really like all this stuff, don't you? The hide-and-seek, the danger?"

Zia smiled but it wasn't a particularly happy expression. "It's a game. Dangerous sometimes, but it's like a test. You put yourself out there, at risk, sometimes in death's path, and see if you can get out of the way in time. It makes you feel alive, Silk. Cheating the Chiller, laughing at him, slapping the knife aside, and dancing to the side as it lunges for you. Knowing you could slip but sure you won't. It's a powerful feeling."

"So I've found out."

She looked at him. "Look, if it's any help, I'm sorry I pulled you into this. Well, not altogether sorry." She slid her hand over and onto his leg.

"I could have thrown you out of my cube when we first met, could have called the police."

"I conned you, Silk. I used your feelings for your dead woman. It's part of what I do." She seemed surprised to have heard herself say this, but it wasn't really a shock to him. He knew. Had known for some time.

"You can't con an honest man." He put his hand over hers and pressed it against his leg. He was tired, exhausted, he needed to sleep, to spend a week on a beach baking in the hot sun and swimming, to eat good food and to shut the world off. But that was the fantasy and this, however fantastic it seemed, was what his reality had become. "I am a professional liar," he said. "A pretty good one, too. I can hear the bell when the truth launches, and I knew you weren't giving me all of it, almost from the first."

"Then why didn't you bail out?"

"I don't know for sure. Part of it was Mac, at first. Part of it was that I felt you pull at me, in a way I've never felt anybody pull at me before. Maybe I was curious to see what would happen. Maybe I wanted to slap the Chiller's face and see if I could dodge him. I don't know. It doesn't really matter, does it?"

"It matters. I thought you were a sucker, one of the sheep, what you call a lily. I thought I was manipulating you, that you were stupid, not a player, but I was wrong. You don't have the experience, but you have the core, Silk. On some level, you're just like me."

He sighed. Was he? Did all this call to him? He had been scared shitless, had never been so close to pissing himself as he had during this mad run, but it had also been exhilarating. He had to admit that to himself, even if he didn't tell her. The chase, the fear, the sex, the entire energy around it all. He had enjoyed it, even when he thought he was about to die, even when he had gone against all his civilized upbringing and killed another human being. He had never felt so vibrantly alive as when he had faced death, faced it and survived.

It was sure going to be hard to go back to work spinning stories for the Port after this. Assuming he lived that long.

Damn.

THIRTY-FIVE

WITH HIS PILOT in a local pub on standby, King went to see how difficult it was going to be to locate his quarry. After a brief meeting with the manager of the hangar and then a cart rental agent, he was somewhat amazed at how easily his story of meeting colleagues had been accepted.

The man and the lovely woman who rented the electric Voss? Why, *sí*, certainly, they had been gone but an hour or so, and if he wished, he could also have an identical cart. No, they had not said where they were going, but should he spot their cart it would be easy enough to determine that it was theirs—the registration plate was but one number less than the Voss cart still for rent. Ah, yes, the *señhor* is most generous.

Most people tended to fall all over themselves to be helpful if given the right story. Most people were idiots.

An hour cruising up and down the streets of the small town failed to locate the cart, there were no public underground parking structures and only a few enclosed private ones. Unless they had rented a house and hidden the cart—for which there would be no reason, given that it was rented and they had not tried particularly hard to lay a false trail—then it seemed likely to King they had left the area. He could not be certain of this, of course, but the town felt empty of his quarry.

He pulled his cart to the curb and allowed it to idle for a moment. Time for a few educated guesses.

If they rented a cart here to travel elsewhere, then likely the destination was nearby, within a few hours, otherwise it would have been easier to have the jet deliver them closer since there were private airstrips capable of landing such craft all over the country.

What was within a radius of, say, a hundred kilometers of this dead-end town?

He consulted his computer map. Outside of a few tiny outcroppings of civilization, there seemed to be little to draw a visitor to this area. There were, of course, assorted plantations cleared from the rain forest; the odd mining operation; scientific study groups; archaeological digs; backpacking camps for tourists who wanted to trek through nature in the raw. There were hermitlike souls who lived in the forest, and, so it was rumored, hidden aboriginal tribes who had moved into the depths of the forest, away from more civilized men. King considered this a modern myth, on a par with the story of the little old lady who raised a cow in her cube by feeding it flowers from her window box.

Within a hundred kilometers to the south were the Amazon River ports of Santa Rita do Weil and Sao Paulo de Olivença. But they could have landed the jet at one of the airports there. To the east lay the town of Santo Antonio do Içá, likewise equipped with an airport of some size.

A policeman went past on a motorized trike that putt-putted with the sound of a small and badly muffled alcohol engine. King glanced at him, then dismissed the man.

To the west lay Santa Clara, just across the Colombian border.

But to the north, there was no civilization of which one could properly speak until Taraquá, on the Uaupés branch of the Negro River, more than three hundred kilometers distant.

King stared at the computer's map.

North. They went north.

The rationale was skimpy at best, King knew that. But he was also sure in his own mind that it was so. They were running, that was true, but they were also running *to* some place. There was a base, a hideaway, something, where the spy thought she would be safe. That made perfect sense, in the same way he had known they were going to Los Angeles had made sense. Call it educated instinct, for want of a better term. When he had leisure to examine it, he could wonder about the why of it; for now, it was sufficient that it worked.

As for holes in the wall, The Scat had hundreds of such places, on this world and others, and another espionage organization would hardly fail to provide its operatives with something similar. True, undercover agents were cheap and generally disposable, but now and again, something of great value must need be protected, and only a totally inept service would fail to provide for such a contingency. The E2 service might not be of the caliber of The Scat but they were not that inept—such would be very bad for employee morale.

And while sometimes the best hiding place was in the middle of a crowd, it depended on what it was one wished to hide. A few thousand square kilometers of jungle could enshroud a great deal.

King pulled the cart back onto the street and turned it toward the north-south road. He would go north. He knew what they were driving, he would check every possible bolt hole along the way until he found them.

"Almost there," Zia said. "Another couple of klicks."

Silk took a deep breath. "Okay."

After several hairpins they came to an even narrower path branching from the road to the right. Zia checked the kilometerage on the cart's odometer and it matched that of her instructions. This must be the place. She turned.

A kilometer along the bumpy driveway brought them to a crude but sturdy-looking steel slat gate blocking the path. Here the dense growth pressed in closer, only a meter or two away from the edge of the dirt lane. There was a cheap keypad lock holding the gate shut.

"I got it," Zia said. She got out of the cart, moved to the lock, and punched in the seven-digit code. The steel gate swung open.

When she got back into the cart, Silk said, "How do you remember all this stuff? Yak or Moff lingo, secret hideaways, codes for a lock halfway across the galaxy?"

"Like going to school, Silk. You cram it in until you can pass a test on it. They're working with viral learning but it's still kind of spotty, you know, get infected and wake up knowing a new language. The lock part is easy. It's an old joke among the E2 agents in the field, unofficial and frowned on, but still used. All nonessential coded locks have the same seven-letter combination: f-u-c-k-y-o-u. Not that hard to remember."

He shook his head.

Another twisted klick and they arrived at the site. In the center of a large cleared area were four prefab hoop buildings, translucent blue plastic tubes sliced in half lengthwise and set upon the spongy ground. The smallest of them would hold a dozen people easily, the largest would hide four 50-passenger buses stacked two high and two wide. The buildings were closed, the doors all shut.

It was quiet in the camp, enough so that the sound of the cart's electric motor seemed loud.

Zia shut the cart's motor off. The quiet deepened.

"Something's wrong," she said.

Silk looked at her, then the buildings. "What do you mean?"

"Most of our agents here are locals, well paid, but native terrans. At least one is from New Earth. If they're here, they know we're here, either that guy on the road or the gate should have signaled them. Procedure says somebody ought to be out here smiling and looking scientific."

"Maybe they are late sleepers."

"Maybe. Why don't you put a dart in that toy of yours."

Silk swallowed, but grabbed the crossbow.

"And how about you let me borrow your knife?"

He handed the tanto to her. She pulled the cro-closure open and pulled the knife from the sheath. Turned the weapon in her hand and got a feel for it, then put it back into the sheath and tucked it into her pants in the small of her back. She left the cro-closure open.

The cart was parked so her side of it faced the nearest prefab Quonset.

"Okay, here's the scenario. I'm going to walk over and knock on the door. You get out on your side and stay behind the cart, keep your weapon down and out of sight but watch me over the roof. Probably all it is is these guys have been here too long and they've gotten lax. But just in case, you watch my back."

"Right."

"You okay with this?"

He nodded. "Yeah."

Zia took a deep breath, let it out slowly, trying to calm herself. But the hormones bubbled in her, popping, filling her with nervous anticipation. *Wrong*, her inner voice told her. *Bad. Leave. Go.*

The part of her that lived in the cold said, Can't do it, sweetie. This is the way home. It could be worse somewhere else.

Her inner voice was not happy with that. *Could be? Not sure about that*, could *be better. Leave. Now.*

The cool part shook its head. Sorry.

Zia got out of the cart and walked toward the prefab's door.

Silk stepped out of the cart, keeping the loaded crossbow held low, the cart covered him to the middle of his chest, and he stood with his left side facing the building. If he had to, he could snap the crossbow up and to his shoulder and shoot over the cart's roof without moving his feet.

His mouth was dry, his heart thumping along faster and louder. Relax, he told himself. Think of it like a match. You know the techniques, breathe slow, center yourself . . .

This ain't no match, pal. What are you gonna do if somebody jumps out of that hut with a gun? You gonna shoot *him?*

I shot the big man outside my cube. They never found the bolt.

You were in a panic then, reacting. This is cold-blooded, this is different.

Listen, somebody jumps out of there with a gun, believe me, I'll be in a fucking panic. But in a strange way, he didn't believe that. He was, however he had come to be here, a player now. No longer just along for the ride.

Zia tapped on the door.

Silk swallowed dryness, blew out half his air, tried to suck in a slow and deep breath.

No answer.

Zia rapped again.

"Nobody moves!" came a voice from behind Silk.

For a place lacking in civilization, this road had more exits than King would have thought. In the first ten kilometers he had been required to pause and examine no less than a dozen such possible hiding spots. He had done so with one hand on his air pistol, hidden under a spare shirt on the cart's seat. The little weapon he had used to delete Pearce was now tucked into the top of a thick sock covered by the thin tropical weight cloth of his trousers.

His caution was warranted, but thus far the results of his search had been negative. Those people he met during the first seven stops had no knowledge of his quarry. At the eighth sidetracking, he spoke with a woman who had seen a cart similar to his pass by earlier in the day, perhaps two hours earlier.

King grinned as he drove away from the woman. His hunch had been correct. He was not far behind them.

If he hadn't been wired on fear, if his personal trigger had not been set to break like a thin icicle in sub-zero cold, Silk might have dropped the crossbow and put his hands into the air. That would have been the reasonable, the rational thing to do. But he was past behaving rationally. He was part of this, now.

He spun and brought the crossbow up to his shoulder.

As time went into its slow fugue again, a thing he *was* getting used to, he saw a man wearing a bright green shirt and yellow shorts standing twenty meters away, pointing a long-barreled rifle at Zia, or at least in her direction. As Silk's vision tunneled and sounds faded, overcome by a ringing in his ears, he saw the colorfully dressed man try to turn and point the gun at him—

You don't have time to aim, the voice inside him said. It was calm, cool, matter-of-fact.

So Silk didn't aim. With his gaze focused on the threat—man with a gun, there!—he let muscle memory take him. He had fired thousands of practice shots with a crossbow over the years, his body knew what the proper position was without having to think about it. Point-shooting it was called, and while it was not good for long range accuracy in the scoring ring, it did work for large targets up close. Silk's brain went into neutral and his body told him when he was lined up.

Shoot! Now!

Silk pulled the trigger. Watched the dart travel in slow motion. Saw it hit the gunner square in the chest and sink in until half of it was left.

The man flung the gun away and grabbed at the quarrel with both hands, pulled on it. His hands slipped, tore part of the fletching off as they slid off the dart. He started to stumble backward—

Zia screamed, a low, guttural yell.

Silk twisted around, almost slipped and fell, saw all at once another whole scenario.

The prefab's door, open. A man standing just outside, a pistol in one hand. Zia, crouched low, her arm extended as if punching him in the chest. The knife in her hand, buried in the man's solar plexus—

"In the cart! Go! Go!"

Silk jerked the door open and jumped into the cart.

Zia came running. He had her door open by the time she got there. Behind her, the man she'd knifed was still falling. She had the bloody knife in her hand.

The cart's motor hummed to life and Zia shoved the accelerator flat against the floor. The cart's wheels threw dirt as the cart slid in a half circle, then found enough traction to shove it forward.

Somebody started yelling behind him as the cart gathered speed.

Somebody started shooting, too. Silk heard that.

Zia drove, trying to think. What the hell had happened? The safebase was anything but that; what the fuck were they going to do now?

She slowed the cart to make the curve. Something hit the back of the vehicle, two quick metallic taps. They were shooting back there, whoever the fuck *they* were—

Next to her, Silk reloaded the crossbow. He was pale, but he'd come through. The gunner dressed like a parakeet would have had her if Silk hadn't skewered him. As it was, the guy from the hut almost got her before she took him out. Shit.

They rounded another turn, she saw the gate ahead of them. Two men with rifles or shotguns flanked the gate.

"Zia?"

"We'll ram it. Buckle your safety harness, duck down as low as you—fuck!"

"What?"

"Motor just died."

She tried to restart it. Nothing. Must have taken a bullet in the wrong place. So much for ramming the gate. They wouldn't be able to coast that far, much less punch through with two shooters blasting at them.

She braked. The cart slewed to a stop.

"Grab your arrows and bail out. We'll have to lose them

in the woods before we circle back."

"Circle back?"

"Yeah. The bad guys have our way off the planet. We're going to have to get it from them. Somehow."

The two men ahead started moving toward them.

Silk stepped out of the cart. Zia saw a laser spot dance up the front of the cart, moving toward Silk.

"Silk—!"

He raised the crossbow as if he had all the time in the world. Shot.

One of the oncoming men sprouted a dart, high and to the left of his heart. He dropped to his knees. The second man dropped prone and started shooting.

"Go!"

Silk ran into the woods. Zia was right behind him.

THIRTY-SIX _____

WHEN KING HAD worked for The Scat, there had been agents who claimed they could smell trouble. He had laughed at them then, but the ensuing years had given their comments some meaning. Intuition was hardly something upon which to risk one's life, but he had to admit that under certain circumstances, it did exist.

As he turned into the driveway, no more than a beaten-dirt path off to the right, King had a bowel-tightening sensation sweep over him. If he could not actually smell it, he could feel it. Something in the air, some kind of . . . vibration. Whatever it was, it signaled danger.

He brought the cart to a stop and shut off the electric motor. The silence brought no clue as to what might be causing the edgy feeling. He sat there for a moment, the window open, listening. If he acted on this premonition and there was no offer of menace, he might feel a bit foolish—though none but himself would take notice of it. If, however, there was some cause for worry ahead on the twisted, narrow tunnel through the thick trees and undergrowth, better he should be prepared than not. A simple decision.

King alighted from the cart. He pulled his pistol, made certain the mechanism was charged and the safety off, and moved to the border of the path. He crept toward the next turning of the driveway, keeping himself only centimeters away from the nearest trees. Did he see something amiss, he could dart into the cover of the jungle instantly. It had been some years since he had trained in such an environment

235

and he struggled mentally to bring up those long-ago lessons. If one must take to the brush, one was best advised to move with even deliberation. It would avail one little to cat-foot along, trying to avoid breaking twigs or stepping on leaves or whatnot; it was better to keep a steady pace, to slip through the growth without thrashing or beating it aside, to—

Somebody screamed.

King clutched his pistol tighter, the grip being damp in the humid air, and dropped into a crouch. The sound seemed to come from ahead, but he could not see the screamer.

He worked his way to the path's turning, squatted yet lower, and duck-walked to a thick-boled tree. Using it for cover, he peered around it and down the path.

Ahead stood a metal gate, blocking the path. On the other side of the gate lay a man on the ground. He was on his back, one leg cocked up, both hands held to his chest over his heart.

A short arrow protruded from the man's grip.

There came too the sound of somebody who had not had training in moving through a dense rain forest, or who now chose to disregard that training, crashing through the brush off to King's left.

Silk! He had just missed them! It had to be!

He hurried forward, glancing quickly back and forth, sweeping the terrain with his gaze for possible attackers. He saw none as he half crouched his way toward the downed man.

He was still alive, if in some distress, when King reached him. He saw King approach and moaned.

"H-help me! I've been shot!"

"So you have."

King nudged a fallen rifle away with his foot and leaned over the wounded man. "Who are you?"

The man tried to pull the arrow from his body, then screamed at the pain of his effort.

"If you want my help, tell me who you are."

"I'm—I'm Nance. KHP . . ."

King blinked at the wounded man. Amazing.

"How did Keep Humans Pure come to be here? What is this place?"

The man, very pale and probably going into shock, pressed his lips together tightly.

"I have an aid kit, back in my cart," he said. "You need it."

The man shook his head. Stubborn lot, these.

"All right. I could put a fléchette into your eye and end your misery and your life. Or I could fetch the aid kit and save you. Which is it to be?"

The wounded man was almost ghostly in his whiteness now. "This—this is the edge of an offworld spy base," he said. "We . . . we have known about it . . . for a long t-t-time. We've been w-w-waiting for the newie bitch to show up here. They, they've got a—" He coughed, groaned at the pain it caused him, withstood it for an instant, then passed out.

King felt for a carotid pulse. Thready, but still there. He glanced away from the man at the path and jungle. The mate to his cart stood silent on the path a couple of dozen meters away. Whoever it was crashing through the forest had moved out of hearing range. Likely this fellow's confederates, chasing after Silk and that damned woman.

King considered his options. Going into the brush after them held no appeal. If they had come this far, there was something at the base they very much wanted. Best if he found out what it was.

He raised from his crouch and began to move along the path. He did so with great care, his pistol held ready to fire at anything that moved other than himself.

Before they had gone two hundred meters, Silk's face and arms were covered with scratches. Twice he had almost lost the crossbow when it snagged on something; once, he had twisted his left wrist when the quarrels tangled in a loop of vine. His sweat was sour and his mouth was dry, despite the humidity.

"Hold up a second," Zia said.

They stood very still.

"Hear anything?"

Silk shook his head. "No."

"Me, neither. We lost them, for now."

"Good. Let's sit down and rest."

They sat.

"So, now what?"

Zia ran one hand through her short hair. "We circle around and find a way to get into the base without them seeing us."

"And then?"

"One step at a time, Silk. First, we have to figure out where the hell the base *is*."

He stood, turned around in a tight circle. "That way," he said, pointing.

She blinked at him. "How do you know that? We dodged and twisted all through the woods."

He shrugged. "I just know. Since I was a boy I could always find my way around a place if I went there once." He sat again.

"Nice trick to have."

Neither of them spoke for a few seconds. Then Silk said, "What are we going to do, Zia? And what is your real name?"

"It really is Zia," she said. "I shouldn't have told you."

"Why did you?"

She sighed. "Damned if I know, Silk."

"What about the other question?"

She leaned back against a smooth-barked tree, her hands laced together around one knee. "Like I said, one step at a time—"

"Fuck that," he cut in.

She stared at him, surprised.

"You're the offworld spy, you want to get that transport and haul your ass into vac where you can catch a ride home. You came to collect Spackler, only he's at the bottom of the ocean, so you're done here, right? You couldn't bring him back, you were supposed to make sure nobody got hold of him to pick his genetic structure apart. I don't guess the fish will much care that he was supposed to live forever and even if they did, they won't be telling anybody.

"But what about me? I know all about it, you told me, so that means I'm in shit up to my eyebrows, doesn't it?"

She didn't say anything. He watched as she unlaced her fingers and casually slid her right hand out of sight behind her right hip. A short reach to where the tanto was stuck into her belt.

"You can't leave me behind. Somebody would collect me, the big guy's pals, who-the-fuck-ever, and they'd pry it out of me, so I'm as dangerous to your mission as Spackler was."

He had the loaded and cocked crossbow balanced on his knees, with his right hand on the back of the pistol grip. He could shift it so it was pointed at her faster than she could pull the knife and get to him, even as quick as she was. Judging from the angle of her arm and shoulder, she had her hand on or very close to the knife's handle.

Could he shoot her? Certainly the act was not beyond him, given the number of men he'd already blasted or spiked. He had gone from a spindoc to a killer, a whole fuck of a lot easier than he would ever have imagined. Yeah, it had been self-defense every time, but what amazed him was how little remorse he felt. He'd heard about policemen who'd killed felons during a crime and who'd had to have psychiatric help for years afterward to keep from going crazy. So far, Silk hadn't worried overmuch about the men he'd killed. Yeah, it bothered him, but on another level, he felt as if they'd had it coming. And if he knew for sure who it was who'd taken Mac, he could put a bolt through the guy's brain without hesitation.

Jesus. That was scary.

So, yeah, he *could* shoot her, pulling the trigger of his weapon was not beyond him. But—*would* he?

No, he realized. He wouldn't. And that was even scarier.

He was no longer the man he had been, in more ways than his new ability to shoot another human. Zia had jolted him out of his life, but in the doing of it, she had become something to him. He wasn't sure if the word "love" applied, but whatever word might fit, killing her was out of the question. If she wanted to pull that knife and slit his throat, he wouldn't stop her.

Jesus, are you fucking crazy? She moves, you spike her, fool!

No.

Silk said, "Here, hold this a second, would you? I need to piss."

He turned the crossbow around and handed it to her.

Oh, man!

Zia took the weapon from Silk and sat there stupidly watching him as he turned his back on her and took a few steps.

He knew.

Zia felt her stomach roil, as if a cold reptile had sprung to life suddenly in her gut and now it wanted out. He knew she'd had the knife gripped in her hand, ready to jump him. He knew she couldn't leave him here alive. He could have whipped that crossbow up before she moved a centimeter and punched her right through the heart.

Could have, but he had not. Instead, he'd given her his
weapon and turned his back, making it easy for her. She
could drop him without even having to look him in the face.

Why?

He wasn't a coward, she'd figured that out. He'd taken out
three or four of the opposition, so he had it in him to kill, but
he didn't shoot her when he had the chance, when he *knew* she
was on the edge of doing him. She wasn't fooling him, he knew
he was a liability, knew she could not leave him here alive.

Oh, *man!*

She heard the sound of urine splattering on the fallen leaves.
Christ, he really was pissing.

He finished, tabbed his pants, kept his back to her for a
moment. Took a deep breath and let it out, then turned around.
He was shaking.

"What is wrong with you?" she asked.

He held his hands wide, palms up in question, still shaking.

"Dammit, are you crazy? How could you do that? You *know*
I had my hand on the knife! Do you want to die?"

He shook his head, dropped his hands. When he spoke, his
voice was quiet, soft, barely above a whisper. "No. I don't want
to die. But I must be crazy, because—because . . . I would rather
die than have to kill you."

It was a time for firsts. It broke her heart. Nobody had ever
done that before.

She sobbed. "You can't *do* this, Silk! I can't *deal* with this!"
She stood, dropped the crossbow, and blinked away tears. "I'm
not ready for this!"

"Me, neither," he said, as he embraced her.

There were two dead men in the compound, one with another arrow in him, the other bled dry from a wound to his torso,
either a bullet or a knife, King figured. He was not close
enough to tell, being hidden in the broad-leafed foliage of
a ground-hugging plant on the edge of the clearing. Distant
rumbles of thunder rolled over the bush where he hid, and
the breeze had freshened somewhat, bringing with it the scent
of rain.

Sounds coming from one of the smaller buildings indicated
occupants. How many? He could not say. He assumed the New
Earth agents who normally peopled this place—if the man on

the path had been speaking the truth—were either dead or
otherwise incapacitated. Likely the voices he thought he heard
from within the building were from KHP operatives. He was
but fifteen or sixteen meters from the entrance. Perhaps the
agents would exit and present themselves as targets, he could
easily hit a man from here . . .

He smiled. Wishful thinking.

But perhaps the gods of chance were once again bored. Ten
seconds later, the door to the prefab building did swing open
and three men and a woman emerged into the afternoon. All
wore jungle camo gear, all were armed with rifles or shotguns.

More thunder echoed through the clearing. The sky had
darkened somewhat and the taller trees swayed in the wind.

"That's all we need, fucking rain," one of the men said.

Another one said, "If you'd done your fucking job and
caught them, we wouldn't have to be worrying about it."

"Eat shit," the first man said.

They all stood still for a moment and looked off in the
direction of the approaching thunderstorm.

King thought about it. Four of them, he would have to
shoot fast. He could do it in a second, second and a half,
and at this range, he would have to be nearly blind to miss.
The fléchettes his weapon now carried were poisoned, even
a superficial wound would be fatal.

Do it.

Despite the darkening skies, it was still awfully bright for
a low-powered laser sight to be useful. He used the backup
notch and post, centered it on the chest of the man farthest
away, took a deep breath and pressed the trigger sharply. The
man had not had time to react before King swung the pistol
slightly and fired again.

The sound of the little gun alerted the others, but before
they could do more than look around in panicked haste, he
fired the third time, at the woman.

The remaining man spun in a circle, blasting with his weapon, a chatter of semiautomatic caseless explosive fire spewing
bullets at waist-height, chewing up tree trunks and buildings,
clipping leaves from bushes, but too high to hit the prone
King.

King lined up on the spinning man and fired again, twice.

Twenty seconds later, all four lay on the ground, dead or
nearly so.

Excellent shooting, Depard.

He held his position, waiting for any others to make an appearance to see what the noise had been, but after five minutes, he detected no signs of more KHP agents. Had he gotten them all?

That would be nice.

A minute later the rain made good on its threat and began to pound on the compound, big, fat drops driven aslant by the wind. The thick sheltering bush kept most of it off King for the initial downpour, but it quickly began to soak and coat the leaves and then drip through. It was warm, though, and not altogether uncomfortable after the heat and humidity of the sunnier morning.

The four agents lay unmoving, and the lightning flashes and almost immediate booms of the thunder following disturbed their slumber not in the least.

When the deluge slashed down at its hardest, turning the world here a thick gray, King slipped from under the bush and hurried to the nearest building. He jerked the door open and jumped inside, gun held ready, but it was a waste of his caution. There were five other people inside, the E2 agents, King guessed, but all laid neatly in a row and all quite dead.

Well, well. The playing field, so it seemed, was now his.

And quite level, too.

THIRTY-SEVEN

SILK WAS USED to rain in Hana, but this was something else. It was like standing under a waterfall. The intense grayness of it was broken only by blasts of wind, strobes of lightning and canvas rips of almost-immediate thunder, bass notes that thrummed all the way through him. He could barely see Zia, only half a meter away, and he had to yell for her to hear him. The trees dipped and swayed under the brunt of the storm, leaves tore free and washed past. It was all very dramatic.

"Which way?" she hollered.

He pointed. Well. At least he wasn't lost.

Her hair was plastered flat to her head, streams of water sheeting down her so that her shirt and pants were also like thick paint. Even so, she was the most attractive woman he had ever seen.

Even more than Mac?

Guilt cut at him, harder than the rain, but he could not deny it. Yes. Even more than Mac.

The two of them slogged through the rain. Once, they had to stop because of a tangle so thick they couldn't penetrate it. Once, a fallen tree, mud still washing from the freshly exposed roots, blocked their way. But they kept moving. The air in one spot stank of ozone and he thought he saw curls of smoke blow past.

During a brief lull, in which the rain merely poured, instead of smashed, Zia said, "Can you find our cart?"

243

"Yes. Why? It's dead, isn't it?"

"So is one of the men who shot at us. Unless the burial detail works in the storm, he's still there."

"Why do you want to see him?"

"I don't. But I want his weapon, if it's still there."

"I have this," Silk said, waving the crossbow.

"And you're good with it. If it still works after a bath. But I'd feel a lot better if I had a gun. We don't know what we're getting into, who these people are, how many of them are at the base."

More killing? Once, the thought would have made him queasy. Now, it was just something that might have to be done. He nodded.

They found the cart, still parked where they had left it. Denser gusts of storm danced across the little vehicle as they watched it from cover.

Thirty meters along the road, near the gate, the man he'd shot lay on his back, unmoving. As they moved closer to him, Silk saw he was dead: his eyes were open and unblinking as the rain fell on them.

"I'm going for the rifle," she said. "Cover me."

Zia crawled on her knees and elbows, scooting out to where the dead man's weapon lay in the mud. She grabbed the rifle and ran back to where Silk squatted.

She sat in the mud and examined the rifle with what Silk saw as an offhand expertise. She did something and a magazine full of ammunition dropped from the rifle into her hand.

"Here we go. 6mm caseless."

She stripped one of the cartridges from the magazine. There was a black cone-shape smaller than Silk's little finger protruding from a white cylinder of what looked like plastic foam, this piece as big around as his thumb.

"Looks like a Black Talon starfish round—it mushrooms on contact, expands into the shape of a starfish," she said. "This white stuff is the propellant, an explosive that drives the bullet."

She reinserted the cartridge into the magazine and shoved it back into the rifle. "Counter says eight rounds. Laser sight is working. The water shouldn't affect anything." She smiled at Silk. "I feel better now."

Jesus, Silk, you're in love with a woman who likes playing with guns.

Yeah. So fucking what?
"Okay. We might as well go see what's waiting for us."
He nodded.
The rain followed them easily through the jungle.

THIRTY-EIGHT _____

KING'S RECONNOITER OF the compound proved to be enlightening, despite the deluge that continued to slap wet hands against him as he moved through his quick reconnaissance. Ostensibly this was a place designed for the study of biological specimens, plants in particular. There were enough trappings of that to convince a layman that indeed this was the function here. In fact, the only real indication of another purpose sidereal to botany was the small vessel inside the largest of the prefab structures. Well, to be technically correct, it was not a starship, so perhaps sidereal was an inappropriate term; still, the craft was sufficiently empowered to break the gravitational chains that bound it to Earth and thus to achieve escape velocity and orbit. For the purposes of one who wished to leave the planet in a hurry, it would do. Of course, Terran Security's radar and doppler net would be thick enough to detect the outgoing vessel, but it was well known that armaments for the atmospheric umbrella that protected the globe from intruders were set up to repel attackers rather than to shoot down someone leaving. By the time the proper codes were used and an appropriate response determined, the ship streaking away would be out of range for most planetary batteries. And unless it was known for certain there was something of a major threat to Earth onboard, politics determined that firing a live missile into interplanetary space was unlikely in the extreme.

Sneaking in was nearly impossible, but sneaking out was relatively easy.

King finished his inspection and determined that he was indeed alone at the base. The rain began to slacken somewhat, the storm pod moving off, and if the tropical pattern held true to form, the sun would out soon and begin to reclaim the water for another cycle.

King retrieved one of the dead KHP agent's rifles, picked a well-covered spot from which he could see the only unsecured entrance to the ship's hangar, and settled into the warm mud to wait.

Did the spy and her consort still live, they would be coming here. No doubt of that at all. Earth was a crowded planet but made small by electronics; if enough people looked for you, sooner or later they would find you, unless you cut yourself off totally from your fellow men.

No, his quarry would come, because they needed the ship to escape. When they arrived, he would be ready for them. *He* needed one or the other of them, preferably alive, so that he could bring this entire affair to a satisfactory conclusion. One way or another, it was going to be done soon, finished, and King could not recall ever being so ready to end an adventure as he was ready to end this one.

THIRTY-NINE

ZIA FELT BETTER armed, but she still didn't feel good. What Silk had done to her was confusing enough; not knowing who was in control of her escape from Earth wasn't any help. She had pretty much figured they weren't Terran Security, at least not in their official mode. TS would have a hundred, two hundred agents swarming all over this place, using high-tech gear that could pick out a particular grain of sand on a beach, the slackening rain wouldn't do anything to hide them.

Thunder rumbled, but it was more distant now, kilometers away. The rain had eased up and was no more than a steady drizzle.

No, whoever it was shooting at them, it wasn't security officials.

Which left . . . what?

Somebody who knew what Spackler represented. Rogue agents, looking to turn a fat profit? A medical type who had stumbled over the tests Silk's woman had done on Spackler and knew what they meant?

Zia wiped water from her face and ducked under a low branch, following Silk. It would make her feel better to know, but in the end, it didn't really matter. Spackler was dead and where nobody would find him, she'd done her job, all she wanted to do now was go home.

Bringing Silk with her.

The man got to her, sure enough, and she didn't know where that would go, or if it would continue or end, but she had to find out. They might not get out of this mess alive but she wasn't going to be the one to kill Silk. No more than he could kill her.

Hell of a business. Not "I love you," but "I can't kill you." Hardly seemed the same, and yet, it meant *some*thing.

Silk pulled up. "About two hundred meters to the perimeter," he said.

"Okay. Let me go first. Keep it quiet and follow my lead."

"No."

"No?"

"You're better armed with that. I go first and you cover me."

He was right. She told him so.

They exchanged places and Silk led them toward the compound.

The clouds began to break up, though there wasn't much sunshine coming into the compound just yet. King shifted in the mud and checked the action on the rifle for the third time. Lying in muck in a tropical jungle had hardly been at the top of his agenda when he'd started this business, but one did what one must. Being fastidious went by the wayside early during the agency's training. He nibbled on a chocolate bar he'd found, sipped at a plastic can of soda water. He needed to urinate again, but recalling how giving into that urge had undone him at the beginning of this debacle, held it in and bore the discomfort. He would remain here as long as necessary.

Zia crept up next to where Silk lay prone. She stretched herself flat next to him and looked at where he was pointing.

"Take a look," he whispered.

She did so.

There were four people lying on the muddy ground. The four wore combat camouflage, three men and a woman, as nearly as Silk could tell. None were moving. Bloodstains, much diluted by the rain, pooled near the closest body.

More corpses.

"Who—?" he began.

"I don't know," Zia said. "My people wouldn't be dressed that way, not if they were supposed to be botanists. These must be the opposition."

"Who killed them?"

"Now there's the question of the hour. I don't know. Maybe they just had our people tied up and they got loose and took them out."

"You think?"

She chewed at her lower lip. "No. Not really. I think our guys are like those."

"Then—?"

"I don't know. Maybe another player we haven't seen yet. Or maybe one of the ones we have seen but don't recognize."

Silk shook his head. This was a big crappy mess.

"We have to assume somebody is in here somewhere and that they don't have our best interests at heart. Somebody who zeroed these guys pretty quick, given how close together they are."

"What do we do now?"

"We look for them. Very, very carefully."

Zia wished she knew what was going on, but more important now was getting out of his hellhole. The escape craft was in the biggest of the prefabs, had to be, if it was even still here. She and Silk had to get to it, light its engines and get away from here without being blasted by whoever it was had blasted the guys in the compound.

Where would she set up, if she were in their boots? If she thought somebody was coming back here to get the ship in the prefab?

Somewhere she could see the doors. There were a couple of them in the biggest building, and if it were her, she'd block one of the entrances shut so it couldn't be opened and watch the other one. If somebody did get to the blocked door and she didn't see them, they would have to circle around to the other way inside sooner or later, or else make a hell of a lot of noise trying to get into the building.

So. Where was a good place to hide to see the two doors?

She led Silk along cautiously, her weapon ready to shoot. The sun peeped through the clouds in places now, but it was still dim enough for her to see the tiny circle of the laser sight on the ground in front of them as they moved.

The brush in the back of the hangar building had been cleared only a few meters away from the wall. Zia crouched low and worked her way toward it. She waved Silk to a halt and crawled another five meters on her own.

After five minutes she was convinced the area was empty, save for them. She wiggled back along her path to where Silk lay.

"I don't see anybody."

"Okay. What now?"

"I'm going to try the door."

He shook his head. "No. Let me."

"Don't be a hero, Silk. I'm better at this kind of stuff."

"Yeah, and that gun you have still shoots eight times. My crossbow only does one. Better you should cover me."

He was right again. "Okay. Go."

Silk crawled to the edge of the clearing, then scrambled up and did a kind of hopping run to the door. He grabbed the mechanical knob and twisted, but the door, hinged on the inside to open inward, did not budge. He scooted back into the bushes and sprawled next to her.

"Locked."

Zia thought about it. If nobody was watching the door— and since Silk hadn't been blasted that seemed a workable thought—then they would have locked it. Using the rifle, she could probably blow the lock open. If they moved fast, they could get inside and into the airship before anybody watching the front could stop them.

Of course, by the time they got the engines on-line, they could be in big trouble. The ship probably wasn't armored and a few bullets in the right place would disable it, maybe beyond repair. The prefab wouldn't stop a high velocity round. And what if there was a barrel of plastcrete or something leaning against the door in the hangar? They'd let whoever was here know they were in town and still be stuck outside.

No. They'd have to go around to the main doors in front.

She explained it to Silk and he nodded.

They began to work their way around the building.

King untabbed his pants, rolled onto his side, pulled his penis free and pissed. The arc of urine was short, a dark yellow that splashed into a nearby puddle. Water still dripping from the trees made enough sound that his own addition to the puddle should go unnoticed, were ears in range of hearing it. He finished, retabbed his pants, and rolled back into prone position, rifle at the ready.

He immediately felt better.

Errant rays of sunshine began to stab down into the compound. The verdant jungle glowed under the light, resplendent after its washing. A fecund place, this. Almost malignantly alive.

Something made a noise to his left and behind him.

King sucked in a quick breath and held it, straining to hear anything else. Would that he had some sensory gear, amplifiers, polarizing lenses, infrared proximity detectors.

Another small sound.

Could that be a vestige of the rain? A torn leaf fluttering down, a small animal clearing detritus away from the entrance of its burrow?

Yes, indeed it could be. It could also be a human attempting stealth. Working his or her way toward his position.

With a certainty that brooked no resistance, King suddenly knew he had been spotted. He had to move!

He crawled from under the bush over the boundary of the clearing. He could move better on the cleared ground, and if they were in the jungle behind him, the angle should keep him invisible as long as he kept to the very edge.

He started crawling on his belly but quickly came up to a hand-and-knee scrabble. Speed was of the essence. He had to reestablish himself in a more secure position, quickly. Where?

"You hear that?"

"Yes," Zia said. "Somebody moving in the brush ahead. Let's try to flank him. Go to the right and circle around, about ten meters, then move in. Don't shoot me by mistake."

Silk nodded. He started to crawl away, then stopped.

"What?"

"Be careful," he said. "I don't want anything to happen to you."

She smiled at him. "Yeah. You, too."

After he moved off, she shook her head. Well, that was better than "I can't kill you," wasn't it? Practically a declaration of undying love.

She didn't feel much like a calm and collected secret operative at the moment. She was tired of crawling. Her shirt and pants were caked with mud, torn in several places and soggy. Her knees hurt and her hands were not only filthy but scratched and bleeding under the grime. She wanted a tub full of hot water and a bottle of good wine and two or three hours to soak in one and drink the other. But first, they had to get out of here alive.

When she reached the edge of the clearing again, she found the spot where the person who'd been watching the door had been. The muddy ground held an imprint of his body, a big man from the size of the impression, and there was a hint of ammonia in the air. Probably peed somewhere close by and with her luck lately, she'd crawl through it.

Silk said, "Zia?" in a hoarse whisper.

She saw him slithering toward her. "He's gone," she said. "Must have heard us coming and bailed out."

He moved up next to her. Stopped and wrinkled his nose. "Gah," he said.

"What?"

"I think I just crawled through a puddle of piss."

She gave him a smile and a soundless laugh. "Come on."

"Where to now?"

"I think he's moved back into the compound."

"How come?"

"He didn't come back past us and I don't think he could move through that sticker bush to the right."

Zia edged into the clearing, glanced to her left. Nothing.

As Silk was emerging from the brush, she looked to her right.

Saw the man crawling away from them on his hands and knees, seventy meters distant.

"There he is!" she said, raising the rifle.

In her excitement, she forgot to whisper. The crawling man must have heard her, for he rolled to his right into the jungle again as she fired. The rifle boomed, but she saw the bullet churn up a furrow of mud past where the big man had dived into the bushes.

"Fuck! I missed him!"

Silk said, "Forget him. Get to the airship! You get it cranked up and I'll guard the door!"

"Yeah, right, good idea!"

They ran.

King let the fear wash over him and then forced it away. They'd shot at him but missed by a couple of meters. He was okay, but they would be going for the airship. He had to get back around to where he could stop them!

He rolled up, took a deep breath, and darted out into the clearing, his rifle held pointed in the direction from which the shot had come.

His sideways run took him into the shelter of one of the smaller buildings without revealing sight of his quarry.

He took three deep breaths, expelled the air, sucked in another deep inhalation, and cut to his right, deeper into the compound. Using the next building for cover, he ran, slipping once in the mud but staying on his feet until he made it into the shadow of the prefab structure. The hangar was one more building away. He stuck his head around the left corner for a quick look, half a second, no more.

An arrow hit the corner of the building as he jerked his face back, hit and glanced off and stuck in the ground five meters away, burying itself at an angle so that only the fletching and butt of the missile showed.

Damn!

King turned and ran toward the right end of the structure. He'd circle around the other way and try to flank Silk and that hellish weapon of his!

Silk saw the man's head pop out from the corner of the building forty meters away, and he snapped off the shot. Too late. The quarrel hit the corner and bounced away.

He snapped the cocking lever down and shoved another dart into place, brought the weapon up and looked for a target. Where had he gone?

"Zia, he's coming this way, how you doing in there?"

"The control board is locked with a keypad code!"

Silk turned his attention back to the compound. No sign of the guy. He worked his way to the corner of the hangar. Maybe he was trying to sneak up behind them?

He peered around the edge.

Saw the big man sprinting in the mud twenty-five meters away, trying to get across a clear spot without being noticed.

"Gotcha, fucker!"

Silk stepped out into the clear and brought the crossbow to bear.

The big man saw him—Jesus fucking Buddha, it was the same guy, the one he'd shotgunned in L.A.!—and fired his weapon from the hip. Silk heard the booms, one, two, three, four. The mud splashed at his feet as he jumped back for cover. Another of the shots dug a groove in the prefab, showering him with plastic splinters—

He was almost there—

Either the third or fourth shot hit him on the leg. He spun away from it and by then was out of sight behind the corner. Shit!

He looked down and saw his pants ripped over the wound. It bled pretty good, but on the outside edge of his thigh, a shallow trench that was mostly skin and only a hair into the muscle. Lucky. Another four or five centimeters and it would have smashed the bone.

"Silk!"

"I'm okay, but he's getting closer. Hurry up!"

Zia didn't have any idea what the code might be. In desperation, she punched in the standard "fuck you."

The holoproj blossomed to life and showed systems controls.

Son-of-a-bitch. They had it!

She said, "Voxcontrol!"

"On-line," the computer's voice said.

"Cycle for lift-off, as fast as you can."

"Cycling for lift-off. Two minutes before ignition sequence is complete."

"Two minutes, Silk!"

"Right!"

Had he hit Silk with one of those desperate shots? That would be a boon, but he could not depend on it, not having paid enough attention to know for certain.

He heard the sound of an engine chamber's throaty prewarm cycle climb in volume as it ascended in tone. She had the ship on-line. Dammit! He might be able to shoot it down, if she got it clear of the hangar and started to lift, but that might kill them and he had to keep them alive. Dead they would be of no real use to him, save to possibly expiate himself from criminal activity the authorities might look at askance. He had to stall the woman and Silk somehow, keep them from leaving until he could position himself to stop them without killing them.

"Silk!" he yelled. He immediately moved to his right and rounded the corner of the building behind the hangar.

• • •

Silk heard the man yell his name. A moment later he yelled again, from a slightly different position.

"Silk! We need to talk!"

Silk ran to the opposite corner of the hangar's front and peered quickly around the edge. He didn't see anybody.

"Who the fuck are you?" Silk yelled back.

"It does not matter who I am. I know who you are, and all about the *ausvelter* spy with you! We can come to an accommodation!"

He was moving, the big man.

"Keep him talking," Zia said.

Silk backed up and looked into the hangar. Zia leaned her head out through the open porthole next to the pilot's seat. "We still need a minute or so to get up to power."

Silk moved back to the hangar's corner. "What kind of accommodation are you talking about?" he called out.

"A business transaction. Do you know what information the spy holds?" Once again, the voice came from a different place.

"I know."

"The knowledge is worth millions! We can share those sums. Plus the secret itself! How would you like to live forever?"

"You're not with Terran Security."

"Not any longer, no."

"What is it you want?"

"You tender the *ausvelter*. In exchange, you get to live and reap the rewards, we share them equally. We can resolve all the rest of it with the authorities. Large amounts of money make a wonderful balm."

Guy talked like a college professor, Silk thought. Tender? Balm?

Then another thought burned through him, one he couldn't keep from blurting out:

"You killed Mac, didn't you?"

The silence was broken only by the sound of the aircraft's engine rumbling.

"You fucking bastard!"

"It was an error. Unavoidable. I regret it."

Not as much as you are going to regret it, pal.

With that, Silk darted from behind the cover of the hangar. He ran toward the building where he figured the big man hid.

• • •

"Okay, Silk, we're ready. Come on!"

The sound of the engines in the hangar was quite loud, but he should have been able to hear her.

"Silk! Come on, we're ready!"

Nothing.

Zia grabbed the rifle and hurried to the exit.

She looked outside.

Where was he?

King heard the sounds of running footsteps splashing toward him. He shook his head. That would be Silk. He should have denied killing the doctor. Then again, perhaps not. The spy would be a better captive, would she not? He did not need both of them.

King dropped the rifle and pulled his fléchette pistol. When Silk rounded the corner he would be but a meter or two away and a long gun might be somewhat unwieldy. The pistol would suffice.

The running footsteps stopped, however.

The man was not as big an idiot as King thought, apparently. Too bad.

King turned and circled around behind the building.

Silk pulled himself up short of the prefab. He went barreling around there all in a rage, chances were the big guy would blow his brains out before he could use the crossbow. He wasn't afraid, but he wasn't ready to die just yet, either. He owed this guy in a major way and he wanted to pay that debt.

He moved more carefully, changing direction. He had lost some of his quarrels somewhere along the way. He had one in the crossbow, two stuck through his belt, points up. It would only take one hit, he was pretty sure of that, but he'd have felt better with six or seven more chances instead of two.

Maybe he could get behind the man and shoot him in the back.

The thought didn't bother him at all.

Zia saw Silk's tracks in the mud and she moved carefully from cover to follow them. They led to one of the medium-sized buildings behind the hangar. She kept the rifle at port arms, ready to snap it into firing position. She thought about

calling to Silk, but decided that wouldn't be too bright, to let
the bad guy know she was out here.

The sun was already drying the ground, but there was still
plenty of mud and more than a few puddles around. She moved
as quietly as she could.

The gods must be getting interested in him again.

King leapt out from behind the corner at the same instant
Silk replicated the action at the other end of the building.
Twelve meters separated them.

King dropped into a shooting crouch, brought the pistol up
with both hands—

Silk saw the big man appear from behind the corner, saw
him snap the gun in his hands up. Once again his vision
tunneled, and this time, the focus of the slowed time was on
the gun, the gun that came up, the gun that would kill him.
Silk could not take his attention away from the gun, it was
all he saw, the man behind it faded and became a blur—

He fired the crossbow—

Zia came up behind them, saw Silk shoot as the big man
pointed a pistol at him. Silk was in her line of fire, she couldn't
shoot—

The arrow hit his hands. It pierced the back of King's
left hand where it cupped his right, tore between bones and
chopped the little finger from his right hand with an almost
surgical precision, hit his right forearm just below his wrist
and sank into the muscle.

King screamed, more in anger than pain or fear. He tried
to pull the pistol's trigger but the finger in the guard wouldn't
work. He tried to yank his hands apart, but the arrow sta-
pled his left hand to his right arm. He screamed again and
jerked, putting his shoulders into it, and the arrow's head
tore free of his right arm, bringing with it a strip of muscle
and tendon. He lost the pistol, it fell, and the arrow remained
through his left hand. He stared at it. It was unreal, there
wasn't any pain, but he could see the damage, knew it would
take a long time to heal and be set right. His rage flowered like a bomb. He leapt at the man who had wounded
him—

• • •

Silk stared at the big man with the bolt stuck through his hand, blinked as the man roared like some big animal and came for him. He fumbled one of the bolts from his belt. Dropped it. Saw he wouldn't have time to pull the other before the man was on him—

"Silk, *get down!*"

She saw him drop flat into the mud. She already had the rifle butt against her shoulder, the laser sight on. The red dot danced up the big man, but he slipped as it centered on his chest and she fired. He was hit, higher, the bullet must have struck his collarbone or close to it. His fall continued, and he slammed into the ground, mud splashed in a concave sheet up around him. He slid to a stop facedown, within a few centimeters of Silk, who was already pushing himself up—

Silk came to his hands and knees and found himself looking at the big man. There was a neat hole next to his neck on the right side and his eyes were closed. Zia had shot him.

"Silk! Are you all right?"

She hurried to him as he came to his feet. "Yeah. I think so."

They both looked at the big man on the ground.

"Looks like you got him," he said.

King was mortally wounded. Dying, he could feel it, the bullet had cut a big path into him, something was ruined in his chest, a lung, maybe his heart or something. He could feel his life slipping away. He had lost the game and was about to pay the final price. Anger boiled, refusing to let it be so.

Not just yet.

He still had two weapons. The arrow through his left hand and the little pistol in his sock. If he was to die, he would bring companions with him on his trip to the next world.

They stood over him, his killers. He had only a few seconds left, he knew.

With strength born of final desperation, he moved. He lunged forward and swung his left hand around, stabbing at the woman's leg with the point of the arrow embedded in his hand. His aim was good enough. The arrow's tip sliced into her flesh. Startled, she dropped her weapon and staggered back—

Good, good, now the pistol—

He clawed at his sock, found the tiny gun, already cocked and ready to fire, and pulled it free. Use the middle finger. Shoot them until he ran out of bullets, shoot them, kill them—

Zia saw the gun, saw she wouldn't be able to get to the rifle in time, screamed in wordless rage—

Silk's crossbow lay in the mud, empty. The big man had done something to Zia, he had hurt her, just as he had hurt Mac, and Silk wanted to kill him! He had half a second to think of a way, and he would never be able to pull the quarrel from his belt and get to the crossbow and load it, never happen.

But as the big man swung his little black gun up to point at him, Silk realized he didn't have to get to the crossbow at all.

The gun boomed, once, twice, and he felt something burn his leg as he lunged, felt another tug as the bullet tore through his shirt but missed the skin and he was there—

Silk came down with the crossbow's bolt in his hand. It was primal, as primal as it could be. This animal threatened him, threatened his *mate!* and what he had was a sharp stick. He stabbed with his weapon, struck as hard as he could. Hit the animal's eye and drove his stick into its brain.

It roared once more, but then it spasmed . . . and died.

He didn't even know its name but Silk was glad to see it dead.

Finally.

FORTY _____

THEY SPENT A few minutes bandaging each other—Zia's ankle, both of Silk's legs—before they moved the little ship from the hangar and into the once-again bright tropical sunlight. Already clouds of flies buzzed and settled on the corpses in the compound's clearing. A quick check of the buildings revealed yet more dead, these being the agents of Zia's world.

Silk felt a great tiredness settle over him as he walked with Zia toward the rumbling aircraft.

"Listen," she said. "You can stay here if you want. Nobody offworld knows about you."

He stopped, caught her shoulders, turned her to face him. "Yeah, but a whole lot of people on *this* planet know about me. You trying to get rid of me?"

"No. I—I just wanted you to know that—that—"

"Shh," he said, touching her lips with his forefinger. "I know."

"What? What do you know?"

"I don't want to kill you, either."

She laughed. "Oh, man. What a pair we are."

"That's true enough. Come on. Why don't you take me for a ride in your rocket plane? Tell me all about this new world I'm going to be living on."

"You sure about this?"

He blew out a breath. "No. I'm not sure about anything. But what the hell, I'd rather be alive there with you than dead or in brainlock here without you."

"You sure know how to make a woman feel special, Silk."

It was his turn to laugh and he did. He took her hand and together they walked to the waiting vessel. He didn't know what waited out there, but he was fairly sure whatever it was, it wouldn't be boring.